THE KING'S WITCHES

Kate Foster

THE KING'S WITCHES

First published 2024 by Mantle
an imprint of Pan Macmillan
The Smithson, 6 Briset Street, London EC1M 5NR
EU representative: Macmillan Publishers Ireland Ltd, 1st Floor,
The Liffey Trust Centre, 117–126 Sheriff Street Upper,
Dublin 1, D01 YC43
Associated companies throughout the world
www.panmacmillan.com

ISBN 978-1-5290-9178-6

Copyright © Kate Foster 2024

The right of Kate Foster to be identified as the
author of this work has been asserted by her in accordance
with the Copyright, Designs and Patents Act 1988.

All rights reserved. No part of this publication may be reproduced,
stored in a retrieval system, or transmitted, in any form, or by any means
(electronic, mechanical, photocopying, recording or otherwise)
without the prior written permission of the publisher.

Pan Macmillan does not have any control over, or any responsibility for,
any author or third-party websites referred to in or on this book.

1 3 5 7 9 8 6 4 2

A CIP catalogue record for this book is available from the British Library.

Typeset by Palimpsest Book Production Ltd, Falkirk, Stirlingshire
Printed and bound by CPI Group (UK) Ltd, Croydon, CR0 4YY

This book is sold subject to the condition that it shall not, by way of
trade or otherwise, be lent, hired out, or otherwise circulated without
the publisher's prior consent in any form of binding or cover other than
that in which it is published and without a similar condition including
this condition being imposed on the subsequent purchaser.

Visit www.panmacmillan.com to read more about all our books
and to buy them. You will also find features, author interviews and
news of any author events, and you can sign up for e-newsletters
so that you're always first to hear about our new releases.

For Dad

20th September 1589, midday
From Andrew Drummond, Harbourmaster
at the Port of Leith, Scotland

A MESSAGE MOST URGENT
To His High and Mighty Majesty, King James the Sixth of Scotland, at Holyroodhouse

Sir – At ten o'clock this morning, a Scottish ship returning from Norway docked at the Port of Leith. Its crew say they almost perished in a tempest raging in the German Sea.

They witnessed vessels of the Danish fleet, which is conveying your intended Bride, Her Royal Highness the Princess Anna of Denmark, to Leith Port, struggling in the weather. The storm has been so violent that the Danish fleet has dispersed, and a distress signal of three cannon shots was heard from the Gideon, the ship carrying the Royal Princess, but the conditions were too dangerous to help, and the Gideon disappeared in a great mist.

There have been no confirmed sightings of the Gideon since then and there is now great concern for all souls on board.

I remain Your Majesty's servant and will provide further news as soon as I hear it.

Chapter One

ANNA

*Kronborg Castle, Denmark
One month earlier, August 1589*

The witch Doritte Olsen is being burned at the stake today and they're making us watch.

I'm going to be extremely brave about it, for she has confessed to the most wicked sorcery and deserves the flames. We're waiting to be summoned out of the parlour and down to the beach, just beyond the castle walls, and Kirsten has snapped and told me to sit down and stop pacing the room. My restlessness is giving her a headache. She doesn't ask if I'm terrified at what we're about to see, or tell me to look away if I need to, but that's simply what Kirsten's like. I sit down gracefully to keep my skirts neat, then pick up my embroidery from the side-table and pretend to sew, for something to do with my hands. Recently I've become very good at pretending.

The burning needs to be done quickly before the Scots get here, and they'll be here any day now. The Privy Council doesn't want the Scots to know we have a problem with witches. Not after all the hard work and negotiations that have gone into my marriage to their king, and the union of our countries. We can't risk having our reputation tarnished with rumours that the wave of witchcraft in the south has spread to Denmark.

Mistress Olsen used weather magic to capsize her husband's fishing boat. When she found out about his whoring, they had the most fearsome row, right in the port. She cursed him for all to hear. And when he sailed into the strait, just as he had done every day for the last ten years with no trouble, a black cloud blew in and the water churned like boiling stew. The boat washed up the next day and so did he. Drowned by sorcery.

She's been in the dungeons, right beneath our feet. Imagine it! I've barely slept, knowing she's down there, cursing us, calling on the Devil. They say it took two days and both her thumbnails, but she finally confessed. I tuck my own thumbs into my fists and try not to think about it.

Kirsten looks up at me again.

'Do I need to send you to your chamber, like a child, whilst we wait?'

Her tone is sharp, but I recognize the flinch in her eyes as fear. She, like me, has jumped at every creak of the floorboards outside the parlour door.

'I can't help feeling agitated,' I reply.

'Then you have not prayed hard enough,' she says. 'Sending Doritte Olsen to her death is the only way to end her wickedness.'

'Yes, but I don't agree that we must all watch.'

Kirsten flares her nostrils and closes her eyes, as if she is counting to three below her breath to keep herself under control. She opens her eyes again.

'We are to watch because we are to learn a lesson from this. All of us. Every courtier and servant – and even you. We are to learn of the dangers of dancing with the Devil.'

Another creak of the floorboards. We wait, our breath in our throats, but the parlour door stays closed. It is getting gloomy. The time is near.

'Can't you ask Mama if I can be excused?' I plead. 'There's still time. Say I feel sick.'

'No one is excused,' Kirsten says. 'Just stand on the beach and pray, as everyone else will be doing.' She lowers her voice. 'The execution of Doritte Olsen is not our biggest concern,' she warns, her eye on the door. 'We have our own problems to worry about. When the Scots get here and your handfasting begins, that is when we face our real test.'

I nod and try to concentrate on my embroidery until she stops watching me, lights the candles and goes back to her reading.

For the first year of my marriage to King James the Sixth of Scotland I will be on trial. They are calling it a *handfasting* – a betrothal – to make sure that we are a true match. But I know it is a trial, and at the end of it I will be judged worthy or unworthy.

James says it wasn't his idea, and that he fell head-over-heels in love with me as soon as he saw the portrait they sent. He insists the Scots will adore me, from the beggars in the Canongate to the lairds at court at Holyroodhouse. He's said nothing of the ladies at court at Holyroodhouse, which bodes ill. They will be flame-haired and rude, with overly painted faces and overly plucked brows. Kirsten says we must try our absolute best to gain their favour quickly. But the ladies will hate me. I know it.

Kirsten is coming with me as my chief lady-of-the-bedchamber because she knows Scotland very well and speaks the language. She spent a year there when she was my age. Her father thought it enlightening to travel. I suspect that if she wasn't so enlightened, she wouldn't have got a place at court here at Kronborg, for she certainly hasn't the temperament that makes a lady pleasant company.

The idea of the handfasting came from the Scottish advisors, James said, the group of red-bearded men who have sailed back and forth these past months negotiating with Mama until all the good wine had been drunk and everyone was in agreement, down to the finest points of my dowry and the confirmation that it would include ten thousand rigsdalers and exempt all Scottish ships of tolls in Danish waters. *I humbly ask your forgiveness, dear heart,* James wrote, *but the handfasting is simply a formality to satisfy my advisors here. I have hung your portrait in my inner bedchamber.*

I'm not sure whether to believe that James didn't come up with the idea, for we haven't met, so I can't know his character. If he's in love with the portrait they sent, then he's bound to be disappointed. The artist was overly generous with my complexion and made my eyes the most vivid blue, at Mama's insistence. And now it hangs in his inner bedchamber. I imagine him standing surveying it whilst his courtiers undress him. I imagine he has skin as white as milk and thin, girlish arms.

The trial will begin with a proxy ceremony, when the ship arrives with the Scottish ambassador who will represent James. The fishermen up the strait have been put on watch for lion-rampant flags and saltires. The sea breeze flutters with their expectant cries. The king could not make the journey to his own wedding as it would be risky for him to leave Scotland for an extended period. Either of us is free to abandon the pledge within one year, should we be unhappy at the match, or if it is thought I am not a suitable queen for the Scots.

The terms of the agreement sound civilized. But if I fail, I'll be sent home in disgrace and put in the convent at Hellebæk Abbey, where the lame and hunchbacked daughters of the nobility are stored out of sight, alongside the ones who are caught being whoreish. It's what happened to Lady Dorothea after she bore a bastard. I shudder again and Kirsten sighs, and I pretend I have pricked myself with my sewing needle.

'Be careful,' she says. 'Don't spoil all the work you've put into that doublet for His Majesty.' All Kirsten cares about is making everything seem perfect and having everything go to plan. She is desperate for my marriage to be a success, but I have long given up trying to work her out or make a friend of her.

'I'm sure it's finished now anyway,' I say, pushing the thought of banishment away and tying off the thread neatly.

'So quickly? Let me have a good look.' Kirsten heaves herself up, as though she is much heavier than her slight frame suggests, and settles on the chair next to me, smoothing her skirts across her lap. I hand her the doublet. Pale-blue satin. I've taken care to keep it pristine. Over the past few weeks I've embroidered delicate marguerites on its sleeves. The flower of Denmark. I marvel at the neatness of my own stitching, given the terror that is sewn into it.

'Will he like it?' I ask, for the hundredth time.

Kirsten studies my handiwork, then nods, seeming satisfied.

'He will like what he likes, and there will be very little you can do about it, except try to please him in all ways,' she tells me. 'That is what the handfasting is all about. But I will be there, to guide you. Now look.' She points with her slender finger. 'There's space for one or two more flowers – here, and here.'

I know exactly what will happen if I don't please James in all ways.

'I'll do two more marguerites by the cuffs,' I say, taking up my needle and thread once more. I always agree to everything. I've found it's the only thing they want from me.

Kirsten goes back to her chair in the window recess.

'They can't leave any trace of the burning on the sand,' she mutters to herself. 'The Scots would see it as their ship comes in, and they might start asking questions. I'll inspect it tomorrow myself.'

When I was shown James's likeness, in oils on a panel, he looked to be positively glowering, as though he had bored of the sitting. He need not have sent it at all, for what would I ever say if I did not like his face? If it was afflicted with pustules, like that of the Austrian prince Mama and the Privy Council were considering? James has no pustules, but a sullen look of contempt that keeps me awake at night. Will he bore of me after a week at Holyroodhouse when he has realized I'm still learning his language and my conversation is dull?

They say he had thought over the matter of marriage for three days and had chosen a union with Denmark over one with France. Catherine de Bourbon, the other potential bride he was considering, is older but terribly sophisticated. She wears a great farthingale and writes sonnets. Apparently she and James still exchange letters. Mama has warned me.

'You'll like Scotland,' Kirsten says. She has laid her book down, just as unable to read as I am to sew. 'You shouldn't fear it as much as you do.'

'Will you not miss Denmark?' I ask. I keep my voice light, for Kirsten rarely entertains emotional conversations.

She shrugs. 'I prefer the Scottish landscape,' she says. 'And you will too. It's majestic, with its mountains and lochs and woodlands. The Canongate, near Holyroodhouse, is very dignified and full of grand houses with gardens. Now, let's have a quiet moment of prayer and ask the Lord for the strength we will need.'

She closes her eyes. I watch her. She's not praying; there's a frown on her forehead that is different from the earnest look Kirsten has when she is at prayer. She is in Scotland, in her thoughts.

What lies there that makes Kirsten Sørensen so unsettled?

I have not smiled in weeks. Not when I'm leaving Mama and Elizabeth, and the portraits of Papa that are so true to life that I can remember him vividly every time I look at them. And the rope swing in the gardens, and the fig tarts on Sundays, and the summer parties to which the girls from the village come and we all do chain-dancing in the hall and take swigs of wine when no one is looking, and I pretend they're my friends even though I'm not allowed to make friends with ordinary girls. And I'm trying to be good and do everything they tell me, because I know how important it all is, but I wish none of it was happening. I wish they had left me alone and found another bride for the King of Scotland. I wish Catherine de Bourbon had seduced him with her sonnets. But she did not. The Danes seduced the Scots with our staunch religious views and our trading links. So Kirsten and I sit quietly awhile, dainty as two silk marguerites on a doublet sleeve, restless in our own storms.

There is a knock at the door and we both jump.

One of the servants comes in and bows.

'You are to make your way to the beach,' he says.

Chapter Two

ANNA

Mistress Olsen is bound to the stake already, a small pile of wood at her feet. Her face is sharp in the evening light and does not hang in shame, but stares back at us as though we are in the wrong, not her. Her gown is clean and white and everything is too vivid and too brittle, and I think my legs are going to give way. We are at the front of a gathering of Privy Councilmen, with Mama on the other side, so I can't see whether she feels as sick as I do. We are at a safe distance, but it still feels far too close.

I can't believe they are really going to do this, but they must.

Everyone knows about the trouble with witches in other places. We've seen the news pamphlets about the mass burnings in Trier. They say it's spreading like a plague. Three hundred witches rooted out in one town alone. Everyone is alert to it now, and they caught a witch in Copenhagen last month. And now this, with Mistress Olsen, who only lived down the road. Everyone is terrified about how many witches there are and what they might do.

Kirsten presses her hand on my back as if warning me not to faint. Bishop Larsen steps forward, his robes dragging behind him in the sand, and asks Mistress Olsen if she has any last words. She spits in his direction. Everyone gasps, even the Privy Councilmen.

'Defiant to the end,' says Kirsten under her breath, sounding almost in awe. We are in the sheltered part of the beach where I used to play with Elizabeth, before we grew up and they stopped us running around and getting our feet dirty. Everywhere I look are memories of seaweed-gathering and shell-hunting and sand-digging, and I am glad she's not here and being forced to watch too. Mama says I'm more demure than Elizabeth, which is why I was put forward for the Scottish king, and they are all supremely confident I will never cause trouble or step out of line. I think I just haven't found out who I am yet. I'm supposed to be a woman, now that I'm seventeen, but I don't feel it.

Bishop Larsen ignores the spittle on the sand and turns around and addresses us.

'Take out your girdle books at Psalm Seven: *O Lord my God, in thee do I put my trust.*'

I reach for the psalter hanging from my waist and open it. But I can barely concentrate on the illuminated script, for I know the men are bringing the torch to the pyre. I hear a crack of fire and Mistress Olsen leaps and strains at her ropes.

'I am not wicked,' she screams. 'You will all suffer in hell for this.'

She jerks her head, her hair flying about her face. She screams again, lifting her feet, as the sticks catch. I can't watch. I look around me. The others are transfixed, ignoring their books, the same look of horror sweeping across everyone's faces. I look down at my skirts trailing on the sand. The laundresses will have an almighty job with our dirty gown-hems. I wish I could put my fingers in my ears and close my eyes and scream as well. I can smell it. I glance up and her gown has caught alight and is burning off her.

'We are going to see her naked,' I gasp, shocked at the shame of it.

'Lord protect us,' Kirsten mutters, ignoring me. Her hand is on my back again, her grip has intensified, the heat flooding through her palm, all her energy rising to the surface like a kettle boiling on a stove. I shift a little to try to release her hand or it will leave a creased sweat mark.

'Let her die soon, Lord,' I pray, not caring who hears me. I look again and Mistress Olsen is howling behind a screen of fire. For one moment the flames die back, as if they are going to burn themselves out, and she looks straight towards me. I cannot look away; it is as though she has locked me in her gaze. Her eyes are dark. Her mouth moves. She is saying something. The fire is blazing too loudly now for me to hear, but as I watch her lips move, it is as if I know what she is saying: *I curse you; you will never be Queen of Scotland.* I don't just see her lips move; I hear her voice in my head. Clear as a bell, as the orange fire consumes her.

Afterwards we are offered a supper of herring and wilted leek, the thought of which turns my stomach, but the Privy Councilmen and Bishop Larsen gather in the banqueting hall, eating so lustily that the servants can barely keep up. Silver plates clatter and wine gushes from jugs. We have brought the stench of smoke into the castle with us. It mingles with the dark wall tapestries and the high tang of the fish. It's so pungent I feel as if we have brought Doritte Olsen with us. I want to get to Mama, to feel the comfort of her, but she is too busy with all the men gathering around the top table. I'm still trembling. My hand shakes as I hold my cup of warmed fruit wine.

'Come,' says Kirsten, 'you've seen enough. I'm taking you upstairs.'

'Bring some more wine,' I tell her and she nods, even though she would never normally allow that.

We escape upstairs, sweeping over the black-and-white tiled floor and up the two steep flights of stone steps to my chamber. I stumble and think I might lose my footing, even though I've walked up these steps thousands of times. When we get to my room, Kirsten undresses me hurriedly in the yellow light of my oil lamps and hangs up my gown, ready for the laundry maid. There is a stain of damp sand along the bottom of my skirts and a faint crease on the back from Kirsten's hand, the only trace now left of her fervour. She waits impatiently, shifting from one foot to the other, as I feed Aksel his little titbits of fruit through the bars of his cage. He peeps and flutters and I envy him his ignorance.

Kirsten pulls back my heavy bedcovers and waits for me to get in, then she curtseys sharply and leaves the room, leaving me to drink the rest of my wine and try to stop the bouts of shaking. I have smoke in my hair as though Mistress Olsen has woven herself about me. I can still hear her cursing me. I focus on the portrait on the wall by the door, the one of me and Elizabeth when we were girls staying with Grandmama and Grandpapa at Güstrow Palace. We stand under the pergola, looking as serious as two little grown-ups, but her hand brushes mine and I remember the tickle of her fingers and her restlessness as we stood there, being sketched, blissfully innocent of the conversations that would come from Mama after Papa died. With Christian sent to boarding school to learn how to be King of Denmark and Norway, and Elizabeth married, all attention was focused on my suitors. *Anna, it is time for you to do your duty. James Stuart has the Scottish throne. If you serve him well, you can help him take the English throne too. It is the opportunity of a lifetime – for you and for all of us.*

I can't sleep yet. How could I? Bright flashes of the burning woman are seared into my eyes. Her howls above the whistling of the fire. The screeching of the gulls as they fled. Her voice in my head.

I get out of bed and go to the window. I can't see the part of the beach where they did it, but Mistress Olsen's body will need to burn for hours yet before it becomes ash. If the Privy Council wanted us to learn a lesson, it has succeeded.

Now we know how savage it is.

The sun is setting now, over the Øresund strait. My belongings, and those of the courtiers accompanying me, float on the dozen or so ships there, filled with everything you can imagine: furniture, a solid-silver coach and my trousseau. Five hundred tailors worked for three months on that. They are talking of my gowns as far afield as Saxony, Mama says. The spectacle of the anchored fleet looms over Helsingør, dwarfing the half-timbered houses and ferryboats and farms. Their cannons, pointing at the harbour from gun-holes, will protect us. The *Gideon* is the ship I am sailing on with Kirsten, and although it sprang a leak on its last journey, they say the best carpenters and blacksmiths have repaired it and now it is even finer than when it was first built. They say it is unsinkable.

'Are you still awake?' Mama stands at the door, a candle in her hand. I am relieved to see her.

'Please come and sit with me on the bed,' I reply, sounding like a child again, for she rarely visits my chamber.

'I know you feel like you will never get over what we all witnessed today, but please know that it was for the best,' Mama says, setting the candle on the stand.

'They should never have made us watch,' I say.

'Bishop Larsen says we must show the Devil we have no fear,' she goes on. 'And you are not to breathe a word of this to any of the Scots. They cannot think we are afflicted with this *disease*.' Mama looks truly disgusted. 'Ordinary women – everyday women – having their heads turned by the Devil. I pray to God that He will save us, and you must pray too.'

'I will say nothing to the Scots,' I promise her. I open my mouth to say that I think Doritte Olsen cursed me as she died, and that I am unfit to marry James as it is doomed from the beginning. But then I think better of it. I don't want that getting back to Bishop Larsen. He might return me to Hellebæk Abbey.

We went there a few months ago, as they were agreeing that we would enter a handfasting and the Privy Council wanted me to understand the risks of failing.

It's a cloistered convent of Lutheran nuns who live a life of prayer, locked away from the world. Some are noblewomen given to the Lord by their families, to keep them in His favour – the ones no one wanted to marry or the ones who ruined themselves. We went with Kirsten, her facial expression stiff, even as the salty sea winds battered our cart and her eyes streamed.

'Life is a journey, just like this,' Bishop Larsen said, settling onto his seat. He pointed ahead. 'We all reach a fork in the road, exactly like that one, do you see? One path goes through the wheat fields and all the way to Copenhagen. The other path leads up to the cliff edge, which is a treacherous place to be. Think about which path you would like to be on, Your Royal Highness.'

'Her Royal Highness wishes to be on the path of righteousness, don't you, Anna?' Kirsten said.

I nodded and I lifted my face to the wind, willing it to slap my cheeks so pink that the nuns would think me excitable and wouldn't want me. The convent was up on a hill, overlooking the village. The women inside it were as hard as the rocks it stood on, and as grey.

We entered a silent cloister and were met by the abbess, who peered at us from under a linen wimple pinned rigidly into place. She nodded. I stood there waiting for her to curtsey, but she did not. My mouth fell open in surprise.

'I bow my head only to God,' she said, and took us on an awkward tour of the kitchen, the refectory and the chapel. Up and down narrow, twisty stairs and past nuns cleaning floors and studying thick books. My legs started to ache. My face was back to its pale shell as I realized how soul-destroying my days would be if I ended up here.

Finally the abbess had shown us the dormitory, where they slept six to a room. Each tightly made bed was exactly the same. It smelled of sweat and pining and despondent dreams.

'We find this a harmonious place, and you would too, should you come here. It would take you a while to get used to our ways. We don't have fine gowns or fripperies here.' She was looking at the emerald pin in my hair. 'But we have humility, and there is more peace in that than you can imagine.'

She poured herself a cup of water from a jug on a bedside table, without offering us a drink.

I could feel Bishop Larsen fighting with himself to avoid looking at the women's stockings airing by the window.

On the way out, in a neat vegetable patch, one of the nuns stood up from her weeding and stretched, her eyes following us as we approached.

'Lady Dorothea,' Kirsten had whispered, 'serving her penance now.'

I had met Lady Dorothea at one of Mama's balls, my memory

of her now hazy. She was tall with sharp cheekbones, and so animated, her fan dancing about her curls. As we passed the vegetable patch she gave the faintest of curtseys, as though she had forgotten how to do it but was determined to try. Kirsten and Bishop Larsen ignored her. I opened my mouth as if to greet her, but Lady Dorothea silenced me with a frown. When I looked back, she was still watching me. She shook her head at me, slowly but purposefully, and I knew what that signified. It meant I must not end up like her.

Mama kisses me now and leaves. I want to ask her to stay, to get into bed beside me and hold me until I sleep, but I don't want to embarrass myself. It's not something she has ever done.

Aksel is silent, roosted on his little top perch. Perhaps the Devil is here, come for Mistress Olsen. I must pray. I must ward him off. Just as I close my eyes there comes the most almighty crash. I let out a scream – I can't help it. The portrait of Elizabeth and me, which has hung on my wall for years, has fallen to the floor.

Chapter Three

ANNA

The Scots arrive three days later, after the sand has been raked and the portrait returned to the wall. Their ship is spotted at first light and I am pulled from my bed and thrown into a pink damask gown, my hair braided into rolls as tight as stale buns.

Kirsten had scolded the servants for the way they bang the door on their way out and said the portrait falling was an accident waiting to happen and it was lucky it didn't get damaged.

I don't believe it was an accident. As I am dressed, I ask her for the crystal pendant from my jewellery trunk.

'And why ever are you matching crystal to a day-dress?' she asks. 'Is this a new fashion I have not caught up with?'

'Crystals ward off witches,' I say.

'The witch has been burned,' she replies. 'No trace of her left at all. And crystal is for evening wear, and we have barely breakfasted. You are to wear the small gold necklace and matching headpiece for the arrival of the Scots. We decided this weeks ago.' She takes the jewellery from the trunk, passing the window on her way back to me. 'They've beaten a storm,' she says, glancing to where a huge cloud is hanging over the strait. 'That has come from nowhere,' she murmurs. 'That is autumn weather.'

I concentrate on my breathing to stop my heart hammering so hard that the maids will notice. After the vows, I am to lie fully clothed on a bed with Earl Marischal, the ambassador representing James at the ceremony, as a symbol of the betrothal. I had to practise lying gracefully when I rehearsed it with Mama and Kirsten, and I lay there very still, squeezing my eyes closed because I thought I might start to cry. I can't do that now, not with everyone fussing about my face and my hair. Everyone is swarming, intent on doing their best. I can't let them down.

'For goodness' sake, try to look happier,' says Kirsten. 'The Scots don't want to see a bride with a face like that storm cloud.'

By midday the Scots have docked and disembarked and we receive them in the banqueting hall, the old kings and queens of Denmark staring down upon us from their portraits. I avoid looking at the painting of Papa. It's so lifelike that he could be in the room. But he is dead and entombed in a cathedral miles away, and I can't bear to think of that. Mama stands next to me, her jaw set for deal-making and hosting, her collar so high that she can barely move her head.

The Scots enter in a fine marching line of beards and bellies and bulbous noses. Sturdy and sea-swept and wild, they cross the tiled floor, leaving footprints right across it. They look stronger than the Devil himself, and that is a reassuring thought.

'They'll be famished,' whispers Mama. 'Whatever the kitchen has prepared for the banquet won't be enough. They will drain us of broth and wine.'

'Indeed,' says Kirsten. 'And our maids will be slapped and tickled half to death. Someone should keep an eye on the servants' chambers tonight.'

'There's Earl Marischal, look,' I reply. He's short and round, with hair and whiskers the colour of mead. Thank God I'm not actually marrying him.

He weaves past the tables to us and bows. 'God has blessed our voyage and brought us here safe and sound,' he says. He smells of damp. There is a film of sweat on his face. 'A momentous day for Scotland and Denmark.'

He kisses my hand and it feels prickly and hot, and I wipe it on my skirts when Mama says it's time for us all to sit down. Although Kirsten is fluent in the Scots language, I am not. She has tutored me these past months and now we'll find out if she has taught me enough to get by.

'Earl Marischal, we're delighted to see you once again,' I say as he lets the chair creak under his weight.

He looks around him, taking in the chandeliers and the high-vaulted ceiling and the wide windows as if he can't quite believe he's here.

'It's a relief to be on dry land,' he says. 'Bad weather.'

I try not to look alarmed, for we return to Scotland as soon as the proxy ceremony is completed and the papers are signed.

'Don't worry,' Kirsten mutters to me across the table. 'The captains know what they're doing, and yours is the admiral of the Danish fleet. Have no fear.'

Earl Marischal tackles his pie and figs as though he has not eaten in days. I sip wine and try not to gulp. As he relaxes, he launches into a long story, full of raised eyebrows and much pointing of his fingers, about his journey. How cold the wind was, and how the sails needed patching, and how delighted he is to eat fresh food again.

I nod, understanding some of it, then losing track. Mama, on the other side of the table, seems altogether lost and keeps asking Kirsten to translate. We muddle through much of the meal like this, with pained smiles and the raising of goblets together, and it hits me fully in the face how difficult the language is going to be in Scotland. How will I communicate with James if I can only understand half of what he says? I should have paid far more attention to Kirsten.

When they bring out the fruit plates, Earl Marischal turns from me and enters into a heated conversation with the man next to him, then turns back.

'Your Royal Highness,' he says. 'This man is Henry, Lord Roxburgh, another of our Scottish ambassadors. Henry is our expert in the Danish language and culture, having studied at the University of Copenhagen.'

Earl Marischal sits as far back as his belly will allow, and I shift forward so that I can get a better view of this Henry, Lord Roxburgh, and find myself, plum in one hand and wine goblet in the other, face-to-face with a man who is quite unlike the other Scots, for he is handsome and dark-haired and young.

I blink.

He smiles.

'Good evening,' he says in perfect Danish. 'I have come here as your language tutor and translator.'

Everything else in the room fades away. I know there's a trio of fiddle players, and I know the Scots have drunk so much their chatter has become a din, and I know the smell of the whale-oil lamps has become high and pungent. The serving girls refilling the goblets look pink-cheeked and sweaty and harangued, and yet all of it is happening in the background, like a smudged chalk-drawing. Henry and I are in the foreground. He understands everything I say, and I understand him. There is no pained smiling or miming of words.

'They didn't tell me I was getting a tutor,' I reply.

'It was decided last-minute. His Majesty wanted to be sure

that you would be able to converse well and have an understanding of Scots history,' he says.

I look across the table at Kirsten, who looks most miffed and is fiddling with her brooch, which is what she does when she can't think of something to say.

'I'll be giving you lessons on our return voyage. Trust me, you'll be glad of the distraction,' he continues. 'There's nothing more interminable than a sea journey.'

I do not speak to men in close proximity very often. They're not allowed near me. Tonight the rules have shifted and no one seems to mind, except Kirsten, who has left her brooch alone, but now toys peevishly with her fruit plate. She is irritated at this unexpected turn of events. Henry appears to be a man around mid-twenties in age, who ought rightly to have a wife and children, but he makes no mention of either when I ask him where he's from.

'Roxburghshire in the Scottish Borders,' he says. 'But I live at court at Holyroodhouse.'

'Then you can tell me what court is like,' I tell him. 'Because that's what I need to know.'

He nods. He understands. 'I will tell you,' he says. 'But now is not the time. Today is for celebrating.'

And he will not be pressed any more on the matter, and I must trust him to tell me when he is ready to. We sit for a while and watch the musicians, but even so I can't bring them into focus, with Henry next to me. We sit in a companionable silence. We share a plate of red berries. I have never before shared a plate of berries with a man.

Chapter Four

JURA

North Berwick, Scotland
August 1589

Feathers are for wishes: the wee white ones are best.
Stones for safe travels, especially smooth ones.
Red berries, all edible sorts, are for passion.

Ma's charmes are like Ma herself. Strange and meticulous and not to be tampered with. There's only one way of doing a charme, to make it work right. There's only one way of being Auld Guidwife Craig. A belligerent old bird, but she'll aye help those who come to our door in need. Usually lassies looking for love inchantments or potions to get unpregnant. If I can be more like Ma and less like those lassies, mibbie life will be easier.

Oh, Ma. You've been dead a fortnight and I'm still talking like you're here. If you're looking down on me, I hope you'll understand why I'm marching quick-smart away from our wee beach cottage, away from Da. But I can't stay there alone with him. Not with the way he sits and drinks all day, repeating himself and ruminating and pissing in his breeks. If I stay, I'll end up just like him. This is a one-way journey.

I'm on my way to the Kincaids, who live in the big sandstone house halfway to the Berwick Law hill. Stuart Kincaid is baillie of the Royal Burgh of North Berwick, collecting rents and managing farms, serving summonses and orders and executing warrants for all of the district. Baillie Kincaid is the most important man in North Berwick. I'll be his new maid. My fortune charme – the one I did the night after you died, Ma – has worked. I know you never liked Baillie Kincaid, but I'll be getting good coin.

I am sweating from the walk, for it's a braw day. You'd call it *a belter*, Ma. The August sun beats down and bounces off the low tide and the wet beach. The gulls are hot and crabbit and swoop and screech, hunting for dead things. My hands ache from lugging my bags already, and I'd aye stop for a rest but the Kincaids need me at great speed. I first heard about the vacancy at kirk; all the lassies were gossiping about it, lifting their psalters and ducking their heads to hide their lips. The Kincaids' old maid ran off in disgrace and Guidwife Kincaid was at her wits' end. *It is better to trust the Lord than put confidence in man.*

After the service I sought out Guidwife Kincaid and found her in the kirkyard. She was standing in a huddle of guidwives all grumbling about their aches and their husbands and their hoorish maids. Her lassie Hazel stood nearby with all the other well-to-do girls, spying on the farm boys from under their caps.

I'd caught Guidwife Kincaid's eye and she'd stepped away, irritated at the interruption.

'I'll come and be your maid,' I told her, mustering up all the bravery I could find. 'I'm guid with brushes and cloths and laundering paddles, and I don't take more than my fair share at the dinner table. And I don't take fright at spiders and mice, but I'll tell you now, I'm terrible feared of wasps.'

She'd looked me up and down and I'd wished I'd washed my face that morning. She wore a cream fustian coif, unfussy but expensive-looking, knotted particularly tight under her chin as if someone might steal it.

'I need a lass about the house who can get out of bed on time and knows better than to complain about everything. But I pay a decent wage, with bed and board, and I provide three kirtles – two for work and one for best. Master Kincaid deals with the wasps, but you'll be up at five doing the hearths. Do you think you can manage that?'

I thought I could manage that.

'And have you a sweetheart? For I don't want any more maids getting themselves into trouble.'

I shook my head. I'd assisted Ma so long that my twenty-two summers had passed with no sweetheart. The way Ma was, odd and missing half her teeth, folk visited when they needed to, not because they wanted to. I hope that's why no sweetheart came, for the alternative – that I am too plain a dumpling to get a marriage proposal, even from a drunkard or an idiot or that lad who cleans the ferryboats, the one with the lugs like jug handles – is no cheery thought.

Guidwife Kincaid nodded, looking satisfied. 'I was sorry to hear about your ma,' she added, her voice low. 'Your ma was a cunning wifie – have you her knowledge?'

I wondered what charmes Guidwife Kincaid had ever needed, because I couldn't recall her come knocking at our door.

'I have some knowledge,' I said. 'But she was still teaching me when she passed, and her healing was never enough to make ends meet.'

'Well, we all must make ends meet somehow,' she said, then she straightened herself. 'You can start with us right away. Guid news, Hazel,' she called to her daughter. 'A new maid, so you won't have to do the scrubbing and the fires.'

The other guidwives laughed and said Hazel Kincaid wouldn't know how to lay a fire, even if it was so cold hell was freezing over. Hazel dragged her gaze from the farm boys and stared at me with open curiosity, before turning to Guidwife Kincaid.

'If she has the cunning wifie's gift,' she said, 'that might be a blessing on us all.'

It takes three raps of the Kincaids' brass door-knocker before anyone comes, and I am beginning to lose my nerve. The front garden is walled and filled with tall, shady trees that nod down at the village, most pleased with themselves. I haven't been in a nice house before, and I'm worrying if I should take off my pattens when the door swings open and I am faced with a short man with curly silver hair and a red bulbous nose, upon which are balanced a pair of eyeglasses, slightly askew, giving his face the appearance of a set of weighing scales.

'No vagrants,' he says, adjusting his spectacles. 'There are alms down at the kirk, and you should take yourself there before I have you whipped for trespassing.'

'I'm not a vagrant, sir,' I stammer, 'I am Mistress Jura Craig, come at the guidwife's summoning to work as your new maid.'

The man runs his fingers over his moustache.

'My new maid,' he says, slowly. He takes off his eyeglasses and lets his gaze slide over me. 'You look like a beggar.'

'I most certainly am not, sir,' I tell him. 'I am from down in North Berwick village and I have never begged in my life.

'Have I seen you in kirk?' he asks.

'I'm there every week,' I say, 'and so are you, Master Kincaid, as I always see you in the front pew, worshipping God Almighty in the most devout way, as I do myself.'

He looks satisfied at this and stands back, allowing me into the cool, dark hallway. The rush mats are clean and the air has the faint scent of lavender, but I don't see any, nor any ornaments or pictures at all, save for a single small looking-glass hung by the door. This is a house without fripperies.

'The maid's chamber is on the top floor,' he says. 'I'll take you up. The mistress and Hazel are down in the town, and Lord knows when they'll be back.'

I don't know what masters should and shouldn't do with their maids, which is why I don't tell Baillie Kincaid that I'll wait for them to get back or ask him to go and find Cook. Instead I let Baillie Kincaid show me up to my chamber, and that is when the trouble with him starts.

Chapter Five

JURA

The Kincaids seem odd to me, but mibbie I'm the odd one and, having been raised in a home with a drinker and a cunning wifie, I don't know right from wrong.

Most I ever see of the mistress is the hump of her back, and that suits me fine. She passes her instructions through Cook, and Betsy the housekeeper, and they have an abhorrence of all things slovenly – which includes dirty fingernails and slouching and sniffing – so much that within the week I have lost all my habits.

Hazel Kincaid is pasty-faced, but with an angry-looking rash on her foreheid that I am desperate to dab a poultice on. She is tutored in reading and writing and numbers twice a week, and has reached the age of sixteen, which is marrying age, yet I hear no talk of any arrangements. The Kincaids also detest beauty and art in all its forms and will not adorn their home with anything but candlesticks and books – the plainer and the holier, the better. I think of the sea-shells and smooth pebbles and bottles and jars that adorned our wee cottage and I consider it most sad, not to like nice things.

Master Kincaid is a problem.

It started in my attic room on that first day. He watched at the door as I took in my new surroundings. The creaky floorboards and the low eaves and the small window that looks right across the Firth of Forth to the Bass Rock and to Fife. A cream wool blanket on the bed and a thin grey shawl hanging over a chair. I thanked him, expecting him to take his leave. He did not.

'The last maid left that shawl,' he said, nodding to it. 'I suppose it's yours now.'

'I'll hang it up when I unpack,' I replied, folding my arms and waiting for him to go.

'She was a wicked girl, the last maid,' he said. 'She was idle and sluttish and let the fishermen have their way with her. We cannot have wickedness under this roof.'

'I don't plan on being wicked, sir,' I said.

'I shall be watching you,' he warned. 'The mistress thinks she's in charge of this household, but she's not. I am the master of this house.'

And he has been true to his word. He watches me. He watches my arse as I clean the fireplace in his study, and he watches my hands as I serve him his supper, and he watches my face to see how much it unsettles me.

I do not let him know how much it unsettles me.

By the time the Kincaids have provided me with new kirtles and Bristol grey soap and two pristine white caps, I hardly recognize myself. The work is no more taxing than looking after a dying ma and a drinking da. I am up at five to do the fires, and I spend most of the day dusting and sweeping and cleaning kitchen pots and chamberpots, and trying to avoid scalding myself on the big pottage cauldron that hangs over the hearth in the middle of the kitchen.

Master Kincaid pays me my wages on a Friday morning, watching my bosom as I count the pennies out, and I keep them in a drawstring bag in the bottom drawer in my room.

It was the same drawstring bag that Ma kept her pennies in, from the people who came to the door. She had to keep it hidden from Da, else he would have drunk it.

'Will you visit your da on your day off?' Hazel Kincaid has an open curiosity about me. Between her and the master, I feel like a specimen in one of Ma's jars.

'Perhaps,' I lie. I could take him some pennies, but I would rather go to the kirkyard and take flowers to Ma's grave, or sit by the beach and think of her and share my grief with the wind that comes in off the Forth, for both elements are wild and can take you unawares.

'Is it true your ma could cure all manner of sicknesses?' Hazel comes closer. She has a way of breathing through her mouth that is unsettling and makes her breath smell a wee bit foosty.

'She knew inchantments and charmes,' I say.

Hazel touches her forehead where the rash is flaring.

'You want a poultice on that,' I suggest.

'Ma's tried giving me poultices. They don't work,' she replies.

'Then you need one of my poultices,' I say. 'I'm going to market on my day off. Meet me down there and we'll have a wee daunder and get something together.'

There's a heaving crowd at Saturday market. I've had my sit on the beach and my think about Ma and I've taken a posy of daisies to her grave. No sign of any blooms from Da. I almost go to the cottage, but I am scared he'll be in such a state that I'll get caught up with his troubles and I'll never leave again. I have a nice yellow kirtle on, the colour of sunshine, bound firm at the bodice. My face shines from the Bristol grey soap, and my hair is plaited under my cap.

Hazel is waiting for me. We daunder to the ribbon stall and buy a ribbon each. She buys a white one and I buy a red one. Red is for love. Ribbons are for binding, but I'm not thinking of that when I buy it; I'm only thinking of my hair, which is a fine shade of brown like chestnuts, if I do say so myself, and about the bonniest thing about me.

Next we buy oats and honey for the poultice I will give her, but I have found the extra ingredient we need on the beach: a stone that leaves white marks like chalk. I show it to Hazel.

'Is it for a spell?' She looks worried. 'I don't want anything divvilish.'

'It is nothing to do with the Divvil,' I tell her. 'He has no interest in you or me.'

We pass the poultry stall before we leave, piled with caged chickens and boxes of eggs. Robbie, Poulterer Bathgate's son, winks at us. Hazel pulls her cap over her rash and blushes so bright I can feel the heat coming off her.

'How about half a dozen eggs for tonight's supper? I've saved my best ones for you,' he calls to Hazel and she blushes even harder.

'We have our own chickens up at the Kincaids',' I tell him.

'Jura Craig,' he says, 'I'd hardly recognized you, looking so smart.'

Hazel bristles.

'It's very cheeky to comment on a lassie's appearance,' I tell him. 'Especially when your boots are covered in chicken shit.'

He laughs and wraps two eggs in a cloth. 'Take these,' he says, 'by way of an apology. But I can't help admiring your fine looks today.'

Hazel flounces off. I take the eggs. I have no shame when it comes to free food. Robbie smiles as he watches me. Brown eyes, bright and light-brown hair turning fair at the tips – a funny combination, like sweet on top of savoury. Hazel has disappeared into the crowd.

'So you are with the Kincaids now,' he says. 'You should watch old Baillie Kincaid. He gets through a lot of maids.'

'I can look after myself,' I reply.

He brushes his fringe out of his eyes. Sweet on top of savoury. I wish I had my new red ribbon in my hair. He lowers his voice, so I have to lean in.

'Come and meet me at start of the Berwick Law footpath tonight and I'll bring you something special that you've never seen in your life,' he suggests.

'Never in a million years,' I say. Everyone knows you don't go there at night unless you're up to no guid, and everyone knows that when boys brag of special somethings, they are talking about their pricks.

'I'll be there tonight, waiting anyway,' he says. 'With a treat.'

'Pff, what treats does a poulterer's laddie know of?' I answer, thinking he'll bring another egg, in full expectation of a grope.

He sees the thoughts behind my eyes.

'I'm a gentleman, I promise you that. But have you ever tasted Tipsy Laird?'

As soon as he says it, I can taste it. Cream and whisky and raspberries spring to my tongue. He sees that thought too.

'My ma makes the best. I'll bring a dish of it tonight,' he says. 'Tipsy Laird under the moon. Nine o'clock. Come on, we'll have a laugh.'

Hazel is up the road ahead of me, but I catch her up.

'What was he saying?' she asks.

'Nothing of any importance,' I say.

I take the eggs back to Master Kincaid's kitchen, crack them into a cup, whisk them and drink them. Fresh and thick and yellow. I decide that I will go to Berwick Law. It's about time I did something with a lad.

I leave just before nine, telling Cook I am off out for a walk. She eyes me suspiciously, but says nothing. The sun is setting, bathing the fields pink. The sheep are settling, and the air is high with the first flutter of bats.

Robbie is waiting with a bright candle-lantern and a glass dish and he looks as daft as I feel.

'I thought you wouldn't come,' he says.

'I'm only here for the Tipsy Laird,' I reply.

He lets me eat it all. Och, it is some tasty dish, that Tipsy Laird! I have never supped the like. I end up with cream on my fingers and lick it off each and every one of them, and I think Robbie Bathgate's eyes will pop out of his heid, watching me do that.

'Don't tell Hazel Kincaid about this,' I say. 'In fact, don't you tell anyone.'

'I'll not tell a soul,' he says, looking friskier by the minute. 'Shall we have a bit of a kiss?'

Afterwards, when I get to bed at midnight, my lips tingling from his kisses, I tie a knot in the red ribbon, to keep him true to me. No lass wants to be unwed at twenty-two. Och, Robbie won't want to marry me, what with him being a poulterer's boy and me being the lass of the cunning wifie. But it's worth a try. Ribbon magic is simple enough to do.

19th August 1589
From George Keith, 5th Earl Marischal

To His High and Mighty Majesty, King James the Sixth of Scotland, at Holyroodhouse

Sir – We have safely arrived, and preparations are complete for the proxy ceremony. Your bride is as I remembered from the negotiations: sweet in nature but quite nervous, which is a trait she will have to overcome. Her spoken Scots is still weak, so it was wise to bring Lord Henry, even though we had our doubts about his maturity for such a task. His knowledge of the Danish language appears to be as good as he claimed it to be, for they certainly seem to have no problem in understanding him. Her own chief lady-of-the-bedchamber, a Mistress Kirsten Sørensen, is also fluent. But she has a shrewdness about her that I cannot quite make up my mind about.

We are now in possession of the dowry, which means the ceremony can go ahead and I am most honoured, Your Majesty, to be saying the vows on your behalf.

I enclose details of the Danish fleet, so that you can oversee the preparations for the welcoming parades and make space at Holyroodhouse.

Kissing Your Majesty's hand, I rest ever your most humble servant.

Inventory of the fleet:
Led by Josaphad *(the flagship)*, Gideon, Samson, Joshua, Dragon, Raphael, St Michael, Gabriel, Lille Fortuna, Mouse, Rose, Falcon of Birren, Blue Lion, Blaa Due *and* Hvide Due.

On the Gideon *with Her Royal Highness: Peder Munk, admiral of the fleet.*

Two Danish ambassadors

Her Royal Highness's goldsmith (he will not travel on any other ship, despite offers)

Keeper of Her Royal Highness's wardrobe

One tailor

Three of Her Royal Highness's ladies

Three servants

One small bird, called a canary, in a cage that travels with Her Royal Highness (this was a last-minute request, and I do feel it is necessary to catalogue all livestock in transit, even pets)

The most valuable cargo will be sent on the Raphael:
Six horses

One riding carriage of solid silver with upholstery of gold and purple velvet, to carry you both from the Port of Leith to Holyroodhouse (this is quite a sensational carriage, Your Majesty. I have viewed it myself).

Other sundry items of Her Royal Highness's wardrobe and chambers (a multitude of gowns, slippers, boots, furs and hats; the jewellery is being catalogued separately by the goldsmith).

In addition: I will travel on the Gideon *with Her Royal Highness, as planned, and I will bring Lord*

Henry, and he will use the days at sea to coach Her Royal Highness in the language.

There had been a concern over the seaworthiness of the Gideon, *but our own carpenters have inspected it themselves and have declared it to be in robust shape.*

Chapter Six

ANNA

Kronborg Castle, Denmark
August 1589

We have the proxy ceremony in the chapel at Kronborg, as though it was a real wedding.

They put me in a gold dress of Italian silk with white sleeves. It binds my chest so tight I have to take deep gulps of air when no one is looking. Even my feet pinch, in white silk slippers that squeeze my toes.

'Act sweetly to Earl Marischal,' Kirsten says, as she leads me to the chapel. 'You will be at his side most of the day. But do not get drunk or touch your hair or check your bosom or your skirts. Be *queenly*.'

I ignore her and check my hair and my bosom and my skirts, for I hate being the centre of attention and can't think of anything worse than people finding a fault and whispering about it, and for evermore the story of my handfasting ceremony being about how I showed too much skin and not enough decorum.

We get to the chapel entrance. Earl Marischal stands ahead of us at the altar like a fat ginger cat, his head nestled in a starched white ruff the size of a cartwheel. Oh God, there is no way back for me now.

'Oh, the ruff on him! The Scots look too admiringly on the fashions of the French. We will not get into that habit,' mutters Kirsten, her breath sour with her nerves, before she hands me to Mama, who has come out of mourning dress for first time in the year since Papa's death.

'You are pale,' Mama says. 'Kirsten, have you not noticed how pale she is? Are you worried about the bedding ceremony? He will not touch you, Anna. He is not allowed. It is in the contract.'

I am worried about everything. I did not feel pale until now, but now I do feel pale and breathless and I think I might faint.

'Fetch her a mouthful of fruit wine,' says Mama. 'Loosen her gown.'

All this is done without so much as a murmur, and the Scots at the top of the chapel wait patiently. Finally Mama pinches my cheeks, to bring the colour back. It stings, but I do not cry out. She marches me down the aisle, to Bishop Larsen. He puts my hands in Earl Marischal's hands and binds them with a white ribbon. James and I are handfasted.

I can smell the smoke from the execution clinging to Bishop Larsen's robes.

Afterwards they lead us to a bedchamber, barely used and thick with tapestries and dust. They wait outside, all of them except Henry and Mama, who stand at the door, holding torches.

I am to go on the bed first. Mama glares at me in the particular way she does when I am not allowed to get something wrong. Henry stares at the floor, as if embarrassed to be part of this.

I take off the silk slippers. They are already grey from dirt. I put them neatly on the floor. The bed is on a platform, underneath tasselled curtains the colour of spiders' webs. I have to hoist myself up. Each creak and rustle is amplified. On the other side of the bed Earl Marischal's belly rumbles and he shifts his weight from one foot to the other. Once I am settled, he does the same as me and sees to his boots. He should have started sooner, because they are tightly buckled and he is so portly, and there is much hoisting himself into position and sighing. I wonder if Henry should come and assist him.

Then he clambers onto the bed. The mattress dips. I fix my eyes upon the hangings, ashamed of their grime.

I can feel Mama's glare.

I can feel Henry's embarrassment.

We lie beside each other. Earl Marischal's belly rumbles again and so does mine. I wish I were anywhere else – even at sea – for then at least this humiliation would be over.

Henry clears his throat. 'My lord, I believe the ceremonial act is complete. It has been five minutes,' he says.

Earl Marischal heaves himself into a sitting position. He swings his legs off the bed and stands. He bows.

'Anna of the House of Oldenburg, daughter of King Frederick of Denmark and Norway, you are now handfasted to King James Charles Stuart of Scotland,' he says.

He returns to his boot buckles. Mama is fiddling with the handle of her torch, unused to carrying things. I get off the bed and put on my slippers and walk to the door. When I get there, tears spring to my eyes. Henry notices and I am horrified. He bows.

'May God bless your union,' he says.

'May God bless the union of Denmark and Scotland,' I say.

These are our lines; these are the words we are instructed to say as part of the marriage contract.

As I pass him, he puts his hand on my arm and lowers his voice. 'There is no need for tears. All will be well. You will see.'

That isn't part of the ceremony.

It's the only kind thing anyone has said to me all day.

I have overheard them debating the proxy marriage, Mama and the Privy Councillors: *It's the best way to protect her. She has a thousand miles to travel. If disaster should strike on the voyage, King James will be forced to send assistance. She is safer as his betrothed.*

And Mama: *But it puts her in peril. What if he changes his mind before she gets to Scotland? Or on her arrival? What if she fails the trial? What will become of her then? No other household will want her.*

The reward, they decided, was worth the risk. They think James will fall in love with me, that I will charm him and he will end the trial early and seal the marriage contract. They are taking a gamble it will be straightforward.

In the days that follow the ceremony, the weather turns. You can smell August bracing itself for September. The whiff of gull carcasses and glaciers and the salty tang of the herring flesh drying in the smokehouses. The sky over Øresund is tarnished silver.

The ships' captains and the Scottish representatives have taken to gathering in the chancellery with Admiral Peder Munk, who has just arrived from Copenhagen and is in charge of the Danish fleet; they are talking of the changing weather and the impending voyage and are consulting their almanacs. I hover, trying to overhear when we will sail.

Henry is translating the men's concerns to one another, and I edge closer into the room so that I can hear what's going on.

'So cold it feels like winter's come,' says one freckle-headed man.

'It will lift. It always does at this time of year. We will have a three-week spell of fair weather,' says Admiral Munk. 'It is written here in this chart.' He points to his almanac, which is spread over the table and has the weather predictions for the whole year written into it. 'The university astronomers are certain in their forecasting.'

The Scots murmur, for there is suspicion about the forecasting of weather. 'Feels unseasonable. Unnatural,' one says. Their hands pull at their beards as the servants refresh the wine goblets. There is more talk, which I don't understand, and then Admiral Munk speaks again.

'We can't delay,' he says. 'Edinburgh awaits us with processions and celebration, the like of which it has never produced. And besides, the winds are currently favourable to sail us out of the harbour. I oversee this expedition and my word is final.'

The almanacs are folded back into place.

Denmark sets sail to Scotland when the tide turns, first thing.

We say our farewells on a harbour that is teeming with men and ropes and barrels of pitch. The rest of the fleet is already gliding up the strait, white sails billowing. The Scots' ship will follow behind the *Gideon*, but Earl Marischal and Henry sail with us.

Mama looks so thin and blowy in her ermine cloak that the gulls might take her for one of their own. We do not want a public display of grief, because a crowd has come to watch, so the goodbyes are as formal and stiff as our new leather gloves. The wind whips my tears away, thank God. I am last onto the *Gideon*. It is a vast fifty-two-gun galleon that dominates the fleet. They only get me onto it using firm arms and hoisting. The planks are slippery, and I am so terrified I think I will pass out, and the first thing I do is use a chamberpot. None of that will be in the official account. The maids are the same: terror-struck in fur cloaks that will soon be ruined from the salt water and wind. Already the bottoms of their gowns are gritty with shell fragments and sand.

They are calling my cabin *the stateroom*, although it is anything but stately, with a ceiling so low I can hardly stand up and barely enough room for a bed, a stool and a chest. Aksel's cage is wedged onto a shelf and tied in place with ropes. The cabin has a window with a shutter, and it is on the castle deck at the stern, high above the waterline. My room is next to the deck, and the ship's carpenter has sectioned me off some space for a private balcony, which is about my only luxury for the next ten days. From the balcony I can see Kronborg and the village that stretches behind, with its snug triangle-shaped houses and calm, whitewashed church. This might be the last I will ever see of it.

On the harbour, at a distance from Mama, stands a circle of women in long, dark cloaks and pristine white caps. They are praying for our safe voyage. I watch them for a minute. I can still feel Mama's gloved fingers brushing mine. I hold onto the tingle of it, for soon the sensation of her touch will fade and be replaced by a longing for home.

I'm dressed in a travelling gown of black Genoese satin with frogging down the bodice, and a sketch has been made of me wearing it, which is to become a portrait to remain in Denmark. But the whole outfit is too thin for the weather, and I feel the wind chill me to my bones.

Mama raises her hands to wave to me.

The women lift their heads and follow the direction of her fingers. Their faces are shadowy beneath their caps. I wave to Mama. I wave to the women, and they look at each other as though they do not know what to do: wave or pray or curtsey.

At a distance to the group, standing at the other end of the harbour, is another figure that I have not noticed until now. It is a small, slender woman. She folds her arms in front of her chest. Her hair has escaped her cap and it hangs about her face. She lifts her head and looks at me, stares right into my eyes.

I swear she looks just like the witch Doritte Olsen.

'Kirsten,' I call, 'come quick.' Kirsten appears at my side, a clothes brush in her hand. 'Look down there, at that woman staring up at me.' The sun is bright, giving us a clear view. 'The small one,' I say.

Kirsten gasps. 'It looks like Mistress Olsen,' she cries. The brush drops to the deck.

'It cannot be her,' I say, dread spreading in my chest like a bleeding wound.

'We watched her burn,' whispers Kirsten. She doesn't even retrieve the brush, even though the planks are hardly clean.

The woman continues to look at me, her mouth opening and closing, and I know it is Doritte Olsen now, for her mouth is the same shape and moves in the same way.

'Has the Devil's consort risen?' I ask.

But Kirsten is silent and, as we watch the woman, I hear it again. It starts with a ringing in my ears and the singing of flames: *I curse you; you will never be Queen of Scotland.*

The men begin the manoeuvres that will get us out to sea, with anchors and lines and shouts. We drift from the harbour, the wind catching the sails. Mama waves. I wave back, but my misery at leaving has been replaced by panic.

'Should we not say something? Stop the ship?' I start to feel frantic. I reach for my girdle book, desperate to recite a prayer, a psalm – anything.

'Get a hold of yourself Anna,' Kirsten says. 'What would the Scots think of us if we start to scream about witches now?'

'Well, what will we do?'

'We will go down to lunch, of course. They are serving beef shin and pheasant, with the best wines. A distraction, I think, so that the ladies-in-waiting do not become even more skittish at the realization that we are afloat.'

'Have we both just seen a dead woman risen?' I ask. 'Witches are capable of all sorts of things.'

'They cannot come back from the dead,' Kirsten replies.

We sway to my left and everything tilts. I grasp onto the rail. Kirsten grasps onto my arm.

'The curse has begun,' I say.

'Nonsense,' she answers. 'We are in the sea, that is all. Come inside. The wind is in the sails, and we have begun our voyage. You must be strong, Anna, or you will wilt and fail and be a useless queen.'

She starts to brush my gown, complaining of the salt on it. Her lips are thin and dry and fluttering. They flutter all the way to lunch, half-admonishment, half-prayer, down precarious staircases and through rocking doors, and do not stop until we are seated with the others at a table that is nailed to the floor, on chairs that are nailed to the floor, and we have all been given wine and are gulping it back in a flurry of flushed cheeks and white knuckles, rolling all the while on the swelling tides.

Chapter Seven

KIRSTEN

*The German Sea
September 1589*

Dear God, we must survive this voyage. The weather turned from blustery to wicked just as we were leaving Danish waters and sailing onto the open sea. The captains of the fleet decided to plough through, led by this Admiral Munk creature, who seems determined to drown us. Now it has been nothing but rocking and retching for two days, with gales howling above our heads and waves smashing at the sides of the ship, pitching us sideways in one direction, then sideways in the other, threatening to capsize us. Barrels of ale and cooking oil have leaked, and sea water has got into the dry supplies, spoiling the oatmeal. A box of herring has spilled, and I have seen three rats already. Moving from one compartment to the next is only possible with arms outstretched, clambering uphill. I am frozen to the bone and permanently damp, even in the cabin they have given me, which is far too narrow for comfort, but at least keeps me next to Her Royal Highness in the stateroom.

The worst of it is that we are not even halfway to the Scottish coast, such is the force of this unholy storm. We can barely see the rest of the fleet. Only this last hour has the weather settled, a graveyard-still lull in which the winds have subsided and the relentless knocking and banging have eased. Earl Marischal has been no use, taken to his cabin with the seasickness that afflicts us all. And he is supposed to be protecting us.

Anna is bearing up, only just, but I will say *bearing up superbly* in my correspondence to her mama, for it's my hope that my letter will be sent when we arrive at Leith Port and will reach Kronborg before she worries herself to death about the success of this handfasting. In truth, Anna is shrinking to a shadow, refusing everything but ships' biscuits, even though there are stocks of every food she could wish for. She will need to do better than this. She can't behave like a child any longer. And that damnable canary is not helping, for he hops incessantly around his cage, giving her even more of the jitters.

There will be an inquiry into this sailing when we are on dry land, if we ever get there. It should never have been allowed to happen.

But I don't think I could have waited a minute longer.

I must get to Scotland.

They need me. They have no idea how dangerous things are getting.

It is mid-morning and the calmest weather yet. I am trying to keep to our normal routine as much as possible. I have coaxed Anna out of the stateroom to stretch her legs down on the main deck and to look at the swirling seas. She has lost the clammy look of the past few days, but remains pale and is still wrapped in the mink cloak that she has refused to be parted from since the minute the weather turned.

'Has the storm eased? Have we seen the last of it?' she asks, her words almost whipped away by the wind.

'I am not an astronomer,' I say. 'I have no idea, but I trust God will save our souls.'

Her eyes are dark and pained, her face childlike without her lace collars and pearls.

'They should never have burned Doritte Olsen,' she says. 'It only made her angrier.'

'Enough of that,' I say firmly. There is no use encouraging her. Doritte Olsen is dead. Burned to ashes. Not lurking at ports. Anna must come to realize that fantastical things are simply not possible. She will learn, in time. But it must come from her own experience of life, just as it did in mine.

Anna turns her head. The young Scot, Henry, Lord Roxburgh, has joined us on the deck, the one who fancies himself as a tutor indeed. As if a spell cloistered away at the University of Copenhagen will have taught him anything as useful as my time in Scotland. He comes at us as if we were long-lost friends.

'Your Royal Highness,' he cries, his hair billowing around him, 'So glad to see you up and about.' His Danish has a thick Scots accent.

'It's a relief to be in the fresh air and not thrown about below deck,' Anna replies.

'We can't stay out here too long,' I warn him. 'We were merely stretching our legs.'

'I've heard they are opening the dining room. Perhaps we should go down together,' he says.

I open my mouth to refuse him, as we have not perfumed ourselves or organized gowns, or done anything of that nature, but Anna speaks first.

'I would enjoy that,' she says. 'I've been cooped up too long.'

And with that, we are escorted down to the dining room, and it matters not a bit what I think.

We sit down to salted goose and plum stew. The plates are pewter, so they won't smash. They water jugs are wooden, so they can't crack. I can only hope that it all remains on the table long enough for us to eat, and doesn't end up sliding to the floor. Earl Marischal is still nowhere to be seen and I wonder how he even made the journey to Denmark, if his sea legs are so feeble. The maids have emerged from their cabins like hatched chicks, damp and wobbly and very unkempt, despite making something of an effort with their dress.

They sit at the bottom of the dining table, a meek ruffle of crumpled silks, nibbling on breadcrumbs and blinking in the gloom, conversing with the tailor and the goldsmith. I will have to keep my eye on them, for etiquette has been blown out of the window, but we cannot let *familiarities* develop on this voyage, even if our bunks are in close quarters and we have all seen each other's vomit-pails. We must try to remain civilized. Anna and I sit with Henry and Admiral Munk. Even the admiral looks shaken.

'I'm afraid this has been one of the worst storms I've ever endured,' he says, chewing on his stew with no great appetite.

'How is the ship bearing up?' asks Henry. 'It feels like it's taken a hammering.'

A fraught expression crosses Admiral Munk's face. 'It's leaking. A small leak,' he adds hastily. 'And it has been patched up. But we need to be able to dock soon, to have it properly repaired.'

Anna's knife clatters to the floor. 'A leak? I thought the

Gideon was unsinkable. That's what Mama said. That's what her secretary said. That's what *you* said, Admiral Munk.'

Henry retrieves the knife and makes a great show of getting her another one. The admiral puts his fingers to his temples and shakes his head.

'I had hoped it would weather the seas better than this,' he says. 'But the sails have taken a battering as well. The crew are working flat out on the repairs.'

'When will we reach Scotland?' asks Anna.

'We are delayed, but if this weather holds, we will be there in a week,' he replies.

'And if it doesn't?' I ask.

'If it doesn't, we are safer heading to shelter in Norway. It's quicker, and you are its royal princess,' he says grimly.

The weather doesn't hold.

The wind rises again as soon as we have finished our meal. If I was a superstitious woman, I would say we are cursed.

'It's time for us to go back to our cabins,' I comment as the maids retreat to theirs, wobbling their curtseys and looking green about the gills again. They can take out their prayer books and lie in their hammocks, and I would rather they did that than talk to the gentlemen.

'Not yet. I am feeling a little better and I wish to study with Lord Henry,' says Anna. 'We've lost quite a lot of time already, and I'm quite happy to try for a half-hour or so and see what the weather does.'

She says it meekly but defiantly. If we were not in company, I might have stood up and glared at her until she obeyed. Instead I pour myself a wine and sit with them as they settle themselves down and begin to converse about Edinburgh.

Lord Henry has a way of talking that makes me almost forget that we are still at sea. He draws a map with his words, explaining what Anna will see when she arrives. From the raucous Port of Leith, crammed with sailing ships and inns, to the marshy loch beneath the castle, which freezes over in the winter. From the Lawn Market, where cloth is sold in every hue and tenement smoke hangs above the rooftops, to the Canongate tennis courts and cock-fighting pits and merchants' houses. The east-coast winds. The morning fog. I sip my wine. Each word takes me back – so vividly I feel myself blink back the tears. *Almost there.*

I confess I am most lost in my thoughts until a great lurch causes us almost to topple backwards. The dining-room door swings open, and at first I think it is the ship pitching again, but then I realize it is Admiral Munk himself.

'Ladies, my apologies, but I must send you to your cabins. I'm afraid we are in for another storm, and the leak is worse. A great fog has come down upon us and we have no alternative but to make for Ánslo Port. Some of the fleet may continue to Scotland, but not the *Gideon* – it is not safe. The leak needs mended urgently. God help us all.'

9th September 1589
From Andrew Drummond,
Harbourmaster at the Port of Leith, Scotland

To His High and Mighty Majesty, King James the Sixth of Scotland, at Holyroodhouse

It is with the deepest regret that I must inform you of a calamity in the Firth of Forth that has resulted in the death of your most respected courtier Mistress Jane Kennedy and her maid Susannah Kirkcaldy. As instructed by Your Majesty, we were preparing to welcome them off the Burntisland ferryboat at the Port of Leith this afternoon, ahead of the arrival of Anna of Denmark, but the boat was carried off in a most ferocious gale whilst midway under sail and collided with another vessel with such force that the boat sank, with the loss of sixty souls. Investigations are ongoing. I am issuing a Notice to Mariners warning against entering the German Sea, as the weather continues to be hazardous.
With the deepest of sympathy, and forever in Your Majesty's service.

Chapter Eight

JURA

North Berwick, Scotland
September 1589

We first hear of the sea-storm when we're told to get to our knees and pray for the safety of the king's bride. The winds that have wiped out summer and whipped North Berwick these last days blow all the way out to the German Sea. That's the sea between Denmark and Scotland, Master Kincaid says. I've never seen a map, so I couldnie agree nor disagree.

He bolts home from an urgent kirk meeting and stands, dripping wet, in the hall whilst he calls us all – family and servants – into the best room, the pristine, bright-windowed parlour at the front of the house. That's the room with the candlesticks that I have to polish till they gleam. The room where I always feel a right untidy dollop.

The king has ordered all of Scotland to pray for the souls of the passengers of the Burntisland ferryboat who perished in the gale that now sweeps across the sea where his bride sails.

Sixty people drowned. One of them was a noblewoman who was going to be a lady-in-waiting to Princess Anna. I cannie imagine it. I think of them clinging onto the ferryboat for dear life, as I kneel behind Master Kincaid, tucking my head as far away from his feet as I can. They pong like the dining room when the lid has been kept off the cheese plate too long.

The wind and rain rattle at the windows. I think of Princess Anna floating like kelp, surrounded by drowning servants. I flip the foreign name of her home over and over in my mouth, like a fish turning in the tide. Is she hanging on tight to the last shards of her ship? She's just a bairn, but she's got the world at her feet. Is she mibbie dead already? Or is she basking in the calm after the storm, puffing her skirts around her legs, feeling the wind on her skin?

'Lord, watch over Princess Anna so that she may come to our shores and please our king,' says Master Kincaid, lifting his words in the sing-song way he only does in the parlour, or for God.

I study his stockinged feet. Small and thin. I cannie see his hands, but they are the same. Yesterday Master Kincaid's hands became too familiar to me. I felt the bony poke of them.

'Lord be with the mariners, Lord be with Her Royal Highness,' Master Kincaid chants.

I cannie help the lost souls, but I can help Princess Anna. I will do a charme to help her. I will take a smooth white pebble to the beach and dip it in the sea, to send calm water to meet her fleet and guide it safely to Leith. Then I'll bring my stone back and place it with the red ribbon.

Then I'll have to think of a charme to keep Master Kincaid away. He has come too close. Yesterday he asked me to bring him supper in his study. When I took the tray in, careful not to spill the pottage and the ale, he watched me place it ever so carefully on his desk. As I left, he stood up and followed me to the door. When we got there, he put his hand on my wrist. His fingers were cool. My wrist was hot and throbbing, showing my nerves. His fingers ran up my arm as he spoke.

'I've not made up my mind about you yet, Mistress Craig.'

I stepped away from him, as delicately as I could, and curtseyed and closed the door behind me. But he will do that again. And worse. Calamitous as these rising winds.

'Amen. Rise now,' says Master Kincaid.

We all rise. Himself, Guidwife Kincaid, Hazel. Then Betsy, Cook and me. We brush down our clothes and cast our eyes up and down one another. We are not often forced together like this, family and servants.

'We will have water for supper – nothing more,' he says. 'We will fast until tomorrow to add intention to our prayers.'

Guidwife Kincaid and Hazel flinch. Hazel looks to her mother with a plea in her eyes.

Master Kincaid sees it. 'Those are the king's orders,' he says. 'And we are a loyal household. Loyal to the king and devout to God.'

We all nod, for how could we not?

I'll get something from the pantry later. It's a Tuesday, so there's ham. The master and the king are fools for thinking fasting will save Princess Anna – God forgive me for saying it. Only the old spells will work in times like these, the charmes that our mothers taught us, and their mothers before them. The secrets women whisper to each other in order to survive.

Hazel has been asking me to do the poultice, but I haven't had a minute yet and we don't want to get caught. They won't like seeing us making a fuss over her face. A girl should not be bothered by a patch of flaking skin when there is so much suffering in the world.

The small looking glass in the hallway is the only looking glass in the whole house; enough to make sure the Kincaids are tidy before they go out, but not big enough to encourage vanity. There's another one hidden away, though. The wee oval hand-mirror Hazel keeps in her top drawer, underneath her copy of the Scottish psalter. A secret market purchase, no doubt, for it is a cheap looking glass with a thin wooden handle and a slender wooden frame, but I say nothing, for I shouldn't have been keeking in her drawer in the first place.

A few days later, when the Kincaids are busy with a supper visit from the minister, Hazel calls me into her chamber and shows me how bad her forehead is getting. Her skin is red, with white patches that look like fish scales. I run and fetch the oats and honey and a cup of milk.

'Wear it tonight,' I tell her, pasting the mixture onto her skin and covering it with a napkin under her cap.

'Will that fix it by morning?' She looks anxious.

'We will speed it up with a trick,' I say. 'I'll inscribe some signs on the floorboards under your bed. No one will see them. But they will help draw out the badness.'

I take the chalk stone and draw the marks that Ma taught me, the ones she would use if I had a fever. They show the selkies where to come. You see, this is the thing with healing: we can all pray to God for our souls, but God is busy and mibbie He's not got the time to answer all our prayers. That's where the selkies and the sprites and the fairies come in. They'll take one look at Hazel Kincaid and whisper their magic to her.

Hazel helps me move her bed and watches agog as I inscribe the marks. Circles and arrows, and other special signs.

'If it works, I'll give you a pair of my silk gloves,' she announces. 'An old pair, of course.'

'Of course,' I say. 'Now hush whilst I say some magic words too.' Magic words make things work better. Ma taught me.

'Whatever it takes,' she says.

So I say them, half-prayer and half-song, with my hands on her arms. The way Ma did it. Asking God to heal, and requesting the selkies to help Him.

Hazel watches me, her eyes growing wider and darker than I have ever seen them before, her arms trembling. She understands the magic, even though she has likely never been taught any of it in her life – not in this house. But she senses it. I can feel her flesh sing with it.

I say nothing about Robbie Bathgate. It's obvious to me that she wants to look bonnie for the boys, mibbie for him, as she blushed so hard at the poultry stall. Not my fault if he prefers me.

Robbie only brought Tipsy Laird the once, but he still brings himself. If you want a laddie to think serious about you, you must never let him touch you under your wylie-coat. You must make him wait for it and anticipate it, and chase you until he'll do anything for you, even asking to marry you. That's what Ma said. She wasn't only guid for charmes, Ma. She knew the ways of laddies, too, having helped plenty a lassie who'd let a laddie under her wylie-coat. I'd hear her dish out the advice when she handed out the herbs to make them unpregnant. Robbie's met me five times now. Mibbie he might be thinking seriously about me.

I leave at the usual time. Cook ignores me as I slip out of the back door. Mibbie she once had a laddie too. I march across the fields, the autumn gale swirling around me, making the trees sing and the bushes rattle. I tighten the ribbons of my bonnet against the rain. The smooth white pebble, for the sea-charme, is in my hand.

Robbie's in our usual spot, sheltering under the rowan, his lantern at his feet. We used to talk a bit, and I liked that a lot. Now he just moves close in and starts the kissing. We are both soaked through with the rain already.

'Not so fast,' I say, shrugging him off. 'Master Kincaid's been lurking around me. I need to get him out of my head.'

'Och, I'm nothing like old Baillie Kincaid,' he replies, trying to take my hand. He finds the smooth white pebble in my palm and looks at it, puzzled. Examines it in the lantern light. 'Carrying pebbles now,' he says. 'What's the point of that?'

'It's for Princess Anna,' I tell him.

He frowns. 'She needs prayers, not pebbles. They say she's guid as deid.'

'This'll help,' I whisper. 'I'm going to dip it in the sea tonight and the calming magic will reach her ship.'

He hands the pebble back, as if it were hot. 'Don't meddle with that sort of thing,' he says.

I laugh. 'I know what I'm doing,' I say.

He looks at me strangely.

'It's true what they said about your Ma, then, that she could make magical things happen. That she wasn't just a healer. Is it true she gave away her teeth to a sprite, so she could have special powers?'

I laugh. 'I have never heard that one,' I say. 'The tooth-puller took her teeth when they were rotten.'

But his kissing is half-hearted after that, like the pebble has lodged in his chest. He leaves when the wind whips up even harder and the rowan whistles with it.

'Too foul to be out tonight,' he says. 'I'm away to my bed. See you tomorrow.'

But I have a funny feeling he won't come. The feeling sits on my shoulders all the way from Berwick Law down to the beach. I dip my pebble and do my charme and hope it reaches the Danish princess: *Stones for safe travels, especially smooth ones.* Her safe journey, and mine too – my journey at the Kincaids'. A household of secrets and fearful prayers, and Master Kincaid presiding over it all, waiting to pounce.

Chapter Nine

ANNA

To Ánslo Port
September 1589

I have given myself over to Fate. They say we are retreating from the storm, but it hasn't felt like that today. It's felt as though the storm has chased us. As if it were actually alive. A creature that can see us and smell our fear, and that grows angrier with every prayer we send up. It lives in the sky and in the sea, tossing gannets and gulls and dolphins and whales in a fury of foam. And I know who rides that creature, seated on its back and howling with laughter. The witch Doritte Olsen!

I have not seen Admiral Munk since yesterday, but the messages that have come back from him, via Kirsten, are that he has steered us through a tempest and blinding fog, and that the weather-forecasting almanacs were sorely wrong. A *tempest*. Until now, that is a word I have only read in books. But now I have lived it. This afternoon hail pelted us like cannonfire. We are not far from land, they say; we are making our way to Ánslo Port and it feels calmer tonight than it did this afternoon, but you can drown even in shallow waters – everyone knows that.

The storm may be lessening, but the leak is not. It's in the hull. They're pumping bilge non-stop to keep us afloat. They're scraping and tarring day and night to strengthen the joints between the boards. I know that, not from the admiral, but from the crew. I can hear them shouting. I have seen the ship's apprentices crying in fear for their lives. I am an expert in eavesdropping and spying. You have to be, when you live in a castle and people only ever tell you what they want you to hear.

It is almost midnight and Kirsten has managed to snatch some sleep. I know, because her cabin is so close I can hear her snore, agitatedly, amid the clank of metal on wood and the whip of sailing cloth on the masts above us. She will not sleep for long. She is like me, catching a few hours here and there and then being dragged from dreams by the shouts of the deck crew as they reef and furl the masts or clear the spill of the waves, trying to avoid being washed overboard. This morning a sailor fell from the rigging. I heard his sickly screams. Kirsten said they sent a boat out to rescue him, but I know she was lying, to stop me getting agitated again.

Aksel has jumped and twittered all night, refusing his treats, and finally tucked his head under his wing in a puff of exhaustion, but I can't sleep. I'm desperate to stretch my legs. They feel stiff and creaky and my back hurts. It has been claustrophobic being in this cabin all day. I've barely been able to step out on the balcony because of the weather. The admiral occupies a far grander cabin further towards the stern, with his own day-room, and I am sure if I were King James's real wife, I would have been given that one. I cannot abide a minute longer in here. Even a walk on the castle deck would give me some air, and no one will ever know. Everyone will be tucked into their bunks.

I pull on a pair of boots and wrap myself in my mink cloak. I unlock my door and step out onto the deck, where the air is immediately wild. But I have found my sea legs, because I can walk without stumbling now, spreading my weight through my feet when I need to steady myself. The whole ship is illuminated by the bruised skies.

The castle deck towers above the main deck and is less busy, with only a few crewmen who see me but don't say anything. The Danish royal party is lodged in cabins on one side, and the Scots on the other. On the main deck below are the doctor and the tailors, and the goldsmith and the ship's carpenter. Below them, in dormitories slung with hammocks, Kirsten says, are the servants and the ship's crew. I walk to the very end of the deck. I find a bench and dry it with my shawl, then sit down on it.

'Your Royal Highness?' It is a question, as though the speaker does not believe his eyes. I know who it is, even in this darkness, because the words are spoken in Danish with a Scottish accent.

'Lord Henry,' I say. Our formalities sound so small and insignificant out here, on the dark sea.

'Are you sure you should be out here alone?'

I laugh. 'I've survived so far.'

He stands stock-still. I can feel his awkwardness, even in the shadows. The way he holds his breath.

'You may sit,' I say.

He sits down gingerly on the bench beside me, taking care not to come too close. I feel the weight of him as he settles on the seat.

'The leak's no better,' I tell him. 'It's the damage from the storm.'

'I've heard,' he says. 'I've tried talking to Admiral Munk about it, but he just keeps saying everything will be all right, and that we'll arrive in Ánslo in the next day or so, where they can repair it properly.'

'Do you believe him?' I ask.

'No, I don't,' Henry says. 'I think he is the worst sea captain I have ever had the misfortune to risk my life with. Last night I thought I might die.'

No man has ever talked so frankly to me. It is a strange, liberating feeling.

'Well, we're still alive now. And you said you'd tell me about court,' I remind him.

'Ah yes. Well, if we do survive this sailing, you will be wonderful at court, so have no fear of that.'

'That's what everyone says,' I tell him. 'But what is the king really like? How best can I please him? How well do you know him?'

Henry shifts his legs, sniffs. 'I know him well,' he says. 'He's been calling on me quite a lot for tuition, as he's keen to learn a few Danish words. He likes to know everything about the world. He'll be intrigued if you can keep him occupied with stories of Denmark. And he is as devout as a kirk minister. He is God's servant on Earth and everything he does is in His name. He will be guided by prayer in all things.'

Well, that's more than Mama or Kirsten has ever told me.

Henry sniffs again. I think he's holding something back.

'I pray frequently that I will pass this marriage trial,' I say, and then I feel embarrassed for being so honest.

'It must be a unique kind of anguish,' he replies. 'Being put on trial like this.'

There is something in the softness of his words that makes tears spring to my eyes. I can't let him know I am upset. He will think I am forever weeping and wailing.

'It's the will of the king, and therefore the will of God, that we are handfasted first,' I say, repeating Mama and Kirsten and the Privy Council.

'Do you know where the handfasting tradition comes from?' asks Henry, his tone brightening. 'It's an ancient Scots custom that a man will take a woman as his wife and keep her for up to a year and a day. If she pleases him, he will marry her and legitimize any children conceived during that time.'

I could almost laugh, were it not so awful.

'And if she does not please him?'

He sighs.

'Is she banished with her bastard? Or sent to a convent? Can she handfast again or is she spoiled?' There is something about the cold, velvety blackness of the night that has given me an edge.

'It rarely goes wrong,' he says. 'All parties usually remain smitten. And I think he'll be utterly smitten with you. If I were King James, I would be so smitten I would marry you on the spot. I would not need to pray over it. Not even for a minute.'

'Oh,' I gasp. He should not say things like that.

'I would never ask you to suffer a handfasting,' he adds. 'I would be honoured that you would even consider being my wife.'

'I don't think you should talk like that,' I say.

'Forgive me,' Lord Henry says.

I am relieved I can't see his face properly, and he can't see mine.

'I think it's time for me to go back to my cabin,' I say.

He stands, saying nothing, and accompanies me back. I hug my cloak around me as I negotiate the deck and the rails and the narrow stairs. At my cabin door he wishes me goodnight and leaves. I stand in the cabin. It must be well after midnight. Yet I am as wide awake as I have ever been.

Chapter Ten

JURA

North Berwick, Scotland
September 1589

Robbie Bathgate has lost interest in me. Master Kincaid has not.

We are doing a Great Wash this week. Today we were laundering sheets and napkins in a tub kept by the stream beside the house. My hands are ruined from the water and the soft soap and the paddling. The rain has hammered non-stop, so we have had to bring the washing in to hang drookit by the fires, and the whole house is steamed up.

The master has been out all day rounding up debtors for the jail. He returns, and I hear him telling the guidwife it has been a long day and he is ready for a decent meat supper. But Cook has not had the time, as she was needed for the laundering, and all we're having is oat pottage; and my nerves jangle from the raised voices as he complains about that.

After we have fed the Kincaids, and tidied up after them, we servants have our supper in the hot, wet kitchen, then Betsy sends me up to bed early as she says I look wabbit and I have another long day tomorrow, with the washing of the ruffs and wylie-coats.

I am climbing the stairs, dragging my heavy legs, when I

spy Master Kincaid on the landing. Hanging there like a ghost. With the slightest tilt of his head, he points me into his study. I walk in, a feeling of dread creeping over me. A tablecloth hangs by his study fire, looking like a ship's discarded mast.

'Did you launder that?' He is looking at me over his eyeglasses.

'I did, sir, in lye soap.'

'It is marked still,' he says, showing me a faint stain that has been there for as long as I have worked at the Kincaids'. It looks to have been flat-ironed in, over the years.

'It's hard to get everything clean,' I say. 'I will try again tomorrow.'

'Cleanliness is next to godliness,' he says. 'But some people are too far from godliness ever to be entirely clean.' He takes off his eyeglasses and places them in his desk. Then he sits in his chair.

'Can I go, sir?' I ask. 'It's been a long day.'

'In a moment,' he says. 'But first there's an opportunity, if you care to consider it.'

'Consider what?' I enquire, confused. My head buzzes. I was exhausted a minute ago, but now I'm wide awake. The room is awful still, save for the rattle of his breathing and the soft tick of the clock.

'Consider giving me some extra assistance,' he says. 'With a personal matter.'

'What personal matter?' Surely he is not going to suggest some sort of hoorish behaviour? There are harlots aplenty down at the ferryboat dock for that. But he does, the auld divvil. And he doesn't even blush.

'You are a healer, are you not?' he says, his voice low and hoarse. 'That's what the mistress says of you. That your old ma had a magical way about her and that you likely do too.'

'Do you ail, Master Kincaid?' I say, looking at the door, desperate to get out or for the mistress to come and interrupt.

'I do ail, Mistress Craig. And you are no more a natural housemaid than I am. The ways do not come easily to you. You're clumsy and unkempt, and you leave stains and your fires smoke.'

'I think I am a decent enough housemaid,' I tell him. 'Betsy is pleased with my work. The mistress never complains.'

He shrugs. 'One word from me and you'll be back with your drunkard of a pa. Och, don't look so surprised – I've made enquiries about you. Now perhaps you'll think on that. And in the meantime, I ail, as you say. I've had a bad week and there is a pent-up energy within me, and there's a coin on the desk if you can give me a quick cure. Healing hands. Do you have them?'

'Do you mean to give me the boot from this job, if I don't do as you say?' I am flabbergasted at Master Kincaid.

'You are better in my guid books than in my bad books,' he replies, unbuttoning his breeches.

I take the coin to the market. First, to see if Robbie Bathgate is there and hasn't dropped off a cliff; and second, to try to get rid of the coin, for it feels dirty just owning it. And since the thing in the study happened, I have not been at peace with myself.

Master Kincaid said nothing afterwards, merely fussed at himself with a kerchief and buttoned his breeches up, and put his eyeglasses on and went back to his papers. But it was in his silence that I realized he means to carry on like that. As though my healing, as he called it, has now become another of my chores.

I feel like I want to kill Master Kincaid, and mibbie I should. But rather than do that, I need something to kill his passion.

Before I get to market, I sit on the beach again and think of Ma and what she might say, if ever she knew what happened in Master Kincaid's study. For that's not what she spent all those years teaching me charmes for. No, she did not. If Ma had known about Master Kincaid, first she would have given me a hiding for being so daft as to let him open his breeches in front of me, then she would have put something in a posset that causes impotence and made sure he drank every drop. And then she would have told me to leave the Kincaids' and go elsewhere. But there will be a hundred Master Kincaids wherever I go, won't there? The only person I know who doesn't live in North Berwick is Aunt Mary, Ma's sister, who moved to the Canongate years ago. I wouldn't even know where to find her.

At a loss about what to do, I dip my pebble into the sea again, to send more calm waters to Princess Anna and calming thoughts to me.

The market teems with the high stink of ferry passengers and fishwives and pottery-sellers. Robbie is at his stall, bold as brass, but when he sees me, he looks away and won't catch my eye and I am flooded with shame.

'I've not seen you at the Law,' I say, feeling small.

'Been busy at the farm. Been too tired to walk out at night,' he replies. He doesn't look tired. He looks as bright as the comb on one of his fat hens.

'Have you stopped wanting to come?' I ask, trying to ignore the guidwives at my back, pushing in.

Robbie's fingers trace the tops of the eggs. He nods.

'Sorry,' he says.

The guidwives nudge me out of the way with their bosoms and their thick arms. Robbie hands them their eggs, relieved at the distraction. I suddenly feel like smashing the lot with my bare hands. Ruining them, like he has ruined my lips and my hopes. I feel like setting his hens free from their cages. But I don't do that. Instead I drift away from him, feeling sickened at the way his feelings have changed. It's because I'm the girl of the cunning wife. I have her mark. I will never be like Hazel Kincaid or the good girls at kirk.

I stop at the haberdasher's stall again. They have a new coloured ribbon I haven't seen before. Purple. It looks like a stormy night. It resembles a bruise. It looks exactly how I feel. It's expensive. I buy it anyway.

Then I go to the apothecary man. Most of what he sells are nonsense potions, but I tell him I need something strong to settle the humours.

'Something to purge or something to lower the bile?' he asks, running his knobbly fingers across the tops of his bottles and jars. 'I'll give you a bottle of this.' He picks up something that looks like cattle dung.

I open the stopper and the unmistakable whiff of cow shit hits my nostrils. 'Did you scrape that off a farmyard floor?' I snort, my eyes watering. 'I'm not an idiot. Have you anything decent at all?'

'Dried dung is a known emetic,' he says, lifting his filthy-looking hat and scratching at a boil on his head. 'Cures all ills.'

'I need something to calm the temperament,' I say, ignoring the grime under his fingernails. I pick up the bottles myself, trying to make out what's inside them. He has all manner of horrors trapped in these, from dead ladybirds to white powders and piss.

'Ground unicorn horn. Dragon's scales. Scotch mist,' he says, waving at his wares.

I inspect the herbs and bulbs laid out on his table, for there are not many lies you can tell about a plant.

He picks up a few small brown bulbs. 'These cleanse the blood, if boiled and mashed into a thick paste,' he says. 'They bring all ungodliness to a head. One to two spoonfuls will do it.'

I am not sure whether he knows what he's talking about, but I know my ma did charmes with bulbs. She swore by them. Said all the energy of a plant is in there: *Bulbs and seeds are nature's essence. Past, present and future in the palm of your hand.*

'I'll take these,' I say.

The next day is another hectic one, with Cook in a strop about mould on the parsnips. On top of all that, it is my time of the month. I have tied a knot in my new purple ribbon, hoping a charme will ease the flow a bit.

'We are short of eggs again,' complains Cook, coming in from the hen-house looking flustered and empty-handed. 'How can I bake anything today? The guidwife wants a fruitcake. Jura, go over to Bathgate's farm and fetch a dozen. I need to get this cake in the oven by four.'

I spend the twenty-minute walk praying I won't see Robbie, for he will think I am chasing him, and I am not that daft. But it is a bad day, so of course he is the first person I spy as I approach the farmhouse. He looks busy enough, carrying two pails, but he stops when he sees me and puts them on the ground.

'I've been sent for eggs,' I say, making it clear I am not

interested in him by the sullen look on my face, although truth be told, when he fixes his eyes on me and sweeps back his hair, I feel a horrible tug of longing.

'How many?' he asks, looking me up and down.

I realize how grubby my pinny is, and how limp and greasy my hair must look.

I give the order and my basket and the money, and Robbie tells me to wait where I am. I stand at the gatepost and look at the bonnie farm his da owns. Fields as far as the eye can see. Sheep grazing on the top meadow, under a line of old oak trees. The whitewashed farmhouse has smoke billowing from the chimney, over a snug slate roof. Robbie Bathgate has everything. He returns with the eggs. I check each one for cracks, for the last thing I want is a telling-off from Cook.

'They are all guid,' he says. 'And fresh.'

'I won't take your word for it,' I answer. 'For your word is not worth much, is it?'

He sniffs. I finish checking the eggs and arrange the cloth over them. I pat it into place with my fingertips.

'What was that you did?' he asks, nodding to my hand.

'Nothing,' I say, puzzled. 'Just tucking in the eggs for the journey.'

'Did you do a charme on them, to stop them breaking?'

'Don't be daft, Robbie. You don't need charmes for everything.'

'Daft?' He grunts at me. 'It's not me who's daft, tempting the Divvil with inchantments and charmes.'

'I have no time for the Divvil,' I retort, raising my voice, 'when I have my own worries, with you asking me up to Berwick Law one day, then ignoring me the next.'

'Away with you. Shoo!' he shouts back, as if I am nothing but a pest come foraging amongst his precious livestock.

'Oh, curse you, Robbie Bathgate!' I yell, kicking over one of his pails, watching with satisfaction as corn spills all over the ground and leaving him trying to scoop it back up. I return as hastily to Master Kincaid's as I can, without damaging the damned eggs.

Chapter Eleven

ANNA

Ánslo, Norway
September 1589

We wash up in Ánslo Port, to the stares of its harbourmen, the *Gideon* a giant curiosity teeming with Danish and Scottish flags and a wretched crew and passengers. The port is high with ships' masts and traders' crates and every strain of fish-stench, from fresh to rotten.

The harbourmaster and Admiral Munk do not spend long in discussion and we are waved urgently to disembark. When my feet finally touch dry land, the relief is a cold, hard slap. I would sink to my knees and thank God, were it not for the fact that the ground is slick with filthy water and the harbourmen are staring in disbelief, and pandemonium is ensuing as everyone scrabbles off the ship.

Ánslo is bright with the promise of a harsh winter coming. The air has a sharpness I have never felt before. Kirsten and I are shown into the harbourmaster's office and served *akvavit* and given blankets for warmth. Messengers are sent to find us lodgings and alert the mayor.

I sit down on a rickety wooden chair at the desk, exhausted. My eyes are dry with sea-air. Kirsten stalks the small, dark room.

'You must write to James,' she says, pushing a quill and parchment towards me. 'We will get letters sent on the next ship out. Hopefully they will find a vessel here that does not leak like a sieve.'

'Have I failed the marriage trial, do you think? If I couldn't even get to him?' It is all I can think of, again. Now that we have truly abandoned our voyage.

'Nonsense. He will be worried to death about you and will think you very brave.' But Kirsten is taut, her eyes swivelling about the room, taking in its maps and charts, as if to try to find a way back to Scotland herself.

She goes off to find out how best we might get my letter to Leith Port, and I set myself up to write, but my hands tremble and I don't know how to start.

The door opens again and I think she must be back, but when I look up, it is Henry.

'Are you all right?' he asks. 'The mayor is on his way. Are you writing to His Majesty?'

'I'm trying, but I don't know my own situation yet, so what can I even say?'

'Shall I help?'

I think, momentarily, about telling him I don't need his help. Which is true, because I have no need of anyone's assistance when it comes to letter-writing. But actually I want Henry here. So I nod, and let him fetch a chair and sit down beside me. Our arms are almost brushing and I know, beyond any doubt, that beneath his thick coat his arm is firm and broad. We both stare at the blank parchment.

'Reassure the king,' Henry says. 'Explain that we did indeed endure a perilous crossing, but that we turned back for our safety, and now we are all in great spirits in Ánslo.'

'Will I tell him about the leak?'

'Not yet; he will learn about that from Earl Marischal. Tell him how quickly everyone came to assist us.'

I nod.

'And tell him how desperate you are to see him. To embrace him.'

We both catch our breaths at the same time, and there is a pause that fills the room. Outside are the faint cries of harbour-men and although I can't hear it, I can feel the creamy swill of the tide.

I can feel heat radiating from Henry's arm. I imagine what it would be like to touch his skin. I think I know what desperate means, now.

The spell is broken when Kirsten returns, bringing a blast of the port in with her through the door. Henry stands up immediately.

'You can write your letter tonight,' she says, eyeing him with the narrowest of glares. 'We're being taken up to the mayor's residence, the Bishop's Palace, and we can stay there for as long as necessary. Come.'

She stands at the door, impatient.

'I'm sorry I can't help you with your letter,' Henry says.

I'm not sorry. I'm glad it's still blank. If I had written a single word on that parchment, it would have been as though James was in the room, standing between us.

Kirsten and I, our maids, Earl Marischal and Henry are all to stay at the Bishop's Palace. Other beds have been begged across town, and the sailing crew will remain on the ship. A captain heading for the port of London tomorrow with a cargo of timber and hides has been persuaded to divert to Leith with our messages.

Trunks of my gowns and undergarments and hairpins and fans, and even Aksel and his cage, have been unloaded from the *Gideon* and carted up the short road – the life I had imagined would be happening at Holyroodhouse unravelling like a dropped spool of thread.

This is what failure feels like. It feels like watching wooden boxes being dragged up a hill that you never knew existed until this week. It feels like the inconvenience of others writ large on their faces. It feels like fear.

The Bishop's Palace is a new large, white building with a high-pitched roof. It stands in sprawling woodlands with gardens to the front and a lake at the back. Mayor Mule, tall and neat and bespectacled, does not know what to do with his unexpected twist of fate and has been falling over himself to be as polite as possible, whilst disguising his discomfort at having his home overtaken.

'Thank God we did not end up somewhere awful,' Kirsten says. We have been settled in a large high-ceilinged room with more windows than I can count, and given a supper of onion soup and ale, spared having to join the Scots and the Danish ambassadors and Mayor Mule, who are gathered in the ballroom deliberating over our next steps. Aksel flutters around his cage, bewildered once again at another new home. He wants out. I can't blame him. I've finally managed to write a letter to James.

'You should hand your letter to the captain yourself,' Kirsten says. 'To be certain it gets to Leith Port. We should walk down to the ship tomorrow.'

'Should we go out walking?' I ask. 'Anything might happen.'

'Nothing will happen,' she says, irritated. She stands up and throws a blanket over Aksel's cage to quieten him.

'Why can't we just hand my letter to Mayor Mule's secretary?

It can go with the rest of the bundle being written by the Scots.'

'I should like to get my land-legs back,' she replies. 'And then, after we have made sure the letter is in the captain's hands, we could explore Ánslo a little. I saw a small square when we came up this afternoon that looked as if it might have shops.'

'We mustn't be seen to be *enjoying* ourselves, Kirsten. We are in the midst of a crisis here.'

'Just a stretch of the legs,' she says. 'For our circulation. We haven't walked properly in days. I should like to write something of our walk to your mama, to reassure her too that all is well.'

'If you think it for the best,' I comment. 'And proper.'

'Everything we do is for the best, and proper,' she says.

I finish my soup. Kirsten leaves hers to go cold and congeal, dabbing her mouth absent-mindedly with her kerchief, which is what she does when she is mulling something over.

Our walk turns into quite the parade. Of course we are not allowed unchaperoned, so Mayor Mule and Earl Marischal join us.

'We should like to meander through the town,' Kirsten says. 'Her Royal Highness wishes to see some of Ánslo.'

'Oh, why ever would you?' Mayor Mule asks brusquely. 'There is nothing much to see in town.'

'It is our request,' she tells him, and he sighs.

'As you wish,' he says. 'But we ought not to spend too much time amongst the crowds.'

Word has clearly got out that we are taking refuge in Ánslo, for we are stared at by everyone we pass. They point at our fur cloaks and hats. We should have dressed less grandly. We

Trunks of my gowns and undergarments and hairpins and fans, and even Aksel and his cage, have been unloaded from the *Gideon* and carted up the short road — the life I had imagined would be happening at Holyroodhouse unravelling like a dropped spool of thread.

This is what failure feels like. It feels like watching wooden boxes being dragged up a hill that you never knew existed until this week. It feels like the inconvenience of others writ large on their faces. It feels like fear.

The Bishop's Palace is a new large, white building with a high-pitched roof. It stands in sprawling woodlands with gardens to the front and a lake at the back. Mayor Mule, tall and neat and bespectacled, does not know what to do with his unexpected twist of fate and has been falling over himself to be as polite as possible, whilst disguising his discomfort at having his home overtaken.

'Thank God we did not end up somewhere awful,' Kirsten says. We have been settled in a large high-ceilinged room with more windows than I can count, and given a supper of onion soup and ale, spared having to join the Scots and the Danish ambassadors and Mayor Mule, who are gathered in the ballroom deliberating over our next steps. Aksel flutters around his cage, bewildered once again at another new home. He wants out. I can't blame him. I've finally managed to write a letter to James.

'You should hand your letter to the captain yourself,' Kirsten says. 'To be certain it gets to Leith Port. We should walk down to the ship tomorrow.'

'Should we go out walking?' I ask. 'Anything might happen.'

'Nothing will happen,' she says, irritated. She stands up and throws a blanket over Aksel's cage to quieten him.

'Why can't we just hand my letter to Mayor Mule's secretary?

It can go with the rest of the bundle being written by the Scots.'

'I should like to get my land-legs back,' she replies. 'And then, after we have made sure the letter is in the captain's hands, we could explore Ánslo a little. I saw a small square when we came up this afternoon that looked as if it might have shops.'

'We mustn't be seen to be *enjoying* ourselves, Kirsten. We are in the midst of a crisis here.'

'Just a stretch of the legs,' she says. 'For our circulation. We haven't walked properly in days. I should like to write something of our walk to your mama, to reassure her too that all is well.'

'If you think it for the best,' I comment. 'And proper.'

'Everything we do is for the best, and proper,' she says.

I finish my soup. Kirsten leaves hers to go cold and congeal, dabbing her mouth absent-mindedly with her kerchief, which is what she does when she is mulling something over.

Our walk turns into quite the parade. Of course we are not allowed unchaperoned, so Mayor Mule and Earl Marischal join us.

'We should like to meander through the town,' Kirsten says. 'Her Royal Highness wishes to see some of Ánslo.'

'Oh, why ever would you?' Mayor Mule asks brusquely. 'There is nothing much to see in town.'

'It is our request,' she tells him, and he sighs.

'As you wish,' he says. 'But we ought not to spend too much time amongst the crowds.'

Word has clearly got out that we are taking refuge in Ánslo, for we are stared at by everyone we pass. They point at our fur cloaks and hats. We should have dressed less grandly. We pass a church, then make our way through a town square alive with fish-sellers gutting and slicing, and stalls hung with animal hides, and windows strung with amulets for sailors.

There is something in the middle of the square that seems oddly out of place, yet horribly familiar. A pile of logs set carefully in a small circle, several tiers of them. In the middle is a single stake. The tang of freshly cut spruce hangs in in the air. I stop and grasp Kirsten's arm. She sees what I have seen and goes pale.

'That is set for a burning,' I say.

'Pay it no attention,' she whispers. 'What they do here is none of our business.'

Mayor Mule has realized we have stopped and are staring. 'Come, ladies, we are not too far from the harbour now,' he says, refusing to look at the stake.

He hurries us along, nodding to the stallholders as he goes, everyone nodding back most amiably, ignoring the most obvious thing in the entire market square.

That stake is for a witch. I can feel it in my bones.

I can't stop thinking about it, all the way down to the port, all the way to the harbourmaster's office where the sea captain is summoned, and all the way through hearing his solemn promises to deliver our letters.

Is there a witch in a dungeon below our feet somewhere? Like Doritte Olsen? Can she sense my arrival? Is she, too, cursing me?

The sea captain leaves, duly impressed with the honour of his task, and I gulp down the *akvavit* offered by the harbourmaster. He raises his eyebrows and offers me another one. I can taste Doritte Olsen's flesh as the liquor burns my throat.

'Excuse me,' Kirsten announces, 'I must have one more word with the sea captain.'

The harbourmaster offers me a third shot of the liqueur and I take it, expecting Kirsten to tell me to stop, but she doesn't. She seems distracted.

I watch through the window as she darts over to the captain. She is a sharp, determined figure. What can she want with him now? My thoughts become idle, blurred with the sting of alcohol this early in the morning.

She catches his arm and he turns towards her. He looks confused as Kirsten talks, then he nods. She passes him something from inside her cape, a small white parchment rolled tightly. Another letter. A letter she obviously did not want to discuss with me.

Who is Kirsten writing to in Scotland? She has never mentioned having any acquaintance there that she writes to. And why be so secretive?

In fact, as the *akvavit* churns, I realize that although Kirsten has talked at length of how marvellous Scotland is – its lush landscape and bracing winds and its wild beaches and smart merchants' homes – she has never mentioned knowing anyone there. Even though her eyes glaze over sometimes as she reminisces.

She turns on her heels as the captain puts her letter with ours. Her face closes in on itself again, as secretive as ever.

Chapter Twelve

KIRSTEN

Ánslo, Norway
October 1589

I suppose we have settled into a routine, of sorts, which is necessary in order to keep going. Life must continue as usual or else we lose our civility, after all. The *Gideon* remains in port and by all accounts is having the most thorough of repairs, if we are to believe anything these sailors say through their dreadful gap-toothed grimaces. But we have no firm idea when we will attempt to cross the German Sea again. Admiral Munk is in no rush. Ho! He knows there will be an investigation when we get to Scotland, and the king himself will demand why he managed to sail us into a calamity.

I have resigned myself to the fact we are delayed. It is no great trouble to be here. We have been visited by a procession of Ánslo ladies, fluttering with ostrich-feather fans and freshly coiffed hair, desperate to see their princess, as they never would ordinarily have the opportunity. The ladies have a tendency towards ogling Anna's jewellery, and their gowns are on the gaudy side, but it is all good for the kingdom, I would say. Her little brother, King Christian, is only twelve and too young to travel yet, so this is the closest they will get to the glamour of royalty. And all of this means that the ladies' visits, of which we have had two already in the week – as well as morning meetings with the ambassadors and afternoon walks around the grounds, plus an evening *akvavit* before dinner – have become our routine.

And as long as I keep pretending to be calm, I will not explode with the frustration of it all and scream at that fool Munk, and grab the bottle of *akvavit* and swill it down like one of those blasted grimacing sailors.

We should have been in Scotland by now.

As soon as I saw the stake in the marketplace, I knew this problem was even worse than I feared.

The stake has gone by the time I take my second walk into town a few days later. All that's left is a dark scar on the earth where the wood has burned.

Who did they kill this time? What trifling thing had she done?

'Let me come with you,' Anna had pleaded, looking sorry for herself.

'I need provisions. It will become too much of a cavalcade if you come too. I can throw on a shawl and go down and back, and no one will notice me gone. You would need to be dressed and accompanied by ambassadors,' I told her. She knows all this, yet she peeped like the canary. 'Take a walk to the lake,' I suggested.

I left, trying to ignore the forlorn look on Anna's face, and went to the market, which is full of stock from the ships. I bought some items to amuse myself and Anna: some crystallized ginger; a bag of pepper, as Mayor Mule's household appears to have a bizarre ignorance of spices; a small bolt of silk that

I might embroider. A few nice things so that when Anna asks, I have plenty to show her.

I didn't want to have to write another letter so soon, but I have to keep up the warnings about how prolific the burnings are becoming. It will fall on deaf ears, of course. No one wants to believe it. I hardly believed it myself until I saw it with my own eyes. Another ship sails for Leith Port in ten days. I left my letter with one of its crew, with a couple of coins for good measure, careful not to show him too much of my face.

You have to be careful who you trust – strangers in particular.

When I get back to the Bishop's Palace I go upstairs, to Mayor Mule in his day-room, on the pretence of asking him about the ball he's planning, to celebrate our unexpected visit. A ball, on top of everything else. As if I don't have enough to worry about. A court without a king in residence can quickly fall into folly and indiscretion. I've seen the way the Scotsmen are eyeing the Danish maids, but that's to be expected, and if there are fumbles in the attic rooms, then I can deal with any outcome as needed.

It's the way Lord Henry looks at Anna. And the way she looks at him. That's what I don't like. That's what worries me. She needs her king. She is primed and ready for him. She has been taught of the bedchamber and seduction, and of what lies beneath a man's undergarments, and in his absence she stirs. She wonders. She imagines.

I say nothing of this to Mayor Mule, of course. I simply ask him if we might decorate the ballroom with Scottish and Danish flags and some ivy and pine branches and pinecones.

'A little decoration might mark the occasion well,' he says. He looks warily at me from his desk, from behind his little round spectacles. We are an intrusion. We've interrupted his comfortable life, but he must accommodate us without any hint of a complaint. He would rather be sitting here, beneath the grand decorated lintel on his mantelpiece, running Ánslo the way he sees fit, without worrying over the welfare of the boy king's sister. His hands flit over his papers, straightening them unnecessarily. He coughs. I sit, uninvited. He looks even more uncomfortable in his high-backed chair.

'Tell me about the execution this week,' I say. 'The burning. We had a terrible shock when we saw the stake in your town square. I would appreciate it if you could let me know what happened.'

'Oh,' he says, 'I'm not sure whether this is a matter for a lady like yourself to worry about.' He squirms a little.

'It's my job to worry about anything that might affect Princess Anna,' I reply. 'Burnings are for heretics and witches. What is happening in Ánslo? Should I be worried on behalf of Her Royal Highness?'

He shakes his head far too vigorously, then has to readjust his spectacles. 'Of course not, of course not. There is nothing for you to worry about here. We have everything under control.'

I lower my voice. 'We burned a witch at Kronborg this summer,' I say. 'The first time a witch has been burned at Kronborg in fifty years. There was a witch found in Copenhagen too.'

Mayor Mule regards me for a moment or two, deciding how much to say. Finally he drops his voice too.

'We've executed two witches this year, with two more waiting in a cellar beneath the market square,' he says.

I blink. 'The witch in Denmark used weather magic,' I say.

'Have you heard about Trier?' he asks. I make my face blank. He clears his throat and takes a deep breath, settling in. Mayor Mule is the sort of man who loves to tell a long story. He just needs a little encouragement. 'The merchants in Trier were a greedy lot,' he says. 'They conspired with the Devil to blight the barley crops and drive up the price, so they could get rich on it. The price of beer was at a premium, but the peasants starved because there was no bread. The merchants got richer and richer until the authorities suspected they were controlling the weather with spells, in order to ensure that half the crops failed.'

'And what happened to them?' I ask.

'They confessed soon enough,' he replies. 'And gave the names of their accomplices. Hundreds have been put to death. But there are lessons to be learned from Trier. We've been too lenient about witchcraft. We've tolerated it for too long. Folk have always been in the habit of using witchcraft to settle their fights and wreak their revenge. But we've allowed it to take too much of a grip. The Devil has taken advantage of our weakness. Here, in Ánslo, we've now introduced the death-penalty for all sorcery.'

'I understand, but our situation is delicate,' I tell him. 'Princess Anna is in a precarious situation and is being trialled as the next Queen of Scotland. If the Scots start to suspect Scandinavia is in the grip of the witch epidemic that has taken Trier, it will certainly go against her. We can't have them thinking of us as wild people, a kingdom of cunning folk. Her reputation is intertwined with the repute of this kingdom.'

Mayor Mule puts his fingers to his chin, understanding my point. 'We will have no more burnings whilst you and the Scots are here,' he says. 'I promise you that. I understand your predicament.'

'That would be a wise move,' I answer. 'I'm sure the Danish royal family and the Privy Council would appreciate it.'

He nods and looks back at his papers. I am dismissed.

Chapter Thirteen

ANNA

Ánslo, Norway
October 1589

To my most darling betrothed, James the Sixth of Scotland

Sir – I hope this letter has made a speedy journey to you, across the German Sea. Firstly, I am safe and well and being looked after at the Bishop's Palace, Ánslo, but it is with the greatest of regret that I must tell you of our failure to reach Leith Port.

If you had only seen the storm that raged against the fleet, you would be in no doubt that Admiral Munk did the right thing in turning back. I sincerely trust that our detour will be temporary and that we will set sail again as soon as we can. Please forgive this extraordinary turn of events.

Your most faithful and loving servant,
Anna, Princess of Denmark

*

I couldn't bear to write the thing Henry suggested – about the embrace. How can I write what I don't feel? I imagine my letter passed from sea captain to harbourmaster, under a leaden Scottish sky. Handed to the swiftest messenger and spirited up to Holyroodhouse with gloved hands and the greatest reverence. Perhaps James is desperate for word and has sent a search party of boats for us. Perhaps he has shrugged at the news we are lost at sea, and is corresponding with his other candidate for marriage, Catherine de Bourbon, already. Perhaps he has found that he enjoys her missives and he's thinking of her, enraptured by one of her sonnets, then irritated by the knock on his inner chamber door with the letter that I'm safe and sound.

Perhaps. But all I care about is the three hours I spend daily with Henry in Mayor Mule's library.

Autumn is turning colder and the library has the scent of musty books and crackling pine logs in the fire, and of the *akvavit* and caraway-seed biscuits we take during our eleven-o'clock interlude, and of something else. Henry has a new fragrance about him, of cedar perfume. He came into our first lesson with it lingering on him, as if it were part of his skin, and carrying a smart kerchief of Holland cloth, trimmed in gold. I guessed, immediately, that he had gone to Ánslo market and bought some fine things, in preparation for spending time in my company. He has dressed to impress. There is no *perhaps* about that. The certain knowledge he is enamoured of me thrills me deep inside, making my heart thump and jump, like Aksel in his cage.

The library is on the ground floor, off the main hallway, with large windows that look onto the gardens. It has been decided that I will study for three hours a day with Henry. Earl Marischal decreed it the best use of our time until the plan is finalized for our attempt to sail again, and Mayor Mule found some books we might use. I am to learn Scottish history and more Scots language, and some studies of nature and James's theory on kingship, which is that kings should be venerated as the images of God upon Earth, even higher an authority than the Church. The last one is something we have avoided studying.

'Kirsten has told me all about Scotland,' I say. It is a morning, mid-week. I have lost track of the days. 'It rains a lot, but in a soft way, and the Canongate around Holyroodhouse is rich with merchants, but the top of the town is thick with smoke, and you eat meat puddings made from sheep's pluck.'

He laughs. 'Every day, for breakfast, dinner and supper,' he says. 'You will come to love sheep's pluck.'

'I will never eat a sheep's innards,' I tell him. 'Not even if that is all there ever is for breakfast, dinner and supper.'

He laughs again. 'Come,' he says, opening one of Mayor Mule's nature books. 'Let's stop worrying about sheep innards and learn some vocabulary.' He points to illustrations of butterflies and bees and birds. I recite the words and scratch them onto my parchment. His tongue touches his lips as he watches me. Sometimes he raises an eyebrow and looks at me in a way that makes me want to reach over and touch him. The room grows warm. I yawn, and he does too.

'I think we should walk the grounds,' he suggests. 'The cold air will revive us. It even has the hint of snow today.'

'Shall I fetch Kirsten?' I ask, thinking she will be irked at having to stop whatever she is doing: matching fans to shoes, or sending my thank-you notes to the Ánslo ladies who have visited us.

He looks at me. Henry's face is shadowy, now the curtain has been drawn, but his eyes have the flicker of fire about them.

'We're not leaving the grounds,' he says. 'No need for a chaperone, is there?'

'No need,' I agree.

We walk through the neat gardens, where the flowerbeds have had their last bloom, into the woodland behind the building. It is freezing, but the velvet dress I am wearing will have to do, because I couldn't have disturbed Kirsten for a cloak without a barrage of questions, or her dragging herself along and making the walk as short as possible.

'Are you warm enough?' Henry asks.

I tell him I am, but he gives me his own cape anyway, engulfing me in cedar. He picks a pinecone and puts it to his lips. I can almost feel its dry scales touching my own.

There is a feeling that I am experiencing, which happened that night we talked on the *Gideon*. It is a feeling of being overwhelmed by him. I can't stop looking at him. It is as though our eyes are drawn to each other's. When Henry smiles, I smile. My heart is in my throat.

We come to the lake, which is glassy and silver, and find a small *hytte* next to it, with chairs set out to watch over the water.

'Let's sit,' he says, and we do.

'What will you do when we get to Scotland?' I ask. 'Will you keep giving me lessons?'

'I would like to,' he replies. 'But that will be up to His Majesty.'

'Sometimes I think we'll never get to Scotland,' I say.

'Imagine if we couldn't. I think it would be magical if we could stay here,' he says. 'Just the two of us.'

I almost laugh. I have never done anything of my own free will. I have spent my life doing what is right and good. But my heart has been unsettled ever since I met Lord Henry.

The air is so thin now that when the first flakes of snow fall – oh, it was inevitable they would – they feel as light as cold feathers. The fall is slight. The skies are not heavy with snow, this is merely an early twirl of it. It will disappear as soon as it lands.

'There is snow on your hair,' he whispers, smiling, then he pauses, his face serious.

Oh God, I think he is about to say something treasonable. I inhale cedar. It curls into my lungs.

'Don't say it,' I tell him. His eyes still have the spark of fire about them, even though we are nowhere near any blaze. Something in the headiness of the woods emboldens me then. It is our solitude. The fact that it is so cold we can see our breath, our words forming in the air. The fact that I know the moment will be over soon, gone for ever, like the snow and the smoke of our breath.

Henry leans towards me and kisses me. His lips, when I taste them, have the tang of crisp air and *akvavit*.

'I must. I'm in love with you,' he says.

His words sink into me, as easily as if they were any old words, but they are not.

'Nothing can come of it,' I whisper.

'It could, quite easily,' he says. 'If you wanted it too. It's your choice. You can make it happen.'

'And how might I do that?'

'By failing your marriage trial,' he says.

11th October 1589
Holyroodhouse

My Dearest Betrothed,
I have received your letter, praise God. What peril you have endured! I have contemplated the matter overnight and I cannot suffer the thought of you enduring the winter in Ánslo. I am on my way to Norway to fetch you. My advisors say I should stay here, as there are factions in Scotland who would take advantage of my absence and plot to overthrow me if they could, but I trust my men here to see off any trouble for the next few weeks.

I take this resolution as a true King of Scotland, in the hope that it inspires your confidence, and the confidence of my countrymen in our Royal Union. I send this letter ahead, in the hope it gets to you in time.

Your most devoted betrothed, awaiting the moment we finally meet, when I can embrace you at long last,
KING JAMES THE SIXTH

Chapter Fourteen

JURA

North Berwick, Scotland
October 1589

Master Kincaid takes his leave for a week, thank the guid Lord, collecting taxes in Dunbar before the winter makes travelling treacherous, flooding the paths with rainwater and allowing only short slivers of weak daylight. He leaves with an escort of rough-looking men who'll guard the coin. As soon as he departs, the household feels lighter. Even the sun keeks out for the morning. Cook whistles as she slaps pastry around with a rolling pin.

'I wish I had ten pairs o' hands,' she calls. 'The mistress is having her guidwives around for knitting and supper tonight and there are not enough hours in the day to get ready.'

Guidwife Kincaid's gaggle of pals are as loud as they are daft and Cook says they aye get together when the master is away, on the premise of knitting fishermen's jumpers, but there is more clacking of their jaws than clacking of needles on those nights. Cook is delighted. She says she'll be invited to join them once the supper is finished, for she always has the North Berwick gossip. I am put to sweeping the dining room and setting out the chairs and lighting the fire to get it warmed for their cold backsides.

'It's been a while since they last got together,' Cook muses as she fills the pastry with herring. She even carves a pastry fish and places it on the top, a flourish she would never do if the master was home. 'I hope they dinnie get too drunk.'

By nine o'clock in the evening they are all as drunk as lairds, and whisky fumes mingle with the scent of their sweat. The knitting lies abandoned in grey woollen jumbles and the pie has been demolished. Master Kincaid keeps his whisky in a locked cabinet, so I can only think the guidwives have brought their own drink. As I have scuttled in and out, filling glasses and removing plates, I have heard enough talk about older women's troubles, and the nightly sweats and bloating they bring, to make me wish I had been born a laddie.

'And the heidaches,' says Guidwife Scobie, brushing pie crumbs from her kirtle.

'And I can't eat bread these days or I'm never off the chamberpot,' says Guidwife Chalmers.

'We should pray for some relief from it all,' says Guidwife Younger.

They join hands – reluctantly, I think – and race through some words of prayer as I open a window to let in the fresh air. Hazel, who has been sitting near the window, has been quietly making her way through a big cup of whisky.

'We should have a sing-song,' says Guidwife Chalmers. 'Start us off, Hazel.'

Hazel stands, a little shakily, hands clasped at her waist, and begins the ballad of Tam Lin, and soon they are all joining in with the old fairie story of inchantment and rescue, of the bravery of a lassie against the Fairie Queen herself, and singing loudly enough to raise the roof. It is a high moment. High enough and light enough for me to stand at the wall, singing along, and Guidwife Chalmers notices me and pours me a whisky, and Guidwife Kincaid nods that I can drink it and join them.

When the ballad is sung, everyone claps, and Hazel looks as flushed and happy as I have ever seen her.

'You're looking bonnie tonight,' calls Guidwife Chalmers. 'What's your secret?'

The guidwives laugh, all except the mistress, for the last thing she wants is a daughter with a secret, I bet. 'Oh, to be young again,' says Guidwife Kincaid.

'But she is looking fresh, is she not? Fair bonnie.' Guidwife Chalmers narrows her eyes and inspects poor Hazel up and down. 'Is it a laddie that's got your skin glowing? Or an ointment?'

'Och, leave her be,' says Guidwife Scobie. 'Hazel Kincaid has no need of laddies, nor ointments.'

Hazel is blushing fit to pop. I don't think she has ever had as many folk gawping at her all at once.

'There had better not be any laddies,' warns Guidwife Kincaid.

'No laddies,' says Hazel.

'Then it must be an ointment,' cries Guidwife Chalmers. 'Which one? Is it from the market? That apothecary?'

Hazel shakes her head. 'Just a poultice,' she says.

'What poultice?' asks her ma. 'What have you been putting on your face and not telling me?'

Hazel is drunk. I can tell from the way she sways and talks too much. She seems larger than she normally is. Uncontrollable.

'It was Jura – the cunning wifie's lass,' she says, nodding in my direction. All eyes in the room swing towards me.

'It was simply a treatment with oats,' I reply, thinking the mistress is going to be furious at the waste of good food. But they are all looking at me with a new admiration, glancing me up and down. I suddenly worry that my plaits are in tangles, and my apron stained like the right dollop I always seem to feel when folk are looking at me.

'Was it now? Well, my Hazel's skin is clearer than I have ever seen it,' says Guidwife Kincaid. 'Not that we should be vain,' she adds hurriedly.

'Have you something for my elbows?' asks Guidwife Younger. 'Dry as sand, they are. I have plenty of money – money's no object. Your old ma had the knack.'

They all murmur in agreement.

'Are you a healer too?' asks Guidwife Scobie.

I shrug. 'Just what my ma taught me.'

They all continue to stare.

'Can you fix a grumbly belly?' asks Guidwife Chalmers.

I look at Guidwife Kincaid, for she is my mistress and I can't be seen to be talking out of turn. She surveys me in a cool way. 'Well, can you?' she asks.

'Mibbie, aye,' I say. 'Tis true. A grumbly belly is easy to soothe. No doubt whatever potions Guidwife Chalmers has been taking will have made it worse. Especially if she bought them from that apothecary.

'We can all pay you,' says Guidwife Scobie. 'That's only fair, isn't it?'

'Well, I suppose you can try,' says Guidwife Kincaid, seeming proud that her maid has a knowledge of cures. 'You can go and help the guidwives tomorrow.'

Everyone is pleased at that, and a fresh round of whisky is served, and Hazel still glows from all the compliments and I am sent to the kitchen for cheese and oatcakes. And if it is a sin to feel proud of myself at this outcome, then I am very sorry indeed, but I like healing far better than I like polishing and sweeping; and mibbie, one day, soothing grumbling guts and easing flaking skin will help me get out of horrible Master Kincaid's house and away from his prick, and able to rent a dwelling of my own.

When I reach Guidwife Chalmers's smart stone house the next day she receives me as though I am a visiting bishop. She is wearing the cleanest apron I have ever seen and she tidies my pattens neatly by the door. A goblet of wine, a plate of ham and a bowl of scented water to wash my hands in. Her guts must be giving her some gripe to be this hopeful.

'Master Chalmers is threatening to take me to a physician in Edinburgh if the pains and boaky feeling don't stop,' she confides, taking off her kirtle. 'And I can't have that. A man touching my belly and inspecting me.'

I'm sure the Chalmers have the means for a physician's visit but, like Guidwife Chalmers, the thought of one poking and prodding gives me the fear too. She lies on her bed and lets me touch her stomach, and for the life of me I have no idea if anything is the matter with it, for it looks like any other old belly to me. I run my hands over it and feel for lumps and bumps, but I can't find anything.

'Have you taken anything from the apothecary?' I ask.

She blushes. 'A drink that tasted of farmyards, which made matters worse,' she says.

I suspect she is eating foods that disagree with her, which Ma always said was a common enough complaint and, when I have finished my examination, I tell her to stick to plain food for a while to see if that helps.

'Oats and chicken and fish,' I say. 'They should soothe. And do not go back to the apothecary.'

'What about my whiskies?' she asks balefully.

'Mibbie your whiskies are causing the problem,' I tell her.

She is gripped by a cramp then, and I can see how much it pains her, so I fetch a rosemary sprig from my bag and hold it over her. And I chant quietly, just as Ma might have done, and ask the Lord to help Guidwife Chalmers. I chant for a few minutes, and eventually she intones along with me, and altogether I consider it a huge effort and I hope that my charme has worked.

The next day I visit Guidwife Scobie and do much the same sort of charme for her bad heid, whilst telling her that she must drink less ale and more boiled water, for there is nothing worse for the heid than too much ale. My Da could tell anyone that.

The guidwives must report back that their symptoms have fair eased, for a few days later I am called to Guidwife Younger and her itchy elbow. That is simple and requires honey poultices much the same as those for Hazel's flaking forehead. All in all, it is three hard days' work, but each of the guidwives gives me a decent handful of pennies.

Then my enjoyment comes to a hard stop, for two reasons. The first is the return of Master Kincaid, who begins to eye me in his hungry old way again, not minutes after walking in the door.

The second reason is news from Betsy – that all hell has broken out on Robbie Bathgate's farm because their hens have been struck by a disease so virulent it has wiped out most of the flock.

Chapter Fifteen

ANNA

*The Bishop's Palace, Ánslo
November 1589*

What if Henry isn't really in love with me, or he changes his mind? If this is just an infatuation and I do fail my trial, and Henry abandons me and I end up in Hellebæk Abbey?

'I mean it,' he says.

We walk in the grounds after lessons every day that we can. I have even told Kirsten we are walking, saying Henry believes fresh air necessary for the mind. The words tripped off my tongue. *How easily I lie! How seductively I kiss. What other talents might I have?*

'You should not walk alone with a man,' Kirsten says. 'Especially a young handsome man.'

'But he is as close to King James as I can get,' I reply. 'He tells me more about King James in our walks than he does in that stuffy study.' *How easily I lie!*

'Very well,' Kirsten says, believing me. 'Walk for no more than thirty minutes and do not catch a chill. Ask him about who the king is closest to. Who you should befriend. Who to avoid. Are you attracted to Lord Henry?'

The direct question catches me off-guard and I gasp.

'I am devoted to King James,' I say. 'And well you know it.'

'I should chaperone you,' she says.

'Then he would not be so indiscreet with his talk of the king,' I answer.

She nods. 'Well, wear your fur cape and hat. Don't let the cold air get to your throat,' she says.

I let the cold air get to my throat.

I let Henry untie the ribbons of the fur cape and kiss my neck.

We are safe, well hidden, in the *hytte*. Henry keeps watch, in between kisses. Everything feels natural out there. The air tastes of snow. The firs have their noses to the sky, waiting for their winter cloaks. We kiss above the sleeping seeds, amongst the deer and hare and shrew and bat, all readying for winter with their mates. I know our time here is momentary. I know I will not see their young in spring.

One way or another, we will be gone by then.

One day I will weep about that, but not yet. I am too thrilled.

It's only when I am alone in bed, hearing Kirsten snore and Aksel's feathers quiver as he dreams, that my thoughts race between the various disasters that I know will befall me if we are caught. I know they could behead us or put us to the fire. But would that be worse than an entire lifetime spent at Hellebæk Abbey? Perhaps I will fail the trial anyway and then I can marry Henry.

'We would marry in Denmark.' He has it all planned out. 'I would leave court and go back to the University of Copenhagen and then come and find you, wherever you are. You could write to me there. They would keep letters for me if I asked them to.'

'How might I fail the trial on purpose?' I ask. 'Without anyone realizing?'

'We will think of something,' he says. 'But it has to come from within you. A reluctance. A coldness.'

I think I can do that, easily enough.

'Don't be frightened,' he whispers. 'Don't think of all the calamities that might happen. Concentrate on our future together. It will be wonderful.'

He ties up my cape ribbons, and I watch him concentrate on the task, his cold fingers fumbling with the delicate threads. He loves me. I know it. I will try to do what he says. I will try to stop worrying.

Tonight we are hosting a ball. Kirsten has been highly occupied with it. Invited are the lords and ladies of Ánslo and beyond, who will all be determined to dazzle, no doubt. There will be fiddle players and dancing. I am going to dance with Henry. And there will be an array of puddings, with the apples and pears from the *Gideon* that might not last the winter on that damp ship; and reindeer stew with mushrooms, which is Mayor Mule's cook's speciality. All the Scots are coming, with Admiral Munk, so there are barrels and barrels of German beer, and sack.

'It is passable enough,' declares Kirsten. We have tiptoed downstairs early and are the only ones in the ballroom, except for the servants. She is inspecting the tables. The gamey scent of the stew is coming upstairs from the kitchens. I pick at a thread in my corset. Kirsten has let me wear a damson silk gown, which ripples in the light of the candelabra, like wine being poured from a decanter. I think Henry will absolutely love it. I have almost stopped worrying and started to enjoy the evening.

We are interrupted by a flurry of knocks at the doors of the ballroom. They burst open, and a servant stands looking as though he does not know what to do next. He does not even bow.

'Is something the matter?' I call, my heart beginning to pound in my chest, for he looks most agitated.

'Far from it, far from it,' he cries. 'Most wonderful news! A messenger has just this minute come to the Bishop's Palace with a missive. His Majesty King James of Scotland is in Ánslo. He is here.'

It is a blessing I am dressed. That is my first thought. Then: *we are going to miss the ball,* but of course the ball will go ahead, this time with real cause for celebration. Then another thought: *Henry — I was going to dance with Henry.*

Kirsten tells the servant to fetch Mayor Mule and send word around the Bishop's Palace. 'Tell the kitchens as well,' she calls after him. Then she sits down. 'He has come for you,' she says. She pours us both a measure of Madeira wine and we take a gulp. 'He risked his life,' she adds, shaking her head.

'I'm not ready to meet him,' I say. 'I'm terrified.' The wave of fear comes back. The wave that I felt wash over me during my last days in Kronborg.

'Of course, you're ready. You're not terrified — you're excited,' Kirsten assures me.

We gulp again.

'This changes everything,' I say. 'Will we even stay in Ánslo for the winter?'

Kirsten puts down her glass and places her palms together as if in prayer, but she isn't praying. Her eyes dart. Her lips purse. She is thinking. She is plotting. 'That will be up to His Majesty. He will make the decisions now.'

*

Even before James gets here, I hear of his adventures, for the messenger is welcomed with beer and stew. He slurps and chews and rattles out the tale whilst everyone crowds around us. It turns my stomach to watch his mouth.

They sailed from Leith Port, but the weather was so dangerous they were forced back within a few hours, only to try again the following day. This time they succeeded, although the sailing was treacherous and there were countless prayers said on board for the safety of the king, for if he had died on that voyage the very future of Scotland and England would have been thrown into chaos.

'All for you, Your Royal Highness,' the messenger says.

All for me.

All as I was falling in love with Henry.

They docked in the west of Norway several days ago and made the trip overland and have only just arrived, sending the messenger ahead. James had written a letter in haste, telling me he was coming, but he has arrived before it.

Dear God, it has been an odyssey.

They put me in the study to wait for him.

It still has the scent of cedar. I can feel Henry's lips on my throat. I think I am going to retch.

Kirsten joins me, ushered in by Mayor Mule.

'I'll come back to the ballroom after His Majesty has arrived,' she tells him. Already a hundred or so people have gathered there. I can hear the excitement throughout the whole building. Gasps and raucous laughter and hurried footsteps.

He nods. 'I will make sure they have not eaten all the stew,' he smiles. 'Or the apple tarts.' He smiles so rarely it is clear he is delighted with this magnificent turn of events.

Kirsten smiles back. She, too, does so rarely. But her face

is alive with relief. I open my mouth to ask her about that letter she passed to the ship's captain, but she whips the smile away and replaces it with one of her thin-lipped stares.

'Stop touching your corset, you will leave grease marks on it,' she rebukes me. 'If we'd had longer, I would have put you in the gold gown. It's far more modest than the damson, in this light.'

She passes me a kerchief. I wipe my hands on it. They feel clammy, even after I've wiped them.

'This wait feels longer than the whole of that wretched sea voyage,' I say. I am about to tell her that I am dreading the next voyage when we spot a line of carriages coming into the grounds, their lamps illuminating the whole procession. He is here.

King James the Sixth of Scotland is *nothing* like the portrait they sent. He is even smaller, slighter and has an unusual air about him that I did not expect.

He strides up and regards me in the way Kirsten examines my needlework. I curtsey as low as I can go. He has dirty boots. I straighten myself up and smile as happily as I can. His eyes have a droop, and they are the colour of weak ale.

Everyone is watching, fixated.

'As you could not come to Scotland,' he says, 'I have come to you.'

Thank God I can understand his accent, for it's broader than Henry's and even Earl Marischal's. But that is the only mercy of the hour, for I feel trapped, and my senses are heightened with the panic of it all.

He takes my hand and kisses it. His lips tickle and his beard bristles.

'Let me look at you,' James says, taking a step back. 'Can someone bring a lamp over here? It's too dark to see her properly.' Within a moment I am awash with light. 'Ah, yes,' he goes on. 'I can see you properly now.'

He makes no comment on whether he finds me pleasing. I dare not even look beyond him to see if Henry is nearby. If I saw Henry now, I would burst into tears.

Our breath mingles. He smells utterly foreign: alongside the staleness of the journey there is a perfume that must be patchouli, for I have smelled that once, on my grandpapa, and James also carries the musty scent of long travel. Of wind and the sea, and the place he will take me to.

'I am overcome,' I mutter, feeling faint. Someone puts me into a chair. Someone else puts a goblet of water on the table, and Kirsten puts it into my hand. I sip.

'Is that better?' he asks, looking fearful that I might fully faint and that would be the story they would tell of our meeting for evermore.

'Much better,' I say, and he looks relieved. I feel as though I am an actor in a masque. I know all the words, and everyone is watching intently, and yet I cannot believe it is real.

'She is quite well,' he announces. I manage a smile, and everyone claps.

The king takes my arm as we walk to the ballroom, and when we sit down together everyone cheers. It makes me want to shrink. Kirsten is relegated to a table of maids, which she will begrudge. Henry is at our table, but far to my left.

I sit between James and Earl Marischal, who is well into his drinking and merry-making and has never looked more relieved, as though the weight of the world has been lifted from his shoulders, which I suppose it has. I am not his responsibility any more.

Opposite us, Mayor Mule says he would be delighted to host us for as long as we need.

'Such kindness, and I am obliged to take advantage of it, but only for a week or so,' says James. 'I can't stay away from Scotland for too long, but now I am here, I want an investigation into the decision to sail and the seaworthiness of the *Gideon*. We must have a full account. Where is Admiral Munk?'

Everyone looks around the ballroom, but the admiral is not amongst us.

'He was supposed to be here,' says Mayor Mule.

'I saw him arrive,' says Earl Marischal. 'He walked up from the harbourmaster's house. That's who he's been lodging with.'

James nods slowly, focusing on nothing but the bowl of stew in front of him. He puts his hands on the table. His fingers glint with rubies and diamonds. He leaps to his feet, tipping over a goblet.

'Send some men out to find Admiral Munk,' he demands. 'He can't be very far. And stop all boats leaving the port.' A flurry of men departs. James sits back down. I don't know whether to try to appease him or stay silent. 'The admiral is trying to avoid me,' he says. 'But he will be called to account.'

'Indeed,' says Mayor Mule, looking nervous. 'Your Majesty, perhaps in the meantime you might enjoy some dancing. We have entertainment planned for after dinner.'

'I'm not in the mood for dancing tonight,' says James. 'I have travelled thousands of miles and now I want to rest.'

And so they don't fetch the fiddle players and we don't have any dancing.

Chapter Sixteen

KIRSTEN

The Bishop's Palace, Ánslo
November 1589

Anna's father was a good and decent king. He had a stateliness about him. He had a sense of humour and a love for life. King James is not like that. Perhaps it is his age – he is only twenty-three – or the fact that he has the fierce look of a man whose boyhood was appalling. He is the sort of man who needs to be utterly in control. His temperament is something we will need to learn to manage. For Anna, it will be a matter of learning what words and facial expressions he finds acceptable and of keeping a tight lid on herself.

She will learn that there are different sorts of kings and different sorts of men. It is a life lesson and she is beginning it.

It is late, around midnight, and we are preparing her in case James visits, as is his right in the handfasting contract. Mayor Mule has given up his own chamber for the king, and I have been put in with the maids, which is hardly ideal. It has been impossible to get word about James's intentions for tonight from any of the ambassadors.

'Perhaps he will be too exhausted to visit upon me,' Anna says. She is having her hair unpinned and brushed, and the finest nightgown from her trousseau has been laid out. Her voice is the meekest I have ever heard it.

'It is better to get the first night over and done with,' I tell her.

'What if I get with child – with a bastard – yet he refuses to marry me?' Her eyes glow wild in the light from the candles. 'Will I be allowed to take the baby to Hellebæk Abbey?'

'You will seduce him,' I tell her. 'As you have been taught to do. And he will marry you. A child is imperative for the union.'

The maids strip her out of her ballgown as though they were skinning a rabbit and dress her in a nightgown of sheer creamy silk. I feel as though I ought to avert my eyes, even though I have seen Anna in all manner of undress, for tonight she looks utterly defenceless.

'Shall I sit here and pretend to read or sit in the bed?' She flutters by the hearth. The maids become hell-bent on tidying and folding and straightening their caps. They are nervous too, at the thought of the King of Scotland striding through the door.

'You will not seduce him if your knees are knocking and your teeth are chattering.' I try to say it gently, for we cannot have Anna getting into a state, but I find gentle words so difficult. I can't help it. Seeing her vulnerable like this reminds me of myself, a long time ago. A memory that I suppress. 'Sit down by the hearth. It is more proper.' I pass her a velvet cape so she might keep warm, but in truth the chamber is stifling. She pours herself a glass of wine. That must be her fourth of the evening, but I say nothing. She sits, gazing at the fire, glowing with trepidation.

Suddenly she turns to me.

'You had better take Aksel, from now on. He will think me a child if I have a pet canary.'

I nod. She is right.

'And feed him his nightly treat, won't you? And sing to him if he looks upset.'

'I will try,' I say, although we both know I won't do any such thing, for I have never sung to a bird and never shall.

I am relieved when finally James knocks. He stands at the door, looking surprisingly small in his white nightgown. Gone are his men and his robes and his collars and his rings. Gone is his bravado. He is just a man, looking as nervous as she does, as though tonight is a task to be got out of the way as quickly and painlessly as possible. I curtsey low as I leave. This is the part Anna must do herself.

James is not there is the morning. Anna is still abed at nine, the maids milling at her chamber door, her breakfast tray of yoghurt and honey and bread untouched, except for the water jug.

'Come in,' she says.

She is a small heap under the covers. I open the curtains and let the winter light flood the room. She sits up. Her hair is all over the place. I have never seen it so tousled. I think he has deflowered her, and with some gusto. I feel guilty, seeing her like this. She does not look right.

'Did the night go well?' I ask. I am embarrassed to ask, but her mama wants word sent on the progress of the handfasting.

'Might I bathe?' she asks.

'I will have the maids fetch hot water,' I say. 'A nice deep bath, would that be pleasant?'

Anna draws her knees up to her chin. Dear God, she looks shrunken into herself. I don't know what to say. I cannot blame her discomfort. But I can't encourage it. That would be treasonous. I sit on the bed.

'It is all perfectly natural,' I say. 'The union of man and woman.'

She raises her eyes from the bedspread. It is a marvellous bedspread, white with gold flowers. I wonder if Mayor Mule begged it from one of his noblemen. I wonder if the Ánslo aristocrats will boast of its use, later, and hang it from a wall like a tapestry. Perhaps it will become priceless.

'It did not feel natural to me,' she whispers. 'I don't like him the way I ought.'

Admiral Munk does not get far, the scoundrel. They find him in the harbourmaster's house. With him is another man, from Copenhagen, whom he insists on bringing when he is summoned for questioning.

I hear all about it from Mayor Mule. I walk into the ballroom to find the chairs being laid out in rows and the flags and foliage being stripped down. The admiral is going to be interrogated. Good. I hope they hang him. I sit on the front row as everyone files in. King James sits at the top, with Earl Marischal at his side. The Scots and Danes who were on the *Gideon* come and take their seats. Admiral Munk strides in and kneels before the king. I have not paid much attention to him before, but he is a tall man, broad-shouldered, with oily-looking hair that sits in silvery curls at his shoulders. His cloak – I suspect it is his best one, for it is an expensive-looking bottle-green velvet – slumps on the floor as he kneels. It looks creased from trunk-storage.

'You are chief of the Danish fleet, are you not?' says James.

'I am Admiral of the Realm and a member of the Privy Council of Denmark,' he replies, mustering his authority, but with a quiver in his voice. 'I am one of the Rigsrådet of regents for King Christian of Denmark.' He throws a glance at Anna at that.

Anna does not notice. She is too occupied with biting her hangnails, the habit she takes up when she is preoccupied.

'You may sit,' says James, nodding to a chair at the front. 'Now, tell me about the decision to sail on the *Gideon*. Was its seaworthiness an issue?'

'It had suffered a great amount of leaking on its last voyage,' the admiral says. 'But leaks are commonplace, and it is a case of mending them and managing them. When we inspected the *Gideon* in the summer, before we attempted to set sail for Scotland, there were no visible problems. It is one of the biggest and finest ships of the Danish fleet. A sailing across the German Sea should have posed us no problems.'

'So why did it?' The king leans forward, a twitch in his cheek. *Good,* I think, *give him an absolute grilling.*

'It was the weather,' Admiral Munk says. He stands up and looks around him. 'Do we all agree that the storm out there on the German Sea was the worst we have ever seen?'

The room comes alive with enthusiastic nods.

'You must have weathered many storms in your sailing career,' the king replies, looking unimpressed. 'Other ships of the fleet reached Leith Port unscathed.'

'And Her Royal Highness has reached Ánslo unscathed,' says the admiral immediately. *Ho, he is good.* 'But we sailed through a tempest that was so fierce I thought it supernatural.'

Supernatural!

'Supernatural?' asks the king.

'Not of this world,' says Admiral Munk. 'A storm of the Devil's own making.'

'So are you saying that the Devil played a role in this ill-fated sailing?' The king simmers, somewhere between disbelief and curiosity.

Anna is paying attention now. In fact there is not a person in this room who is not rapt.

The Devil has a habit of bringing everyone to attention.

'I am saying that there are forces we don't understand,' says the admiral. 'The *Gideon* is more than seaworthy. I made sure of it myself before we set sail. The timbers are the best oak. The pitch is best-quality. The rope is the finest manila hemp. I have all the receipts in the logbooks.'

Then the passengers give their testimony. The goldsmith is no use: he spent most of the sailing in his cabin, praying for his mortal soul. Crew members say that as soon as one leak was patched, another appeared, until it made no sense to continue as it was quicker to get to Ánslo. In all, three sailors died during the voyage.

At the end of the day, when the servants are bristling by the doors to get the tables and chairs back in order for dinner, King James sits in conversation with Earl Marischal. He stands up and everyone else does too.

'I have decided this,' the king declares. 'That you did your best in an impossible situation, Admiral Munk, and that we must try to put this episode behind us, for the sake of the union of our countries.'

There is a palpable sigh of relief amongst the ambassadors.

'But perhaps this might be a good opportunity for you to retire yourself from sea service,' he adds.

The admiral looks aghast. It's a humiliating order.

'Perhaps,' says Admiral Munk, 'I might offer the testimony of an acquaintance of mine.' He points to the man from Copenhagen. 'He is not a sea captain, but a scholar. I wrote to him when we were forced to land at Ánslo and he agreed to make the journey here. He has been here two days and we have talked of a most serious matter.'

The king looks annoyed until the man stands up. He wears a heavy black cloak with a modest white ruffled collar and a thick gold chain, every inch a university man. James nods. He is the type to be impressed by scholars.

'Your Majesty,' he says, 'I am Dr Neils Hemmingsen, a theologian from the University of Copenhagen. I am an acquaintance of Admiral Munk and was most intrigued by the letter he sent me, describing how the fleet was driven back by contrary winds.'

'Continue, Dr Hemmingsen, but be brief,' says James, motioning for a refill of his wine goblet.

'Is it also the case,' asks Dr Hemmingsen, 'that a recent storm capsized a ferryboat in the Scottish Firth of Forth, drowning its passengers? And one of them was Mistress Jane Kennedy, on her way to Holyroodhouse to attend Princess Anna?'

'Yes,' says the king, taken aback, his wine goblet full, but momentarily forgotten. 'Midway under sail, a tempest so fierce that the boat sank and most of the passengers drowned, including our dear Mistress Kennedy, who'd attended my own mother and was bringing precious heirlooms of plate and hangings for Holyroodhouse. All lost.' There is much sorrowful shaking of heads around the room at this.

'I heard about the Firth of Forth drowning from the scholars at Copenhagen. They are particularly interested in disastrous weather events. We have seen a similar case in Copenhagen. We believe, Your Majesty, that there may be sorcery afoot, and that these recent storms are not simply a turn in the weather, but deliberately conjured by witches.'

It's as though a lightning bolt strikes the room. Everyone gasps – me included. All eyes swing to the king.

'Witches?' He narrows his eyes. 'Folk magicians?'

'More than that, much more,' urges Dr Hemmingsen. 'Our Copenhagen case is a most unusual instance of a drowning caused by weather magic. A woman by the name of Ane Koldings, who is known as the Mother of the Devil and who killed her neighbour with a storm. This is far more than the simple curses of ungodly folk. We are talking about pacts struck with the Devil. Murder.'

Admiral Munk stands up. 'Is it not the case that some would have objected to the union between Scotland and Denmark, Your Majesty? The theologians suspect there were malevolent forces behind the storms in the German Sea, intent on preventing the royal union.'

Dr Hemmingsen nods. 'It is not beyond the realms of possibility,' he says.

'And in that case, there was nothing any man could have done,' offers Admiral Munk. 'And we have a greater problem on our hands than just one ill-fated voyage.'

The king looks terrified. The room falls so silent you could hear a pin drop. 'I must know everything about this Ane Koldings,' James says. 'Ask the Copenhagen court to write to me.'

No one mentions the burning of Doritte Olsen for an almost identical crime in Kronborg: sending a storm to capsize her husband's fishing boat. But that is only going to be a matter of time. That was a burning done discreetly, but that secret will get out. I wish I could say something. I wish I could stand up and tell them this is all nonsense. But that would only make things worse. They might think I was trying to defend these women. They might accuse me of being a witch myself.

Chapter Seventeen

JURA

North Berwick, Scotland
November 1589

The Bathgate hens were bold and bushy a week ago. Then, one by one, they stopped laying, started gasping and their combs purpled. The Bathgates, who have kept poultry for generations – flocks passed down from father to son – have never seen the like. The few surviving birds are now barricaded in the barn, for Master Bathgate believes there are poisonous miasmas on the winds, whilst Guidwife Bathgate is blaming the water from the pond. In any case, it is an almighty disaster.

'They still have their geese and ducks and three fields of wheat,' says Master Kincaid. 'They are luckier than most.' He and the guidwife are settled by the fire whilst Hazel sews her sampler. I am sweeping the hall. The parlour door is ajar and, when I hear them talk of the Bathgates, I stop and listen.

'Yes, but two hundred dead hens, Stuart. We must have compassion for them.'

Master Kincaid snorts. 'We cannot have compassion for everybody, Isabel. I'm sure the Bathgates have plenty of coin tucked away for emergencies like this.'

I wonder, as I go back to my sweeping, at what point in his

life compassion left Master Kincaid. Was he mibbie beaten roughly as a bairn, so it never had the chance to form? For he aye seems to take a pleasure in others' pain and discomfort. I feel sorry for the Bathgates, even though Robbie's nothing but a dirty divvil. But sleekit wee Hazel Kincaid loses no time in persuading her ma they should be paying the Bathgates a visit.

'We should take them a jar of our rosehip jam. And a cake or somesuch. Just to show our sympathies – it's such a shame for them,' I hear her say to her ma the next day.

'Aye, mibbie one of the wee jars,' her ma says. 'Guidwife Bathgate's never done us any harm. And half a dozen scones.'

'I'll put on my new my kirtle,' I hear Hazel say, as she thunders up the stairs. 'Jura, help me do some hair rolls.' I know she will be reaching for that wee wooden-handled mirror in her drawer. Checking her skin is still looking good.

Och, she is plenty taken with Robbie Bathgate.

When the pair of them return, they are full of the horrors. The dead hens had to be put on a pyre and a stench of burnt chicken still hangs over the place, charred feathers whirling like blossom. Guidwife Bathgate has taken to praying all day long and Master Bathgate has resorted to drink.

'They will not last the month if they carry on like that,' says Guidwife Kincaid. 'Leaving poor Robbie to do all the work.' They are sitting in the kitchen sharing the gossip with us, everyone tutting as Cook pours out small cups of sack.

'Poor Robbie,' murmurs Hazel, winding her curls around her finger.

'If only there was something more we could do to help,' says Guidwife Kincaid.

It takes Hazel all her strength not to jump up at once. 'I

could assist,' she offers. 'I could go and help Guidwife Bathgate around the house.'

I close my eyes and try not to laugh. Hazel Kincaid would not know which end of a broom to sweep with.

Guidwife Kincaid chews her lip, thinking.

'Go over there tomorrow,' she says. 'I pray the Lord will witness your good deed and think favourably on us and save our home from any pestilence.'

The next day is shuddering cold. After I do the hearths and set the breakfast table, I stand at the window of my wee room, hugging myself warm with the other maid's shawl, watching the waters of the Firth shift to and fro under a sunrise the colour of gold. Winter has set in. I mind how you hated the winter, Ma. The foraging for rosehips and haws would leave your hands red-raw, but the cottage was aye cosy and warm, with the fire burning bright. I know there's plenty of firewood for Da. He'll not freeze to death. I know I should visit him, Ma, but already it feels like it's been so long he'd just be angry.

Master Kincaid calls me into his study again after Hazel has skipped up to the Bathgates and the guidwife has gone a-calling on one of her daft pals.

'Come upstairs and help me organize my quills and ink,' he says when he finds me alone, mending stockings in the back sitting room. He stands there, looking shifty.

'I don't want to,' I say.

'You'll do as I tell you,' he orders.

I don't move. My palms sweat onto my darning. I will ruin the wool.

'Are those my stockings?' he asks.

'Aye, sir.' My voice has a quiver in it.

'There was a maid whipped in Haddington last week,' he says. 'Right in the main street, for stealing her mistress's fine silk stockings. I authorized the payment for the flogger myself. They stripped her to her bodice, even though it was freezing cold.' His voice is cool, but his eyes glitter, savouring the memory. 'Come, Mistress Craig, and let's dwell no more on punishments for errant maids.'

I go upstairs.

I do as he says again.

When I return to the back sitting room, the stockings are still faintly damp with my sweat, and the scent of my fear lingers.

That night I am feared about so many things I can barely sleep. Whippings. The fear of Guidwife Kincaid finding out what goes on in the study. I wish I'd never asked her if I could be her maid.

I can't go back to Da.

Master Kincaid warned me, as he tossed me another coin. 'If you try to leave, I'll have you brought back by my men.' He'd said it casually, as if we were discussing a trivial matter.

I'd said nothing, just closed the study door as quietly as I could and stood on the landing, listening out for anyone close by. Luckily, it was all clear. But luck runs out.

In the morning, after I have done the hearths again, I go back to my room and find my charme box. I have given up knotting ribbons for now, and Hazel's skin is better and the king has gone to rescue his princess, so I have not had much use for my charmes. But Master Kincaid needs his passion culled. The brown bulbs from the apothecary are in there. I take them out and look at them, racking my brain for the proper way to use them. Och, mibbie there's only one way I can really use them. Put them in his food. For I can hardly slather a paste on him, can I? They'll be bitter too, so I'll need to put them in something sweet, like the honey posset he takes with his breakfast.

That will do it.

And there's time yet to prepare it this morning. I'm the only one up.

8th November 1589
From Douglas Murray of Kirkbrae,
at Holyroodhouse

IN THE STRICTEST OF CONFIDENCE
To His High and Mighty Majesty, King James the Sixth of Scotland, at Ánslo, Norway

Sir – I trust that you have arrived safely in Ánslo and are with your betrothed. God has overseen your journey, so I write with the utmost faith that the future of Scotland is now secure with the union with Denmark and that you will be blessed with children, and soon.

Unfortunately, your wicked cousin has been out of prison no more than a few weeks and is already back to his plots to grab your throne. My sources tell me he is organizing his men and ordering more arms to replace those we seized when we arrested them. It is imperative that you return as soon as you can.

I remain your servant and await any messages, but mostly I await your return. Not only so that you can bring your cousin under control, but also so that we might embrace each other once more, in the manner to which we have become so dearly accustomed.

Chapter Eighteen

ANNA

The Bishop's Palace, Ánslo
November 1589

Witches are determined to murder us – an entire gang of them. No doubt Doritte Olsen too. That's why I heard her voice as she burned and why we saw her apparition in the port at Kronborg.

Thank God for Dr Hemmingsen and his knowledge. For he means to help protect us now. The problem is that we must set sail for Scotland again immediately. The weather is wintry, and witches hunt us, yet sail we must, for it has become imperative that James returns to Scotland. His cousin Francis Stewart, Earl of Bothwell, is at large.

Bothwell is trying to avenge the execution of James's mother Mary, Queen of Scots, by invading England. James wants none of it, for there can never be a union with Scotland and England if the countries are at war, and he believes his mother was immoral and her execution justified. The longer James remains in Denmark, the more likely it is that Bothwell will raid the border or, worse, plot to seize the throne. So the *Gideon* looms over Ánslo Port, patched up and teeming with an agitated sailing crew who will be kissing their caul amulets, for rumours of the witchery that hunts us down will have spread like fire.

But this time, under Dr Hemmingsen's instructions, we are taking a guard of bishops on board, who will pray continually to ward off any wickedness. We must outrun it and sail to Scotland safely.

'Will you write of these events in another of your books, Dr Hemmingsen?'

James and I are sitting in the small chamber we dine in together, but this evening Dr Hemmingsen has been invited. He has been asked to remain in Ánslo so that James might seek his counsel. Tonight he imposes on our intimacy with no embarrassment at all. James is fascinated by the scholar. Were it not for the fact that I am passing the *smørrebrød*, I would be invisible.

Dr Hemmingsen nods. He tucks in, heaping his bread so high with pickled herring and egg that I think it will spill, then looks at me.

'Indeed. I have been taking notes. Witchery is endemic now, in these parts, and it will be in Scotland too,' he replies. 'The threat to the Church has never been greater. If we Protestants only ever worry about the threat from the Catholics, then we miss the point entirely.'

James is captivated. He looks at Dr Hemmingsen in a way he has never looked at me. He has not touched his food. I have only seen one witch, Doritte Olsen, but Dr Hemmingsen is the expert, I suppose.

'Have you heard what is happening in Trier?' Dr Hemmingsen asks.

James shakes his head.

'Trier is six hundred miles south-west of us. But what is happening there should serve as a warning to us all. Trier has been plagued with pestilence and famine and bad weather. The problem has been found to have been caused by witches.

Dozens have already been caught. They believe the problem is so widespread they have appointed special inquisitors and judges to deal with it.'

James shakes his head. 'And how do they find the culprits?' he asks.

'Their neighbours have been persuaded to report them, and they have been rounded up and tried and burned. A hundred executed already. They confess, but only under torture.' Dr Hemmingsen shrugs. 'But the problem is that this evil is not only limited to Trier. As I have explained, it is everywhere.'

'Well, if it is endemic in Scotland, that means I must get a grip on it. We cannot risk any threat to our crops and our cattle,' James says, straightening up in his chair.

'We all must,' agrees Dr Hemmingsen. 'For demonology spreads like disease. They believe themselves more powerful than God. And that is when the Devil swoops in, and that is when the pacts are made and when chaos reigns.' He takes a large glug of his wine. I wish James would eat something.

'But how does the practice spread from one country to another?' James asks. 'Six hundred miles is a long way to travel, even for a witch.'

Dr Hemmingsen shakes his head and looks around the room, as if checking for witches in the bookcases and candle sconces.

'In the sky,' he says earnestly. 'In the sea. It does not matter. They have methods of transport that we can only imagine.'

'Of course,' ponders James. 'The Devil can help them fly.'

'He can indeed. He can come to them in any form – man or animal. He can come in the form of a bird or a bat or a cat, well disguised. The witches smear themselves in special ointments to help them fly. They congregate at their Sabbaths! From all corners of the world. They feast and dance in the sky! Thousands of them! They have *intercourse*, then as they bid each other farewell, they kiss the Devil's arse. Right under his tail!'

I blush furiously, but James does not even notice.

'We are theologians, you and I, are we not?' Dr Hemmingsen goes on. 'Men who pride ourselves in our *extensive* understanding of religion?'

James nods.

'Well, the study of demonology is as vital as any lesson in theology,' Dr Hemmingsen says. 'Witches are cunning and have hidden themselves in plain sight. And in my view,' he pauses here and spreads a thick smear of pork-liver paste on his last slice of bread, 'in my view, they are our biggest threat. How familiar are you with the *Malleus Maleficarum*?'

'*The Hammer of Witches*,' says James, 'makes it clear sorcery is a crime that should be investigated with torture and punished by death.'

'Indeed. Witches should be treated in the same way as heretics,' replies Dr Hemmingsen.

The conversation continues in this vein over red-berry pudding and I am largely ignored, until Dr Hemmingsen puts down his spoon and addresses me directly.

'Your Royal Highness,' he ventures. 'As an example of what I am saying, was there a witch-burning at Kronborg in the days before your voyage? Since my arrival at the Bishop's Palace I've heard rumours, but you know what rumours can be like. Admiral Munk never mentioned it, but it might be something that was kept secret. It might have happened before the admiral arrived at Kronborg.'

Of course he would find out. He's the sort of man to rely on a network of tale-tellers. How else would he get his facts for his books? James looks aghast.

There is no point denying it. I pick my words carefully. 'I

believe you are correct, Dr Hemmingsen, but I was not privy to the case, of course. I am sure someone would give you the details.'

'I will ask them myself,' says James, glaring at me. I think I understand that look. It is a look that says I ought to have been honest with him. I ought to have told him this. It is a look that says he doesn't trust me.

After supper, James sends me to prayer, saying I do not pray often or fervently enough. He has decided I must spend extra hours doing just that, kneeling at the side of my bed so that I can pray for our prospects, as well as myself. I wonder if he is concerned for my soul or is punishing me, letting it be known that I am not to keep secrets from him.

After prayer, it is time for the marital act.

James has already got us into a routine so rigid that you could set a clock by it. First, we lie in bed and talk. He frets about the Catholics, for there are conspirators everywhere in Scotland. He fears God's wrath; he frets about the fire and brimstone he faces if he incurs God's fury and fails to govern Scotland well, for as he has been appointed by God Himself as king, with the honour of serving the Lord, so comes the threat of eternal damnation if he does not. If he picks the wrong wife, for example, he says, looking at me with his pale-brown eyes. And then, of course, he frets about the witches.

It is quite terrifying, all of this, in bed, but I believe it means James is confiding in me, for that is what Mama said he must feel he's able to do, if I am ever to become his wife.

Next James takes two confections from a silver tray and hands one to me. He has a nightly habit of sucking on a rose-water sweet, which he calls a *scorchet*, for its medicinal benefits. They are made by a sugar-man in the Canongate, and James brought a box with him on orders from his physician. We take them with the last of our wine.

After we have taken our *scorchets* he moves towards me awkwardly, the pillows creaking under his shoulder.

He smells of patchouli. I yearn for cedar so hard that I ache. I hate the way he touches me. I want to push him away. His manner with me, when we are intimate, is strange. It is not like Henry, who was entirely full of longing when we kissed by the lake. James is mechanical, like a clockwork doll that was once brought to Kronborg by a travelling showman and moved surely but stiffly through a simple dance, as if it were on strings. And so, I suppose, we are both mechanical, moving through the motions of intimacy that we've both been instructed in over the years, by courtiers set with the task of ensuring we produce a royal lineage. Like a court dance, like a slow *pavane* or sometimes a rapid *galliard*, but never anything out of step or from the heart. *I can do it* – that's what I tell myself, fighting the urge of nausea, the stench of his wine-breath, the stab of pain below. *This is the thing you were born to do.*

But it is not just me who is uncomfortable. I think James is telling himself the same. I think he suffers it as I do.

Afterwards he mutters words of prayer. I lie back and think of Scotland.

I have been allowed to continue my lessons with Henry. It keeps me out of the way whilst James meets his men and strategizes over plots and organizes our arrival procession, which must be as ostentatious as possible. But we no longer walk, unescorted, to the lake.

'We can't,' Henry says, knowing by the way I am looking at

him over our books that I am desperate for us to go. Desperate for us to be alone, and for me to rest my head on his chest and let him envelop me in love and warmth. We are sitting in the study, stifling from the log fire, and neither of us can concentrate on the collection of English poetry he has brought down from the bookcase.

'But it's our last day in Ánslo. Can we not say our goodbyes to the *hytte*?'

'If we go out there, alone, then I will want to hold you in my arms, and if we are caught, I will be drowned in the lake and you banished to Hellebæk Abbey.'

Instead he calls for *akvavit,* and reads some of the poetry aloud to me.

Outside, servants are heaving the last of our crates onto carts bound for the port. Inside, the wood crackles in the grate. All is unsettled. Outside, sails are being unfurled and ropes tested for the final time. Inside, Henry finishes reading and puts down his book.

'Your handfasting is the talk of the courtiers,' he says. 'They are keeping watch so they know when to look out for signs of a pregnancy. And I will not ask you about your time with him – not about the details. But I do need to know whether you feel bonded to him.' Henry looks as edgy as I have ever seen him, worrying at a flaw in the cover of the book with his finger.

'There is nothing much to say of the details,' I tell him. 'There are barely any details. It is perfunctory.'

He sips his drink. His face looks drawn.

'Have you been dwelling on it?' I ask.

'It's the fact that you have no choice,' he says. 'It makes me sick to my stomach. I have never thought about it before, in all the marriages at court.'

I start to feel the rush of horror that I have been holding back. I have been doing such a job of keeping it at bay, but it was always going to come out eventually. My pulse races and I feel hot, but I can't leave the room because they would notice how upset I am, and anyway I don't want to leave Henry.

He stands up and opens a window, letting the air trickle in. He sits back down and clutches my hand across the table.

'I would embrace you, but someone might walk in,' he says.

Our hands clasp each other on top of the book of poems. Henry's grasp is firm, his hand large and reassuring.

'Is it unbearable?' he asks.

'It is our duty,' I whisper.

'Have you thought any more about what I suggested?' he says. 'That you should try to fail your marriage trial?'

I think about it constantly. But it is one thing to imagine something and another to take the risk.

'I have thought about resisting him,' I tell Henry. 'But I'm frightened of what James might do. And I'm frightened you might change your mind about me, and then where would I be?'

Henry squeezes my hands.

'I would never leave you,' he says. 'When we get to Scotland you must find a way of deterring the king, lessening his interest in you.'

'He hardly has any passion for me,' I say.

Henry nods. 'Then we must find a way of gently spoiling this union, so that it ends with no blame on either side and you can walk free to be with me.'

'I can't imagine how we might possibly do that. I'm not very cunning, or artful,' I say.

'And that is why I love you,' he replies. 'But this is a task so delicate it needs all our conviction and prayer. Or even magic.'

'Don't say that,' I say, shuddering at all the talk of sorcery I have been hearing. 'You will tempt the Devil.'

Henry lets go of my hands, just in time, for Kirsten walks in without knocking. Although our hands have separated, our tension is obvious.

'This lesson has overrun,' she says. 'It's time for you to come and get ready for luncheon.'

Then she stops, almost sniffing the air, blinking once, twice, as if she is trying to get the sense of something that lingers, as though she has caught the scent of our passion. Her eyes flick between Henry and me. Her lips knit into a tight little purse.

'Come, Anna,' she continues. 'We must dress you for your final luncheon in Ánslo with your beloved betrothed.'

November 1589
From Hans Hansen, Chief Assessor
of the Court of Copenhagen

To Dr Neils Hemmingsen

In response to your enquiry for further information about our Highly Unusual Court Case in Copenhagen. Here are the details for you to pass on to His Majesty King James of Scotland, in order that he has a full account of the case:

The prisoner Ane Koldings is a woman of around fifty years of age, of average height and build and with grey-to-brown hair. She has the strength of a beast and has to be held in chains. She is known, locally, as the Mother of the Devil and has been accused of witchcraft three times previously, although nothing came before our court on those matters.

On this most recent occasion she was accused of creating weather magic that caused the sinking of a fishing vessel off the coast, as part of a personal vendetta against the boat's owner, who is also her neighbour, Captain Jacob Oxe. There has been a long-running argument between them over land ownership.

She has confessed, under examination, that she is a witch who raised weather magic against Captain Oxe's boat. She is prone to prolonged outbursts of nonsense-speak and, since her conviction, refuses to use the slop pail given to her. She has, in short, been a most impossible woman.

Mistress Koldings was apprehended in Copenhagen in July and has been sentenced to death by fire, the sentence to be carried out on the first of next month to allow for preparations to be made. But we can delay the execution if His Majesty the King of Scotland wants us to examine Mistress Koldings on any suspicion of further sorcery.

I must advise you that she needed much interrogation before she confessed, and torture methods had to be deployed. She is, as I have said, a most impossible woman.

November 1589
From His High and Mighty King James
the Sixth of Scotland, at Ánslo

To Mr Hans Hansen, Chief Assessor of the Court of Copenhagen

Sir – I write to you in haste on the matter of Mistress Ane Koldings, indicted on charges of weather witchcraft.

My advisors have reason to believe she may have knowledge of, or have been directly involved in, an attempt to raise a storm to sink the Danish royal fleet, causing it to abort its journey in September.

I understand from your letter to Dr Hemmingsen that Mistress Koldings is to be examined on these matters. I am writing to tell you to keep me informed, by letter, of her confessions. There may have been another witch in her acquaintance, a woman by the name of Doritte Olsen, lately executed for weather sorcery at Kronborg Castle. I am keenly interested in seeing whether there is a wider plot afoot.

I am bound to return to Scotland within the coming days, as I cannot remain away from court any longer, but I have instructed Dr Hemmingsen to travel to Copenhagen and oversee the examinations and then report to me.

In the name of Almighty God,
James VI

November 1589
From King James the Sixth of Scotland,
in Ánslo

To Douglas Murray of Kirkbrae, at Holyroodhouse

D – A brief note to let you know that all is well, and we begin our return voyage in the coming days.

I cannot wait to leave this dark part of the world. I had thought Scandinavia to be a land of scholars and kirk men, but some of its secrets are ungodly.

Anna of Denmark is a fair match. You will see for yourself that she is intelligent and eager to learn, and pleasant company. She will need the guiding hand of our court, of course, but I believe she has potential. I fear I am not enough of a force against the Devil.

I need the sanctity of marriage and a wife to strengthen me. I hope that we will, in time, find love and affection in our union.

Oh, Douglas, how I miss you and wish it was you in my chamber. It aches that you can never be betrothed to me, but that is the pain we must endure.

In great anticipation of our next meeting and your counsel,

J

Chapter Nineteen

KIRSTEN

*The King's Wark, Leith Port
December 1589*

Finally, we have disembarked, but into a wicked Scots winter. Wind and hail and darkness even worse than the weather we fought at sea. I have made up my mind that I will never set foot on a ship again. The fear that disaster is never more than a gust or a wave away is one I never want to repeat. But I have arrived, thank God. I am here. Washed up like a broken crab. They led us off the ship, on a wooden walkway lined with Turkish carpet, through shrill crowds and cannon salutes. Past trumpeters and violin players and kettle drummers who beat a rowdy march for hours, before descending into bawdy songs.

There was nothing stately or dignified about it.

Now I can do what I came here to do, with not a moment to lose.

Leith is as I remember it. But the port is bigger and busier, and we are being kept in rooms at the King's Wark for several days, ahead of our formal procession up to Holyroodhouse, although the caw of the Scots tongue rising from the harbour is so familiar I feel that this is my homecoming. This morning, as the sun rose, I stood at the window and watched crates of wool and coal and fish being hauled onto ships, and crates of wine and pottery and cloth being unloaded. Stray cats and dogs sniff at piles of sacks. Masts tower over it all, set with foreign flags.

We will make a formal entry procession into Edinburgh town, with Anna riding in a solid-silver carriage. There will be pageants and performances and feasts. All the households of the Canongate have been told to send their best table linens to Holyroodhouse for our banquets. I have barely had a minute, what with all the hanging and airing of gowns and consulting the goldsmith and the Scottish royal jeweller.

And underneath the jewels and the silver, the royal betrothal is weak.

I have tried to spend time with Anna, but she slipped about the *Gideon* like a freshly caught fish. When she was not in prayer, or with James, I could barely find her. Sometimes I would catch the tail of her skirts whispering up a set of stairs. Or the faint lilt of her laugh. I suspect she has an infatuation with Henry Roxburgh, and he with her. Their language lessons continued, and seemed to take longer and longer each day.

And if I am right, she is playing a most dangerous game.

'Remember you're still on trial,' I told her, finding Anna standing at the prow one morning, letting her cape fall below her shoulders, despite the unbearable cold. Despite the sailors being in full view.

'What do you mean?' she snapped. She has never snapped at me before. Never dared. The wind whipped her hair. She bit her red lips and tilted her head back, jaw clenched, daring me to question her further.

'You've become a woman now,' I said, as delicately as I could. 'It has, perhaps, emboldened you. But you are being watched. The Scots are judging your every move. They are still deciding if you are worthy of the king.'

'Perhaps I am also deciding if a royal marriage is what I want,' she replied.

I hid my shock by putting my hand on the rail and looking out to the horizon. 'Oh, shall you go back to Kronborg and pack a chest of your plainest clothes for Hellebæk Abbey?'

'I am never going to Hellebæk Abbey,' she said. 'I have decided that.'

'So you have decided you have *options*. Whilst the Scots construct platforms for your procession, and practise their dances and songs and send their best fattened livestock for our feasts, you are deciding whether you will be their queen.'

She flinched at that. I took my eye off the horizon and looked at her.

'When I was a young woman, about your age,' I told her, 'I met a charming gentleman who told me all sorts of tall tales, and I believed him.'

Her face grew serious. 'Go on.'

'I never usually talk about these matters,' I said. 'It's an undignified habit, to reminisce and ruminate over old matters of the heart. But I will tell you this. There are men who will fall in love with women at the drop of a hat. And then, when they have got what they want – whatever that is – they will fall out of love the next day, as if nothing had ever happened between them at all. And their promises and kisses and admiration simply disappear as they move on to their next conquest. Why, Anna, the air of the whole world is full of the ghosts of the promises of handsome young men. Your betrothed, King James, is not one of those men. He is a man of God, of honour and decency. He may not be the man of your dreams. You may never fall in love with him. He may never fall truly and deeply in love with you. But he is your best chance of making something magnificent of yourself.'

She nodded, then pulled her cape about her shoulders again. 'Perhaps,' she said.

'I will leave you here to think upon these matters,' I told her. 'But I expect you back in your cabin before too long. I don't want you getting waylaid by any of the other passengers. Particularly by Lord Henry. It would be unseemly for you to be caught chattering together outside your lessons.'

And sure enough, just as I spoke, the very man himself appeared. Almost as though they had arranged to be on the prow at exactly the same time. When he saw me, Henry stood, awkwardly, waiting for me to leave.

'Kirsten,' Anna said, as I was curtseying my leave to her, 'the gentleman you mentioned. The one you met when you were a young woman. The one with the promises. Did he break your heart?'

I straightened up and took a deep breath.

'It is undignified to talk of such matters,' I replied.

After we landed, the Scots, including Henry, went straight up to Holyroodhouse to get back to the business matters they'd neglected these last weeks. We remain at King's Wark for the next day or so, as they ready the carriages and assemble the courtiers. The procession will last all day. We will be showered with confections and will watch masques and wave until our arms ache. All the girls of Leith and Edinburgh and the Canongate will wish they were royal, envying us, blissfully ignorant of the sacrifices we have to make.

I am hoping the palace is vast enough so that we Danes can live our own lives and mingle with the Scots as infrequently as possible.

If there is anything between her and Henry Roxburgh, he

will tire of her when he realizes he cannot have her in any meaningful way.

At least that is what I hope.

Anna bled this morning, perfectly on time too, which means no royal child this month.

'Arrange linens for Her Royal Highness,' I tell the maid, Hanne, and she scuttles off to find where such things have been packed. She will be back in ten minutes, empty-handed, and it will become my problem to search them out, but until then I will relax, sitting on a chair by the window, and breathe freely at the relief I feel that I am here.

As I sit, pulling a blanket over my knees, another maid knocks and delivers a note. If she is surprised that I have received a letter, then she does her best to conceal it. I thank her and do not open it until she has closed the door and I am sure she is not lingering outside:

> *Kirsten,*
> *I hope this letter gets to you. The things you warn of sound terrifying enough, but there is no hint of it here in Scotland. We are safe enough. This is a civilized country. You fret too much. Enjoy your return. It has been a long time coming. Come and visit when you can.*

Chapter Twenty

JURA

*North Berwick, Scotland
December 1589*

Snowdrops to ward off evil. Their flowers are fragile, but their bulbs are dangerous.

I never meant to do Master Kincaid terrible harm. Mibbie the apothecary got them mixed up with something more poisonous. Mibbie snowdrop bulbs are more poisonous than I thought. But after I boil them up and put them in his posset, he falls deathly sick. They speed up his pulse and give him wild daydreams, seeing divvils and witches and fairies dancing around his bed.

Hazel has not left her father's bedside for two days, convinced he will slip off his mortal coil in the midst of a fever dream. Robbie Bathgate's farm having been abandoned, she sits in the fug of her father's sick-chamber, apologizing for all the times she has thought ill of him for making her learn respect and obedience, and other skills that she now realizes are vital if a girl is to become a wife.

A physician came twice and could not determine the cause of Master Kincaid's illness. At first I was relieved, but on the second visit he sat with Guidwife Kincaid for so long in the parlour that I could not help but hover at the door and heard him say, 'I have never seen the like – 'tis a grave matter indeed. He seems under a spell of some kind.'

That's when my own stomach began to churn.

The guidwife herself took to standing with her hands on her hips at the window, gazing at nothing, whilst her husband rolled around in his bed. I could not settle anywhere. I could not eat or drink or sleep or rest. I thought I could even taste the bitter snowdrop bulbs myself, sticking in the back of my throat. I gagged on them. I gagged on my own thoughts. *I have poisoned him.*

Hazel guessed. She guessed it after a visit from Robbie Bathgate on the third day when they put their heads together.

I am drying the breakfast dishes when she comes and speaks to me. It is the fourth day after the snowdrops. Master Kincaid is sitting up in bed now and has managed some porridge. The household has held its breath, tiptoeing, and with the news of his clean porridge bowl, it has let out a sigh of relief.

'Did you do something to my pa?' Hazel stands at the other side of the kitchen. Her rash is back and is raw-looking too.

I shake my head. 'Why ever would I do anything to him?' I ask.

'Robbie says you don't like my pa,' she says.

'He is a decent master to me,' I lie.

She chews on her lip. 'Did you ever do anything with my pa? Robbie says he thinks you tempted him.'

A jolt of anger rises from my gut. I swallow it down. Hazel cannot see me angry. Then she would realize. 'That is a shocking thing to say,' I tell her. I should never have told Robbie about Master Kincaid hanging around me. It was a secret, and now he has spilled it, the rogue.

She stops chewing on her lip. Her hand flits to scratch her rash, but she makes it stop at her collar instead. 'Robbie says you tempted him as well,' she goes on.

I put down the dish cloot, laying it carefully beside the drying rack. Hazel fiddles with her collar.

'Robbie Bathgate is a disgrace,' I say. 'You should watch yourself with him.'

She stands at the doorway for a few more moments, looking at me in her sullen way, then takes her leave. The kitchen is quiet, as quiet as it has ever been, which gives me a moment to think hard. I wonder if I have enough money saved to run away from here and never return. Aunt Mary can't be that difficult to find. How big can the Canongate really be? Master Kincaid might send his men, but they would never find me there – it's too far away. He would never even think to look.

Master Kincaid makes a fast recovery, which they all put down to the power of their prayers. He is soon bristling around the house again, admiring the way his shirt hangs looser after days with no food, and pulling at his eye-bags in the small looking glass in the hall.

Hazel Kincaid makes no eye contact with me at all and utters no words. It is as though I no longer exist. I know it is time. I have so many coins saved up that the bag weighs heavy in my hand. Tonight, when this strange household sleeps, I will slip out of the back door like a shadow.

I have no real plan, just a jumble of hopes as I march along the pathway through the fields. I imagine Master Kincaid jumping out of the shadows at me demanding, *Where do you think you are going?* There is no answer. I only know that I must put distance behind me and the Kincaids. My life spreads before me like spilled wine. It could go anywhere.

In any event, the only route to anywhere decent is the road into Edinburgh, and the only person I know outside North Berwick is Aunt Mary in the Canongate, so I follow that. Hazel has talked of Edinburgh – of how there will be parades for the arrival of Princess Anna, when she gets there from Leith Port. Of sugar banquets and cannon salutes. Men are building timber scaffolds for the plays: masques with dancers and torch-bearers and flower garlands. There will be work for me. When I am established, I could set myself up as a healer again, for there is a guid living to be made in effective tinctures. I have a bag on my back, packed as fast and stealthily as I could, with as many of my belongings as I could carry, but I had to travel light, as Edinburgh is three hours' walk, so I left some items at the Kincaids.

It's a freezing cold night. The wintry wind tugs at my kirtle. My bag is already too heavy. The further I trudge, the more I feel my fear. I had thought leaving North Berwick would get rid of it, but the opposite is happening. Feelings that I had suppressed heave their way out of me. *Master Kincaid would have come at me again. If he had died, it would have been my fault. I am wicked! Master Kincaid is wicked. Robbie Bathgate is wicked.*

If I am ever caught running away, what will they do to me?

Chapter Twenty-One

JURA

The Canongate, Scotland
December 1589

I could never have imagined the likes of Edinburgh and the Canongate, even in my maddest dreams. Houses four storeys high and lined up side by side, so that the street is in shadow. I take one daunder down the burgh of Edinburgh and that is enough. There are so many beggars I have to keep my belongings clutched into my kirtle and my head down. But then I arrive at the Netherbow Port, a great gateway set into stone walls, high as a castle, with turrets and spikes. I pay my toll and enter the Canongate and I know I have arrived somewhere magnificent.

The Canongate is green and grand, for it is an extension of the royal court. Shops with squeaky-clean windows and polished brass door-knockers sell the best wines and cheese-rounds, and gold. In the centre is a tollbooth with a handsome bell-tower. Big houses with dark timber frames dominate the back streets, where the jewellers and merchants live. Everyone else lives in the tenements lining the main street. Tennis courts and orchards and cock-fighting pits and bowling greens line the outskirts. And to think I lived all these years in North Berwick knowing nothing of this. Within a day I have eaten an orange and watched a game of pall-mall played by gentlemen on a long strip of pitch made of crushed sea-shells and been winked at by boys carrying water from the wells to their masters' houses.

It does not take me long to find Aunt Mary, for healing folk have an understanding of each other. I enter an apothecary shop near the tollbooth and I ask the man there if he knows an auld Mary who might come to him for chamomile, mint and garlic and who has a good cure for heidaches, for that is about all I remember Ma saying about Mary. That and her gift for future-telling with cards.

He points me to a building across the road. I climb two flights of winding stone steps that get narrower as they get higher.

Aunt Mary is unsurprised when she opens the door to me and I tell her who I am.

'The cards told me you were coming,' she says, sitting us down at her kitchen table as though I had written her a letter in advance, warning her of my visit. The kitchen is clean and tidy, with copper pots hanging from pegs. Light pours in through a wide window and there are vases of herbs and flowers around the room. She pours us both a drink of wine and raises her cup to me. 'I've had strange readings these past weeks and I knew something had happened in North Berwick, but that I was not to come and meddle, but wait for my time to be useful.'

'A lot has happened,' I tell her. 'Enough for me to run away.'

'Has my sister died?' she asks, but she already knows the answer – whether from her cards or from the fact that I am here with all my worldly goods.

'I made it as easy for Ma as I could, at the end,' I say. 'She barely suffered.'

Mary sighs and sips. 'And your da used to enjoy this stuff too much,' she says, nodding at her cup.

'He still does,' I reply. Then I tell her that my master, Baillie Kincaid, tried to have his wicked way with me.

That, she does look surprised at.

'Kincaid – I remember him well. He was always a monster,' she says.

Ma had told me that Mary was different from other people. *Folk say I'm off my heid. A mad cunning woman. But you should meet your Aunt Mary.* Ma also told me how kind she was, and she was right. Mary says I can live in the rooms on the opposite side of her stair, which have lain empty for months. They are fine too. A small bedchamber and a wee kitchen.

'Did your ma teach you the craft?' Mary asks.

'I learned a fair few of her charmes,' I say. 'And it's what I'm guid at. I think I have her skills.'

A troubled look passes across Mary's face. I don't like that. It gives me a bad feeling.

'What's the matter?' I ask.

'You'll not know this, being from out on the coast, but there's talk in this town that cunning women are putting themselves in danger by practising their craft,' she says.

'What sort of danger?' Mary is a canny woman, aged half a century or so, and if she is worried about something, then mibbie it's worth worrying about.

'There are rumours that we are being linked with the Divvil,' she says.

'Well, that's daft,' I reply. It sounds like the sort of thing Robbie Bathgate would say. 'Why ever would we be tampering with anything like that?'

She shrugs. 'It's what I've heard, that's all. So you might want to be careful.'

'I'll be careful, I tell her. 'But this is what I'm guid at.'

'Aye,' she says. 'It's what I'm guid at too. Now, before you even begin to think about what you're going to do with yourself here in the Canongate, let me give you a card-reading. We could both use a little guidance.'

I have never had my cards read before. Ma did not like the notion of it, but it seems to have done well for Mary, for she lives far better than we ever did.

She pulls her shawl about her shoulders, shuffling her cards before spreading them across the table, over a silk cloth.

'Mibbie I don't want to know what's in the cards for me. I like to live in hope,' I tell her.

'The cards can help you,' she answers. 'Let's see what they say.'

I hesitate. Is it wicked to seek a future-telling? If you know the future, might you try to change it and interfere with God's plan?

'Pick three,' she says. 'One card for the past, one for the present and one for the future.'

The first card is the Knight of Cups, upside down.

'You've been tricked by someone – a man,' she says. 'Given false promises, or maybe there's someone in your past who has trouble with the truth.' I think of Robbie, or even Master Kincaid, for both of them were trouble, were they not?

The second card is the Queen of Swords.

'Independence. Intelligence. You're in a position of more power now than you've ever been,' Mary says. 'That's guid news. Very guid news.'

I nod. My fingers hover over the pack again. The next card will be my future, and she has not been wrong yet.

'One card will call out to you,' she says. 'Concentrate as hard as you can.'

I choose my card and turn it over. It is the Divvil himself.

'Am I to go to hell?' I cry. I can't take my eyes off the ugly beast, all horns and tail.

Mary looks troubled. I do not like this at all.

'Let me think,' she says, closing her eyes.

Oh Lord, what a dollop I was to go along with this.

She opens her eyes again. 'The Divvil is not evil – not in a reading,' she tells me. 'But it does mean you're in the dark about something. And you'll find out soon enough.'

I am not sure I believe her. What if we've conjured him up, just by talking about him? But Mary makes it clear we are done with the reading. She puts the Divvil back in the pack and shuffles the cards, as if to try to lose him. Put him off our scent.

December 1589
From Dr Neils Hemmingsen, in Copenhagen

To His Majesty King James the Sixth

Sir – I write to you in great haste. I have, this evening, returned from the Interrogation Chamber at Copenhagen Prison, where Mistress Ane Koldings has been examined on the matter of an International Sorcery Plot.

Sir, I will spare you the details, but it is sufficient to say that Mistress Koldings required the most intense measures before she would finally deliver the truth, but so eager were the councillors to get to the bottom of the matter, they did indeed examine her for the entire day. In Copenhagen we have the use of a torture rack, and this was brought into commission in order to ascertain certain facts from Mistress Koldings. And they are as such:

Mistress Koldings does not act alone, but convenes regularly with witches from other countries. They convene by means of magical flight and meet at beaches and ports. She was an acquaintance of the witch Doritte Olsen, of Kronborg.

When asked if she has ever convened with witches from Scotland, she admitted the fact.

The point of these conventions has been to conspire against common enemies, including Your Majesty and the Princess of Denmark, in an attempt to prevent the royal union of the countries and the ascent to the English throne.

You remain at risk. There are numerous witches involved with this plot. Mistress Koldings will be put to death, but she is only one of Satan's many servants.

Enclosed with this letter is a gold amulet that I recommend you wear at all times. I have had it engraved by a man in Copenhagen who knows certain signs and symbols to ward off evil.

Your faithful friend,
Dr Hemmingsen

Chapter Twenty-Two

ANNA

The King's Wark, Leith Port
January 1590

The New Year dawns, in a salty wash of grey sky and grey sea. James has gathered an army of kirk men and courtiers to stamp out the Devil and anyone else who might want us dead. He tells me of Dr Hemmingsen's letter when he travels down to King's Wark to visit me for our marital act. I wish he had not told me. I wish I knew nothing of this horror that has chased us across the waters. I wish I knew nothing of witches gathering at ports.

'Any threat to me is a threat to you, and to the future of Scotland,' he whispers, trembling so much I can see his shadow quiver on the wall. We are in my bed, taking our *scorchets*. The only warmth in a Scottish January is the yellow flicker of the sconces and the sweet melt of the confections.

'Will you protect me?' I ask him. It feels strange, but urgent, to ask such a thing. It is the king's sworn duty to protect me, now I am in his care, but they were not thinking of sorcery when they were drawing up the betrothal contract.

'I will protect you,' he replies. 'I will protect Scotland. I am a holy man. A loyal man. I abhor wickedness of any sort.' His pale-brown eyes glisten. His arms are thin under his white nightgown. A gold charm swings on a slender chain from his neck. I have never desired anything less than what is to come.

He becomes more passionate than before, as if he feels stronger now that he has a war to fight. He kisses me with wet, bristly pecks and makes guttural sounds. I lie back and do my duty. There is something arousing him that I cannot understand. Is it the talk of the witches? Is he stirred by the notion that the Devil has called him to war? All the while I can only think one thing: *I want to find Henry and run away.* We could escape from the witches and from the men in black robes. If I was not betrothed to James, the witches would leave me alone.

I have never known so much about sorcery. Afterwards, James bursts with the detail of it. Their filthy orgies, where men and women and beasts all unite in sexual congress, bringing infants to be cannibalized – and all so that they can have whatever they want on this Earth. But it is mostly women, for we are the weaker sex and more susceptible to the Devil. It is our frailty that makes it easier for the Devil to lure and trap us.

And then he takes me again, almost immediately, as if somehow I could save him and our union will protect him. I did not know a man could do that. Kirsten never said anything about doing it twice in one night.

Is that even godly?

I pray, afterwards. I pray so hard I fall asleep muttering my amens.

My grand entry into Edinburgh on the silver carriage is delayed so that the men carrying the canopy over it, and those performing the masque beside it, can be vetted to make sure they are not sorcerers. They are being asked about their godliness and made to recite prayers ahead of the procession. We will stop at three churches on the way to ask for God's blessing. The timings have been amended to allow us extra prayer.

Meanwhile the Port of Leith is inspected for sorcerers and spies. Then a minister comes with courtiers to bless my chambers, and they find Aksel in Kirsten's room.

We are standing at the door when it happens. They have pushed past us, with looks of holy intent on their faces, brandishing candles and incense.

'Aksel is my pet,' I tell them. 'Kirsten looks after him for me, so that he does not disturb His Majesty.'

They are standing around his cage.

'The Devil can disguise himself in many ways,' says the minster. He is called Reverend Thompson. He has been appointed as my guardian. Never mind the Lutheran bishops we brought, who now await their return voyage. We are in the custody of the Scots kirk now.

Reverend Thompson opens the cage. His hands are trembling and he looks terrified of the little mite. He takes Aksel in his hands and breaks his neck with the lightest and most sickening crack. Small yellow feathers float about the cage.

I scream, and think I will scream again, but Kirsten grabs my hand, squeezing it so tightly it hurts. Her fingers are hot with sweat. I know what she is telling me: *Do not let them see you scream. Do not let them see you have weaknesses. Agree with them.*

Everyone is looking at me. Aksel is now just a lump at the bottom of his cage.

'I have never seen a yellow bird in all of my days on this Earth,' says Reverend Thompson, his voice shaking. 'I am sure they are common enough in far-off lands, but not here. Here they are unnatural, and we cannot have anything unnatural coming into Holyroodhouse. We cannot give the Devil any opportunity.'

I remember the day Papa gave Aksel to me. He came from a hot country. A merchant brought him as a gift. He looked like a tiny ray of sunshine, as if you could hold the sun in the palm of your hand.

I take a deep breath. My corset digs into my chest. 'I am sorry for bringing such a strange beast to Scotland. I pray that you will keep me safe,' I tell the reverend. Kirsten's hand relaxes.

Reverend Thompson nods, but his eyes roam the room, searching for more signs of wickedness. He spots a red cape; the one Kirsten was planning to wear for the procession.

'Red is a colour for whores,' he says.

I hear the click of Kirsten's throat. It is the sound of dry fear.

'I will dispose of the cape, Reverend,' she says.

After they have given our chambers the all-clear for rats and mice and spiders, we go downstairs and assemble for refreshments in the dining room. But this is not a luncheon. It is a war committee.

They serve sheep pluck, and I think of Henry and how we laughed at it. Reverend Thompson watches me pick my way around it: lung and stomach lining and kidney. Kirsten eats heartily, as though she has not eaten in weeks, and nods intently at every word the reverend says. It is incredible to watch her pretend to be compliant like this. She has depths that I had no idea of.

'His Majesty has summoned Dr Hemmingsen,' Reverend

Thompson says. 'I've dispatched a letter with the next ship to Denmark. We need his counsel for what is to come.'

'What do you think is to come?' asks Kirsten.

The reverend looks at her, puzzled at being quizzed by a woman.

'His Majesty's biggest enemy is his cousin, Bothwell,' the minister says. 'Bothwell is a murderer, and he will fight anyone who crosses him. Hates the English and any notion that James might unite the crowns. He tried to seize the king some months back, but so far he has failed in his attempts to cause chaos and disorder. It is our opinion that any attempt on the king will have Bothwell behind it. And now there's been an attack on the king from sorcerers. We suspect Bothwell has asked for their help.'

'And so the enemy is not just brandishing swords, or coming in fleets, or poisoning the royal feasts.' This is another man talking now, a man who has stood up at his place near the minister. He is tall and so striking-looking that I cannot help staring at him, fair curls rising from the crown of his head in every hue from golden to white.

'This is Douglas Murray of Kirkbrae,' says the minister. 'Murray is His Majesty's closest confidant and comes here today as the king is unable to be spared his duties until suppertime.'

'Bothwell has incited witches to act in his name. He will have communed with the Devil – of that we are in no doubt,' Murray says.

Thankfully, the servants remove the plates. We are served whisky. I suddenly crave *akvavit*. Kirsten excuses us and I can feel the men watch us exit the room. She stands in the hallway, looking agitated. For a minute I consider walking out of the door and going to the port, or sending a messenger to

Henry or stowing away on the next ship, regardless of its destination.

The men are still drinking whisky and talking in their low Scots rumbles. I can hear them. I think it is the reverend speaking.

'There was none of this wickedness until the Danes came,' he says.

Chapter Twenty-Three

JURA

The Canongate
January 1590

The king and Princess Anna make their grand entry as the tollbooth clock strikes noon, and I manage to catch a magnificent glimpse, despite the crowd being so thick. Mary said she would watch from the window, but I wanted to be in the crowd, as close as I could get, even though it's freezing out here. Mary is used to seeing royalty to-ing and fro-ing. I find a wall to perch on near the Netherbow Port, behind a gathering of scruffy laddies. I buy a hot, fresh scone spread with salty butter. The wall isn't high, but I don't dare stand on it until the moment comes, for those laddies would have my kirtle up, if the wind didn't get there first. They roam our little spot, restless. They eye my scone, as though they might grab it from my hands. I stuff it down, just in case, wiping my greasy hands on my sleeves.

'How long do we need to wait for the Danish bitch anyway?' one of them asks.

'Shh,' says another, looking around warily. 'Don't call her that. They'll take your head off.'

'I don't see the point in standing here,' says the first lad.

'There's nothing else to do, is there? I want to see the Danish princess. See if she's worth all this fuss,' his friend replies.

'She's a foreign whore who isn't worth the lives of the sailors who died bringing her here,' the first man comments. 'They say the families got paid compensation from the king himself, to stop them making a fuss. She'll never be accepted.'

The lads make me feel ill-at-ease, for they are looking for a bit of trouble, so I am relieved when the crowd falls silent and I hear the clip-clop of horses' hooves, which means the procession is close. I hop up on the wall and am well rewarded with the view.

It is true, what they say: her carriage is of silver. You can tell, for it shines in the winter light in a marvellous way. Heavy and light, all at the same time, draped with gold cloth and hung with purple velvet curtains. He rides ahead, the king. I have never witnessed a man sit so straight. And Anna of Denmark has the highest hair I have ever seen, topped with a sparkling tiara.

I am all set to be satisfied with a view of the queen in profile, when the procession halts right in front of me, whilst a group of performers dance for the king up ahead. No one in the carriage seems to know what to do, for they can't see the performers. The lads nudge each other and call out for the princess's attention, but they aren't daft enough to call her a Danish bitch. The horses' tails twitch.

There is a guard sitting next to the princess and he seems worried, scanning the crowd as if we might all take a run at the coach. She turns her head and surveys the people on my side of the street. I'm suddenly embarrassed by our rags and filth. I urge her to smile, for that would be a blessing on us all. But she does not. Perhaps she is not allowed to smile. I am desperate for her to look at me, to notice me.

There is another woman sitting opposite her in the carriage, whose face I can't see properly for she won't look out at the crowd, and a man at her side who must be a minister, for he has a white collar and a black cloak. I'm sure they all have thick furs over their knees in that coach to keep them warm.

Finally she waves. Everyone cheers, even the scruffy lads. I wave too and her eyes meet mine briefly, for the carriage starts to move again and she is gone.

I feel my shoulders sag with disappointment. Did I expect something to happen? For her to smile at me or make me feel special? I can almost hear Da scold me: *What is it about you, Jura, that makes you want to be better than yourself? Hoping the royalty of Scotland will bother with the likes of you? Why are you not content with your lot? Why trouble yourself, when you could just sit down with me and have an ale? Come on, lass, have a drink.*

But I am not like my old da – I want a part of this wondrous Canongate. I want an apothecary shop, with a gleaming window and my name on the front in gold letters, and a queue out the door. *By Appointment to Her Majesty the Queen.* On Sundays, after kirk, I would play pall-mall.

Mary says women like us are being hunted down, like animals, but I have never heard such a thing. Mibbie in far-off lands, but not here in Scotland. I shall be the finest healer Scotland has ever known.

Ribbons are for binding. I have a ribbon in my hand, brand new, white, from the haberdasher's. As I watch Anna of Denmark, I knot the ribbon three times. Once for her, once for me and once for us both. I have bound us together now. My Anna will come to know me, and I will serve her.

20th January 1590
From Sophie of Mecklenburg-Güstrow,
Queen Regent at Kronborg Castle, Denmark

To Princess Anna of Denmark at Holyroodhouse, Scotland

Daughter – I thank God for your safe arrival in Scotland and I am eternally grateful to His Majesty for rescuing you. I am told he raised the funds for the voyage himself, such was his desire to be with you, and I am going to reimburse him and also send an extra gift of eight thousand rigsdalers for your safe passage.

I come now to the matter of your handfasting, which has fasted long and hard enough, in my opinion. How have you come this far and suffered such peril and not received an offer of marriage? You may want to raise the matter, with delicacy, with His Majesty. I always found the best way to approach sensitive topics with your dear late papa was when we were abed. A couple's bed is a sacred place and is where they are at their most intimate, physically and spiritually. And now that I have mentioned the physical aspect of the bed, I pray you are trying your hardest to get with child.

I had a visit from the Abbess at Hellebæk yesterday, asking if I thought you would join the convent. She spoke very highly of the cloistered life. Women make their own rules and set the rhythm of their own days, which all sounds quite amenable, if I am being honest. You might even enjoy that. In any case, arrangements are being made for a place for you there, just in case.

Chapter Twenty-Four

ANNA

Holyroodhouse
February 1590

I've always been a prisoner of sorts. At Kronborg, guards patrolled the gates and Kirsten monitored my every move. But this life at Holyroodhouse is a different kind of incarceration. My inner bedchamber, deep within the newly furnished Danish apartments, forms the centre of a labyrinth, past long, criss-crossing hallways hung with oil portraits that are so dark you can barely make them out; around corner after corner; up winding staircases.

I exist here, a kept creature peering out at windows onto the Canongate at one side and onto Arthur's Seat at another. Visited upon, and not only by James. Reverend Thompson comes after breakfast for religious study. Then a procession of Scottish court ladies comes a-calling. They are all of the same flock. Hair curled into the thinnest of spirals. Soft white necks that crane at me. Hardly able to walk or sit in their fearsomely wide gowns that barely fit through the doorway of my day-room. Hell-bent on wearing the gaudiest of hats. On the surface, of course, they could not be happier that our entourage has arrived. *Oh, we have waited months! Oh, how we prayed!* But their eyes dart about me, in judgement. What brooch am I wearing? How foreign is my accent? Sometimes their foreheads crease in puzzlement when I speak.

My menses come again.

Kirsten has been watching out for bloodstains on the linens and, when they come, there are tuts and sighs and the rolling of eyes. James keeps away when I bleed and I am allowed to sleep alone for five nights, and that is an utter relief.

Finally the day comes that I have been desperate for, since I arrived. My lessons with Henry resume. I had told James I needed to go back to my books; that I was struggling to understand the ladies, and they were having difficulty understanding me. He nodded and said that could not be allowed to continue, for the ladies and I are to take afternoon possets together as often as possible and walk around the grounds when the weather is better.

They put Henry and me in the music room, which is on the first floor and has a view over the Canongate. I arrive early, but Henry is already there, playing a melody at the clavichord. The minute I see him, everything feels right again.

I walk over and watch him play, watch his fingers dance over the keys. His skin is the colour of honey. His fingernails are short and clean. I am back in Ánslo once more, with his hands playing with my hair, ducks skimming the mirror-like lake, snowflakes falling.

He stops playing as I take a seat at the table. I pour us both a glass of wine and sit down. For a minute or so, we just watch each other.

I take a deep breath. 'I hate it here. They killed Aksel. James talks of witches,' I tell him. 'Mama is still threatening me with the convent.'

Henry rubs his face. He looks as though he hasn't had a good night's sleep in days. 'I think of nothing but you,' he says.

'Is that really true?' I ask, remembering Kirsten's cautionary tale of men who make promises to women and then disappear. 'It would be far easier for you if you fell in love with anyone other than me.'

'Don't you think I've thought of that? Many times,' he says. 'There are lovers at this court who are happy in their secret relationships. But I don't want something hidden. I can hardly sleep sometimes, knowing you are sharing a bed with another man.'

He stands up from the clavichord and sits opposite me. He opens a book, but neither of us look at it. I am vaguely aware of Henry getting out parchment and quills.

'I want us to run away,' he says.

'They will execute us if we are caught,' I reply.

'We would be over the English border before they even realized we were gone,' he says. 'Or to Leith Port, and then on a ship to wherever you want.'

I can't concentrate on anything now.

He sips his wine, never taking his eyes off me. He is deadly serious.

'Are you sure you would take such a risk?' I ask him. My voice is so low I can hardly hear it.

'Do you not feel it too? This love for each other. To me, it feels more powerful than anything I've ever experienced. Or would you rather stay here, marry James when he proposes and live in Scotland. Perhaps England one day too. Do you want the throne?'

'I've never wanted any of it,' I tell him. 'All I've ever wanted is to live my life surrounded by love.'

'Then you will,' he says.

'When he comes to my bed it is insufferable,' I whisper. 'For both of us. I think he hates it as much as I do. He makes his way through intercourse as though it were a set of exercises prescribed by his physician. The only time he seems to seek comfort in me is when we are talking of terrible things like witchery and he grows afraid.'

'He's in love with Douglas Murray,' says Henry. 'I have no doubt he dislikes the task as much as you do. But you must produce children. Many of them. The bedding will continue until you have produced at least three or four living heirs. That is the life you will have, if you stay here. The whole world will worship you. But you'll be miserable.'

'How can he be in love with Murray?' *How is that possible, for two men to love each other?* It makes no sense to me, but Henry shrugs.

'They love each other as we love each other,' he says. 'You can't legislate for love. It just happens. But that is exactly the kind of relationship I don't want. I want us to be together all the time and to share our beds with no one else.'

A low cloud of mist hangs over the town. The gloom of the outside world seeps in, fingers of damp that carry the stink of the Canongate. It's a smell that pervades everything here. Sulphurous and sweet. Ale-tainted piss, dank water and rotting meat and old dung. I even smell it in my dreams. I imagine how rancid it will get in the summer. Fruit-flies and bluebottles gorging on it all.

'If James loves Murray, then he can never love me,' I say. I imagine the two of them embracing. *How does it even work? Do they kiss? I suppose they must do, many times.* I once saw two men kiss: two showmen from a travelling troupe at Kronborg. I had come into the banqueting hall early, when they were getting ready. It was shocking and stirring, all at the same time, and I slipped out of the room, unnoticed. I had assumed it was only showmen and artists who might embrace like that. Not a king. Not a courtier.

'James will treat you well,' Henry says. 'But your marriage will not have true love. And you will come to find, quite soon, that Murray has power in this court. It is Murray to whom James goes for advice. Murray's opinions will count for far more than yours ever will.'

Kirsten fetches me promptly at midday, saying I must rest because of my menses.

After that, I am called for a private meeting with Murray and Reverend Thompson. It takes place in the gallery, where portraits of the kings of the Scots hang. We start at a painting of Fergus, the first monarch of Scotland, who fought with the Scots against the Picts and the Britons.

'I thought you would benefit from a tour of the Scots kings,' says Reverend Thompson. 'I come to the gallery quite often myself. It gives me a sense of perspective. We are all just small creatures in God's grand plan.'

King Fergus is a giant. Broad and bearded, and muscular and leaning on a huge sword.

'He's an impressive man, is he not?' Murray is admiring the portrait too. 'That sword will no doubt have seen off countless enemies.'

'He is a man to be revered,' I reply, trying not to glance at Murray and wonder at him and James together.

'In those days Scotland needed a king who could fight on the battlefield,' says Reverend Thompson. 'But we are in different times now. Scotland needs a king who is wise and scholarly, and who can remain one step ahead of his enemies, in order to keep well away from the battlefield.'

'We are fortunate to have James,' I say. I have become so used to saying what they want me to say that I barely notice I am doing it.

'He is the very man we need in these dark times,' says the reverend. 'For there is devilry afoot. You will know all about that of course. For have there not always been witches in Scandinavia? A tradition that has descended from the pagans in your dark lands and never really died out?'

'I know very little about witches,' I say. 'Except that I pray daily, to ward them off.'

Murray has been studying me, fingers brushing the edge of his ruff all the while. Perhaps he is curious about me too. 'Come,' he says, and we walk past portraits of more great men, all with black hair and black beards and ruddy cheeks.

'And you have never been tempted with sorcery yourself?' asks the reverend. He enquires casually, as if the answer would be irrelevant to him, either way.

'That is a shocking thing to ask,' I say.

'I am sorry to have ruffled your skirts,' he says, 'but it is a matter of most gravity, and I can't help but worry that you Danes have brought something of the Devil with you, on that ship. We are hearing the most fearsome tales of sorcery in Denmark.'

'We are people of God,' I tell him. 'I am His most loyal servant.'

'And are you praying that your union is blessed with a child?' he asks.

'With every breath in my body,' I reply.

'A child would sanctify your union,' he says. 'It would prove you are worthy of the crown. It would show us all that you are a woman of God, sworn to give her life to the kingdom. I believe you should make this your priority.'

'Indeed,' says Murray. 'An heir will help James secure his claim to the English throne. And that is in all of our interests.'

'I will produce an heir,' I tell them.

They bow. I am excused. I look Reverend Thompson in the eye and remember him cracking my canary's neck. I smile as well as I can, and imagine running out of this hideous place with Henry and never seeing any of them again.

On the sixth day after my menses, James returns to my bedchamber after my prayers.

'I have missed having our conversations,' he muses as he passes me a *scorchet*, making himself comfortable on the cushions.

I should be delighted he has said this, thrown me this offering, but, oh God, I have not missed our conversations. I have enjoyed having my own thoughts, unmuddied by his. I have enjoyed not being overwhelmed by him and his firm belief that he is the most important person in the whole world. I have even enjoyed the sweet sadness of longing for Henry.

'Reverend Thompson spoke with me,' I tell James. 'He asked me if I had ever dabbled in sorcery. I was very upset that he asked such a thing.'

James looks at the ceiling, avoiding my eye.

'The reverend is the holiest of men and asks such questions only because he must. He understands devilry like no one else.'

How is that true? I wonder, sucking on the sweet and stretching my feet, now they are out of my uncomfortable slippers. How can one person understand wickedness more than another? I saw the devilry in the storm – I am not an idiot. Devilry likes to make itself known, does it not, for isn't that the very purpose of mischief-making?

'Has the reverend sensed any devilry about the place?' I ask.

'He is undecided,' James replies, sighing as he battles with the cushions in the way he always does. 'He is wary of some of the characters outside – the hawkers and the fish-sellers on the Canongate – as he believes some of them are watching us. And he says that any collections of twigs or leaves, or petals or stones, are to be removed from the grounds, if they are found, as these are likely to be curses.'

There is a quiver in his voice as he recounts all of this, and he still cannot settle. The floorboards creak outside the door and I know it will be one of his men or Reverend Thompson, and in that one moment I ache so much for Henry that I have to bite my lip to stop myself crying out.

Then it is time for our union again. We are doing it during the afternoon today, as there's a late evening dinner planned with some of James's men, which I am to attend. The act is even more vivid in the daylight – the cushions discarded, the pierce of him. The grit of my teeth. The heave of him as James goes through his motions. I try to ignore the gold amulet, its strange flower engraving around his neck. With his rocking, comes a chant in my head: *You can run away with Henry. You can escape all of this.*

The dinner is going to be interminable. I would rather eat with Kirsten in her chamber, but I have been summoned to entertain James's friends.

As they sit talking amongst themselves, largely ignoring me, I wonder if I have conceived this time. How long do these things take? Some women seem to be always with child. And if I do conceive, I know I will have to remain here. I could not leave a child and run away with Henry. I am running out of time.

Which would be the worse fate: dying of a broken heart or being executed with Henry for treason? For that is what would happen if we were caught. When I'm with Henry it seems obvious that we should try to make a life for ourselves, but the minute I'm back with Kirsten or James or Reverend Thompson that all seems impossible.

'Do they eat such marvellous meats in Denmark?' The man sitting across the table, interrupting my thoughts and pointing at the roast venison and duck, is Lord Lothian, a friend of James's from out by the east coast of Scotland.

'They mostly eat fish over there,' says Earl Marischal, who is sitting next to the man.

I don't open my mouth to disagree; or say that sheep pluck is the vilest food I have ever mouthed. I take a slice of duck breast and wonder if Mama is thinking of me, sitting at her own table, which will be bursting with roast pork cooked in apples, and round breads and rich wines. I imagine she is. I imagine she is worrying at the grey hairs sparkling at her temples and is willing me into bed with James, and is wondering whether to ship fine Italian silk undergarments out to me or French wines to pour for him in bed.

'This must all surely be a great treat for you, especially after such a terrible journey,' says Lord Lothian. He is pointing at the meat again and then at the fine decorations strewn around the dining room: ivy and white candles and table linens and silver plate that have been begged and borrowed from the Canongate merchants. Incense burns in the corners, to ward off evil.

I nod, hoping they will bore of me soon enough.

They do. 'On the subject of that terrible journey,' says James, putting down his cup with a most dramatic flourish, 'officials in Copenhagen have unearthed an International Sorcery Plot.'

Every bushy eyebrow in the room rises upwards an inch.

'My good friend – a Danish scholar by name of Dr Hemmingsen – writes to me regularly on developments. We were deliberately targeted by witches intent on destroying me.'

I do not point out that it was me, and my ship, that the witches tried to destroy. There are murmurs and blessings uttered all around the table.

'There are witches,' James continues, 'acting on the direction of our enemies, to engage supernatural forces against us. Bothwell is behind it, no doubt.'

Everyone nods.

'Bothwell would stop at nothing to claim the Scottish throne,' Lord Lothian says. 'He would happily sell his soul to the Devil for it. It makes absolute sense.'

'Having failed with force, he has now raised an army of witches,' Earl Marischal says. 'Women – their weakness lures them into such bonds, but they can raise storms with the power of God Almighty. I have witnessed them myself.'

'A witch can't raise a weather storm surely,' Lord Lothian says.

'The Danish witches are powerful,' James replies. 'Descended from pagans. Scandinavia is a harsh place, my men. But do you recall what happened? First, we suffered the loss of the Burntisland ferryboat. The same contrary winds then almost capsized the *Gideon*. These women are coastal sorceresses.'

I try to swallow the thick wedge of duck meat.

James continues, 'The worst of it is that they are recruiting witches from these very shores. We must set Scotland to more fasting and prayer. We must alert all the kirk ministers. We must make it clear that sorcery will not be tolerated.'

One of the men at the table is listening, rapt. He raises his hand.

'Your Majesty, if I may be allowed,' he says. 'It may be nothing, of course, or it may be something. But you say the witches involved in this plot were coastal sorceresses?'

Everyone turns to him, a plainly dressed man with beads of nervous sweat at his upper lip.

'That's right,' says James. 'Do you have any observation to make, Baillie Kincaid?'

'Only this,' says the man. 'A few weeks ago my serving girl in North Berwick absconded from my home after a series of strange events, which we believe were witchery.'

James blinks. His hand strays to his amulet. 'There is sorcery everywhere,' he says. 'But the sorcery of a serving girl is a trifling matter compared to what I am facing.'

Baillie Kincaid's voice trembles, but he presses on. 'This serving girl started off by healing women of various afflictions. Her mother was a cunning woman too. But then she killed a flock of hens after an argument with a poulterer's son. And I am certain that she tried to kill me with some kind of spell.'

'Typical sorcery,' says Reverend Thompson. 'Where is the girl now?'

'She ran away,' replies the baillie. 'But some suspicious items were left in a box,' he continues. 'My daughter found the box and brought it to me after the girl had left, and we went through it. Some of the items were certainly used for sorcery. Stones. Twigs. The tinctures that were used to heal the women. But there were coloured ribbons too.'

'Ribbons are highly prized by sorceresses. Their colours can be used in a very direct way,' Reverend Thompson says, looking absolutely rapt.

'Indeed,' says the baillie. 'That is what my wife and daughter told me. They are not witches, of course,' he adds hastily. 'This is just common knowledge in folklore.'

'Your wife and daughter are correct,' says Reverend Thompson. 'Colour is important in witchcraft: red for love, and so on. Tell me, what colour were the ribbons in this witch's box?'

I wonder briefly what colour of ribbon I might wear to deter James, to avoid conceiving, to escape Holyroodhouse.

'Well, we found a red ribbon, which we suspect was used for a love spell of course. An orange one, which is thought to have been used to curse chickens, for it matched the colour of their feathers perfectly.

A shiver runs around the room now.

'But then we found a most unusual ribbon and we could not understand what it was used for. It was full of tight knots and pins. Its colour was purple. My wife said it would be most unusual to find a purple ribbon in the possession of a serving girl of course, for that is an expensive dye, as you will know. The most expensive. My housekeeper said that in all her days she has never seen a serving girl wearing a purple ribbon.'

'A purple ribbon? And what was that for?' James asks.

The man nods at the king. 'Purple, Your Majesty, is for royalty. Now that I have heard your concerns, it all makes sense. Our maid was prone to night-time wandering. Our cook said she left the house many an evening, and for no good reason. She was seen down at North Berwick beach around the time of the great storm, acting suspiciously by the water. I believe that purple ribbon was used to raise those storms.'

Chapter Twenty-Five

JURA

The Canongate
February 1590

I have started hawking at the bottom of the Canongate. Mary says I am to be careful. Sell cures, not charmes. Keep to dock leaves and oat poultices. Mint teas. But I will never be a grand apothecary unless I go out there and start. And there are enough boils and pustules and scabs and rashes to keep me busy. Scalps that flake and knuckles that swell, and bellies that gurgle and bairns that gurn and gurn. In fact there's enough sickness in the Canongate to need a gang of cunning women. It is the closeness of human flesh and animal flesh that does it. The fevers spread. The water from the wells is dank. Despite the wealth, the royal commissions and the tournaments, they all throw their own vomit and shit out of their windows and doors onto the streets. Even I have not been immune to it – I have developed a cough and an ache in my knees.

It's a freezing cold morning. Messenger boys dart from inn to inn. Housewives balance water jugs, leaving a stream of dank droplets, from the wells to the closes. Bairns chase away the pigeons looking for crumbs. Gamblers stand jittery at the gate of the cock-fighting pen, waiting for it to open. I set out my wares in my usual spot. There is a lot of commotion at the gates of Holyroodhouse, with carriages coming in and out and guards bowing non-stop. A party of fine-looking men set out on foot, and I can tell where they are going as soon as I see them: they are going to Holyrood Abbey for a morning service. I wonder if the king and Princess Anna will follow suit, and I fancy I might catch another sight of them.

As they draw closer, the urchins gather, stretching out their bony hands for coins, so I have to stand and gather my blanket to avoid everything being trampled upon or stolen. I think about dodging away, but there's something about the grandness of the men that fascinates me, so I stay to watch.

And that is the biggest mistake of my life, for when they draw close, at the moment when it is too late to turn my head, I recognize one of the men. I recognize him as soon as he claps eyes on me, and his face opens in shock.

It is Baillie Kincaid.

I duck into the crowd, dipping my head and pushing past urchins and flag-sellers and girls hawking flowers. I thump against elbows, clutching my blanket tightly. I push to the back of the crowd, bolting up the Canongate. There is already so much cacophony that I don't know if I'm being chased. I dodge down a close, sending chickens fleeing and startling a goat tied to a stump. The end of the close turns into a courtyard, with other closes leading off from it, so I pick the nearest one. I am parallel to the main street now, with two high walls on either side of me. The stench of piss and shit is overpowering. I am too terrified even to look behind me.

Finally I reach a gate that leads into another courtyard. It has a bolt that has been left unlocked. I open the gate, slip into the courtyard and bolt the gate behind me. In the corner of the yard there is a pile of all manner of things under a canvas roof: filthy straw, rags, logs, bottles, planks and barrels. I don't know if it's someone's rubbish dump or someone's makeshift home. But I don't have time to worry about it. I dive behind a barrel and hide.

February 1590
From Dr Neils Hemmingsen, in Copenhagen

To His Majesty King James the Sixth

Sir – I write with the latest developments in the Danish sorcery plot. We have now embarked upon a Great Witch Hunt.

Before she was executed, and in exchange for the promise of a swift death by strangulation at the stake before the fire was ignited, Mistress Ane Koldings gave up the names of two men and nine women that she said were acquaintances of hers in sorcery, amongst them the wife of the Mayor of Copenhagen and the wife of one of the royal weavers. They are all now in our custody, and we expect to keep them in custody over the coming weeks as we ascertain the extent of our problem. Your Majesty, we are on God's mission to stamp out all the wickedness in this land.

Copenhagen Prison has been modified so that we can accommodate these prisoners. We now have two large women's cells, having transferred some of our existing male prisoners out to Helsingør. We have fitted the Interrogation Chamber with a strappado by which to suspend a suspect with ropes, in order to have an additional method of torture. The bishops visit on a rota, to bless the premises and ward off any demons.

We have employed the services of a Witchfinder from Trier, who is on hand to examine those brought to the Interrogation Chamber. According to him, a witch can be discovered by pricking her body with a bodkin, as witches possess a Mark, given to them by the kiss of the Devil, through which they can feel no pain. By pricking the skin all over the body, the Devil's Mark can be found. This is a great advancement in our understanding of this exceptional crime. The Witchfinder is a learned scholar of the Malleus Maleficarum *and has explained how women – the weaker sex – are more carnal and less faithful, and that is why they are more susceptible to witchcraft. They are more corruptible. I admit I had a passing knowledge of the text, as we discussed in Ánslo, but I have taken to studying it with aplomb, as you may wish to do yourself.*

We face a great battle with evil. But we will triumph. In the name of our Lord Jesus Christ, Amen.

15th February 1590
From Sophie of Mecklenburg-Güstrow,
Queen Regent

To Mistress Kirsten Sørensen at Holyroodhouse

Dear Kirsten,

I write to you directly on the subject of the Royal Betrothal because, frankly, you are best placed to answer my concerns.

It appears to me that King James of Scotland is enjoying my daughter's company so much that he has entirely forgotten to commence his plans to marry her.

He has up to a year and a day, but time is marching on and no hint from him about wedding preparations. I had doubts about this Scottish 'tradition' of a handfasting and I should have listened to my conscience. I hear rumours that Catherine de Bourbon in France is still unwed and is planning a visit to Queen Elizabeth's court in England, where James occasionally visits, along with her ambassadors. Heaven forbid they attend at the same time, and before any wedding. She would outmanoeuvre Anna in any battle for a man's attention. It is imperative that Anna does whatever she can to consolidate her position at Holyrood. Assist her to seduce King James as often as possible.

The problem, Kirsten, is what we would be able to do with you, should the betrothal fail. You are under contract to return Anna here to Kronborg and, after giving the matter due consideration, I believe that if the worst was to happen, and no proposal comes, the best course of action would be for you to go with Anna to Hellebæk Abbey and live there with her. She would need you, Kirsten. She would not manage the convent life on her own. I have spoken with the abbess and she has said you could both share a private room; you need not be in the dormitory with the others. I have made a substantial donation to reserve the space.

Yours, in the hope that you will do everything in your power to influence matters,

Sophie

Chapter Twenty-Six

KIRSTEN

*Holyroodhouse
February 1590*

I put Sophie's letter in the drawer and sit at my desk.
I will not respond straight away. She can't threaten me like that and expect a submissive reply. Rain drives onto the windowpanes, wavering between grey slashes and white sleet. From what I have seen of King James's character, he will not be in the mood to contemplate a wedding if he feels he is under threat from witches. He will want to win that battle first. He will not want the Devil lurking. Marriage is sacrosanct.

I'll deal with Sophie's letter when the more immediate problem has been addressed. The one I feared would happen as soon as I heard that Doritte Olsen had been taken into custody in the dungeons at Kronborg, with the ludicrous accusation of raising a storm. It's one thing to hear of hysteria in far-off lands and quite another to see it unfold under your own roof.

People knew of Mistress Olsen's medicine skills. I had need of them, once. It was summer. I was young. I knew something of the ways of men by then, but not everything. I was in grave trouble. I knew Mistress Olsen could help me, because I'd been told about her over the years – her name dropped carefully into conversation by aunts and friends. Women whisper secrets to each other; it is how we survive. *If you ever need help of a sensitive nature, go to Mistress Olsen. She lives in the fishermen's cottages, and you must only visit her when her husband is at sea. Don't let anyone spy you on the road to her house. Don't tell anyone you visited her.*

It was a bright June morning, the pathways sparkling with marguerite flowers all the way from the village to the fishermen's quarter. The sailing boats were out on the horizon somewhere, teeming with herring and men and boys – fathers showing their sons the ropes. One of the boys out there was Peter Lund, who had put me in this position. I was carrying his child. He was out there trying to forget I ever existed. He would be on the biggest fishing boat; his father owned a fleet of them. A few weeks ago we had promised ourselves to each other. He'd said he wanted to marry me. When we made love, I told him to be careful. I knew what could happen if he wasn't.

When I told him I was pregnant, he asked if the baby was definitely his. *How can you be sure you're pregnant? How can you be sure I'm the father?* I knew I was pregnant because I had not bled, and I'd felt sick each morning for a week. I should have taken something to prevent it, and not trusted him. I should have been more careful. But I thought Peter would marry me.

'Of course the baby's yours,' I told him. 'So we will need to hurry the wedding along.'

We'd even talked about the wedding; Peter had said his father would pay for everything. He had turned eel and plaice and cod and sole and silver herring into gold coins by purchasing fishing boats. My father would be appeased by their wealth. It would help him come to terms with the fact that I would serve a husband, and not the royal court he had ambitions for.

Except that Peter changed his mind. He did not want a baby. He did not want a wedding. He did not want me as his wife.

Mistress Olsen didn't only provide abortions. She provided the firm shoulder and fleshy arms that girls need comfort from, when they take the medicine to end their pregnancies. It is a terrible thing to go through. If it had not been for Mistress Olsen, I would probably have ended up at Hellebæk Abbey. They have a nursery for babies. They are kept there until they are weaned and old enough to be handed over to childless couples.

When they took Mistress Olsen into custody, in the dungeons at Kronborg, I went to her. I found my way down one evening, making sure no one noticed. I gave the guard a coin to let me speak to her, and another to make sure he told no one of my visit.

I had never been in the dungeons before. Above ground, Kronborg is imposing and majestic. Its spires rise to the heavens. Its black-and-white tiled hallways are pristine. Its oak cupboards and tables gleam with beeswax polish. Below ground, it is cold and dark. It's where they store the ice and the prisoners.

'I remember you,' she said, when I stood at barred doorway to her cell. They had put her in a room with a ceiling so low she could barely stand up straight and with merely a shaft of light and air from a grille at the top of the wall. I had a box of candles. I gave them to her.

'I will help you if I can,' I told her.

She shook her head. 'There's nothing you can do. People are frightened of me. Have been for a long time. They've made their minds up.'

Then she started talking about Trier. Hundreds put to the stake in the city. Purges of Protestants and Jews and then of witches, who were blamed for the failed harvests. Those who tried to stop the persecutions were also burned. The executioner has become the richest man in Trier. I knew some of it from the pamphlets in the library, but Mistress Olsen knew more.

Women whisper secrets to each other; it is how we survive.

'Those in Trier passed their warning messages to those in neighbouring towns, and now the hunts have arrived in Denmark,' Mistress Olsen said. 'No woman is safe. Men are using it as a way to get rid of troublesome women.'

I visited her one more time. She insisted that I stay away. But I'd heard she'd confessed to raising the storms that killed her husband and I wanted to see her for myself. I brought bread and milk. Her thumbs were bandaged with bloody linens.

This time, she was weaker. She was not like the bold woman who had offered me a way out of my predicament, with no judgement and no blame. She was shrunken into herself. She was starved and sleep-deprived and tortured.

'I told them what they wanted to hear,' she said. 'If I'd carried on denying it, they would have done worse. They had pincers and knives.'

I shuddered, feeling distraught.

She was sitting cross-legged on the floor. She still had firm shoulders and fleshy arms, but her body sagged now, broken.

'When they burn me, they will make everyone watch, just like in Trier,' she said. 'But you must not give yourself away. Do not cry, as you are doing now, or gasp or try to catch my eye. Who knows what I'll scream, when the flames catch me. I'll be desperate. I don't want to say your name, or the names of the other women at court that I've helped over the years. I don't want to beg you to save me, so avert your eyes and pray for me. Blend into the crowd.'

'Is there anything I can do for you?' I asked.

'Yes,' she said. 'You must pass the warning on. To anyone you know who may need to be warned. Anyone practising healing, particularly women. They are coming for us all. They don't understand the craft. They think healers are working with the Devil. No one is safe.'

That night, I wrote to Scotland.

Every whistle of the wind, every screech of a crow, has the court on edge.

Only kirk men and courtiers and well-trusted merchants are allowed past the gates of Holyroodhouse now. I have only ventured out into the Canongate once since I arrived, and I dare not go where I want to, because I could easily be followed. Instead I wander past butter merchants and salt men and dawdle in shops. A masque scheduled for this evening has been postponed. Instead we are gathering in the dining hall to pray. The chairs have been lined up in rows. Candles and incense burn. Everyone is talking of the news that the Danes have caught more witches, and that the one who cursed Baillie Stuart Kincaid and tried to drown us has been spotted on the Canongate.

Baillie Stuart Kincaid. Now that is a name I have not heard for a very long time.

'The Danes are ten steps ahead of us – they have found almost a dozen witches and we have captured none.' I can hear James deep in conversation with Murray. They are sitting in the front row of our prayer session. I have managed to get myself into the second row. I need every opportunity to hear what they are up to.

'The wickedness came from Denmark, so is it any surprise? They are desperate to show us they have a grip on it.' Murray speaks to James as though they are familiar friends, not king and subject. Their hands stray onto each other's arms as they talk. Murray has long fingers set with sparkling rings. They look like expensive gifts. Love tokens.

'But the Danish witches weren't working alone,' says James. 'There must have been a coven manipulating the waters in the Firth of Forth to capsize the Burntisland ferryboat. I am sure they had it within their sights as the storm took it. It's imperative we catch this North Berwick housemaid, for she will know all about it. For all we can tell, she could be outside as we speak, cursing us again. Why else would she have come to the Canongate if not to murder us?'

'I am sure Bothwell is behind it all,' says Murray. 'It's terrifying to think how many others might be involved. He must be paying them handsome coin.'

'The Devil has no need for coin. He will be rewarding these witches with other riches,' replies James. 'Magical powers and sexual gratification, and promises that they may reign with him when the kings and queens are all murdered.'

'You're terrified, my lord,' says Murray. 'You're shaking.'

'I have faith,' says James. 'But I can't pretend that I do not fear the darkness.'

He *is* terrified. His shoulders tremble and he looks about him, agitated, until Anna arrives and takes a seat next to him and then he holds his head up straight.

Reverend Thompson stands up and begins his sermon.

'Merciful God, help us,' he says. 'Help us to root out the witches. Help us to find them in their hiding places.' There are murmurs of amen. 'Grant us the strength we will need for the task ahead. For there will be blood spilled in Your name.'

James stands and walks to the front of the dining hall. 'A purse of gold coin for anyone who can find the North Berwick witch. And more purses for anyone who can locate the coven who bewitched the Firth of Forth and the German Sea. Bring them to me.'

Chapter Twenty-Seven

JURA

*The Canongate
February 1590*

*Feathers are for wishes,
Stones for safe travels,
Gold rings for the highest level of protection.*

I have no gold rings. Mibbie I should have saved enough coin to buy one before I left the Kincaids. My mind travels back to the pictures in Ma's charme books for other high protections. Crystals? Rubies? Nothing I could afford anyhow.

I wait a few hours until I think it is safe to go home and, when I finally do, with straw sticking to my kirtle, my cough has worsened and I am feverish. I go and see Aunt Mary. She is at her table, looking worried.

'Where've you been?' she asks.

I cannie tell her that I've been spotted. What if she throws me out? Where would I go?

'Just daundering,' I tell her.

'You've been away all hours,' she says. 'I had a notion you'd run off, except you'd left your good bonnet.'

I take off my damp clothes. I am trembling and my legs

and arms are all goosebumps. I put on my night-shift, as it is the only other garment I own, and hang up my clothes by the still-warm fire.

'Promise you've not got into trouble out there,' she says, handing me a blanket. 'We cannie be getting ourselves into trouble.'

I'd spent all day in the corner of that courtyard, ears primed for the march of soldiers. Remembering Master Kincaid – his dirty ways. Now he knows where I am. I would run away again, but where? Perhaps he might decide to leave me alone. After all, the stories I would tell about him would not be pretty. I think I'm safer here.

I go to my chamber and get into bed, still feeling cold under the blanket. I will give it a few days. I will lie low here. Mary can fetch me food and make me a tonic for this cough.

By then Master Kincaid will be long returned to North Berwick.

Hours pass and the fever worsens. I see Mary come and go in a haze. She bends towards me, whispering charmes and pressing hot stones to my chest.

She feeds me a thin broth. I should not have stayed out so long. I should not have run away from North Berwick. I see other faces too, of folk who are not even here. Guidwife Kincaid – I can even smell her Bristol grey soap. Hazel promising me her silk gloves, then never giving them to me. Robbie Bathgate trying to get his hands under my wylie-coat. There is a night and a day, another night and a day.

I fall in and out of sleep. More faces come. Master Kincaid. And some other men I do not recognize. I feel myself lifted out of bed, and I think I might be flying. I feel something hard slap my head. At first I think something has fallen onto me. When I open my eyes I see Master Kincaid again, only this time it is not a dream. I know that, for the spittle on the sides of his mouth and the way his whiskers curl up to his ears, and the way his spectacles are askew. He is too real to be a fever-dream.

I'm wide awake and the baillie is here.

'Caught you at last, bitch,' he says.

He doesn't say how they caught me. He must have sent men up and down the Canongate with a description of me, asking if anyone knew of me. They bundle me onto a cart. No one tells me why, or where we are going. It is an abduction done in silence, as though they are working to a plan.

'What are you doing with me?' I ask them – Master Kincaid and the other men. But none of them answer. When I scream, one of them slaps me so hard across the face that my ears sing. I don't scream again.

They tie my arms with a rope that cuts into my flesh. I am only wearing my night-shift. They throw a blanket over me. My body loosens with the fear and I smell shit and realize it's my own. Two men sit on either side of me in the cart. Master Kincaid is seated opposite me. His silence is worse than his words.

I am taken down the Canongate and along the side of Holyroodhouse. I think we are going to ride past it, to some unknown destination, when the cart stops and a side-gate opens. Then we are driven through the gates into the grounds of Holyroodhouse itself, and I realize I am in the almightiest trouble. We stop at a small barn lit by torches. Master Kincaid gets out first and watches as the men pull me down from the cart. The last thing he does is rip my guid red ribbon from my hair.

Chapter Twenty-Eight

ANNA

Holyroodhouse
February 1590

We've finished the *scorchets* and no more have been sent for. I would ask James, but it makes me feel like a child to beg for confections. Perhaps I'll ask Kirsten. It seems trivial, but the *scorchets* were the only thing I enjoyed about James being in my bed. Perhaps I will write to the sugar-man myself.

Henry is late to our lesson. It puts me on edge. I am not used to lateness. I am used to being waited upon. I stand at the window of the music room, watching over the Canongate. A crowd of men has gathered by the gates. They are carrying Scottish flags and looking up at the vast windows of the palace. There is a knock at the door and I turn, assuming it will be Henry, but it is not. It's Murray.

'I was expecting Lord Henry,' I tell him. 'Is there a problem?'

'No problem,' Murray says. 'I've asked him to run me an errand and I'm keeping you company in the meantime.' He joins me at the window.

I feel my skin prickle at his proximity to me. He smells of patchouli, the same scent as James. Earthy and powerful and exotic. He's handsome and sophisticated. He's everything I am not.

'Ah,' he continues, nodding at the crowd. 'The troublemakers are here.'

I can hear the men shouting; their cries rise above the narrow street, but I can't make out the words.

'What are they saying?' I ask. All my senses are on edge now. Murray has come in here, at this moment, on purpose.

'I can't hear exactly what they're saying, but it won't be pleasant. Unfortunately they don't like you,' he replies. 'They don't want the Danes here. They don't want any foreigners here. They don't trust that you are a true Protestant. There is anger at the sums of money that might be spent on your wedding and your coronation.'

'Oh,' I say, shocked.

'It is just the way of the world,' he adds. 'People don't like change. I'm sure they will come to like you, in time, once they accept you.'

I have never been disliked by strangers, so I puzzle over the idea, examining it.

'Do they mean me harm?'

Murray shrugs. 'They mean all of us harm. But they can't get near us. The question is: what can you do about it? Can you help in any way?'

I wish Mama was here to help me with this conversation. She would know exactly what to say. Or Christian; if my brother was here, I wouldn't have to talk at all. I wish Papa was still alive.

Murray is waiting for me to say something. I have never felt more alone than I do now. My family has sent me here to fight for my survival without telling me how to do so.

The men outside are jostling, their flags rippling in the sleet that never seems to stay away for more than a few hours.

'I'll help in any way I can,' I respond. 'Of course I will.'

He folds his arms and gives me a coy smile.

'I think you are the perfect bride for James,' he says. 'But Scotland does not know you yet. I believe you should be seen in public. Go out and distribute alms. Let them touch your hands. Make yourself popular. Make yourself a true Queen of the Scots.'

And that would make James more popular too, of course.

'And when you go out to the public, you would look marvellous in a farthingale-hooped gown,' he whispers. 'All the ladies at court have been wearing them – the French fashion has really caught on here – and I think you would blend in better if you started to wear plaid and wider skirts.'

I nod. 'I will look like a true Queen of the Scots,' I say.

'But much sweeter and more discreet than the Frenchwoman he was considering for marriage,' Murray says. I realize, from the tremor of his chin, that he is as nervous of Catherine de Bourbon as I am. 'They say she's very worldly-wise and quite demanding. I don't think she would like me,' he adds. 'I don't think she'd like how close James and I are. Our friendship.'

'Perhaps she wouldn't like James distracted,' I venture. 'Perhaps she would want him to be more attentive to her.'

'Perhaps,' he says. 'But you are not demanding at all. It is admirable.'

It is my meekness that serves all of their purposes: Mama, James, Murray. My obedience. The quality that was instilled in me by everyone. My *agreeableness*.

But it does not sit comfortably with me any more. Perhaps the Devil whispered something in my ear as he danced around the *Gideon* in the German Sea. *Never mind what they want. What do you want?*

I want Henry. A whole life with Henry. A life of love and embraces and joy. I want children conceived in love. I want to go back to Denmark, my home, but perhaps we couldn't do that. Perhaps we could go to Ánslo. The place we fell in love. I want to go back to the *hytte* by the lake and drink *akvavit* with him and watch spring bring the forest back to life. I don't want to be Queen of Scotland, or Queen of England, or wear a crown or live in a convent, or bite my tongue around Kirsten or listen to men talk in dining halls and nod along.

Murray is scrutinizing me. I cannot let him know that I am thinking any of these thoughts. I must play along with him.

'Your mama and brother would be proud of you,' he says. 'We can arrange a portrait of you wearing plaid to send back to Denmark.'

'I think it is time for my lesson now,' I reply.

'Enjoy your time with Lord Henry,' he says.

I wonder if he knows about Henry and me. I wonder if he cares. I wonder if any of them care, so long as I do my duty with James. I have ensured that my family's interests are taken care of, have I not?

The mistake they all made was assuming that my interests and theirs were one and the same.

My lesson with Henry passes too fast.

'You must keep telling James you need to continue your language instruction,' he says. 'Murray has hinted he thinks you have learned enough.'

'Does Murray know how close we are?'

'It's his business to know everything that might affect his position at court,' Henry says. 'But he won't tell James.' He blushes. 'In any case, James won't want to know unless it affects the lineage, and Murray realizes that neither of us is stupid.'

'We can't live like this,' I whisper. 'Are you sure it will be safe for us to run away?'

'I've thought it all through,' he replies. 'The safest plan is for you to return to Denmark, even if you have to go to Hellebæk Abbey for a while, and for me to come and fetch you. We can't run away together.'

The abbey. The place I dread. He watches my face fall, but he carries on. 'They'll send you back if you don't conceive,' he tells me. 'I've heard James discussing it. That's why he hasn't proposed yet. He wants to make sure you're fertile. He needs heirs if he is to take the English throne.'

'I can't refuse him when he visits upon me,' I say.

'Then you need help – medicinal help to stop you conceiving,' Henry says. 'How well do you trust your lady of the bedchamber? Could she find you a tincture or something?'

I do not trust Kirsten Sørensen at all in this matter. She is hell-bent on making this union work. She has personal business in Scotland and that is the entire reason she has come on this endeavour with me.

I only wish I knew what that business is.

I try to talk to Kirsten that afternoon. She is organizing my dinner dress, matching navy fan to navy shoe, bustling about my chamber. I am lying on the bed, stretching my legs because my knees are stiff from bedside praying.

'I think my gowns are a little unfashionable, compared to the way the Scots ladies wear their skirts,' I say. 'I am thinking of being fitted for a farthingale hoop.'

She stops, a curl of hair falling onto her face.

'A wide dress, like the French and Scots ladies? Why ever would you want to dress like them?'

'And I would like a plaid shawl,' I go on. 'For wearing outdoors when the weather is better.'

'Where are you planning to go?' she asks, putting the fan down on the bed and staring at me, perplexed.

'Out of the gates, to distribute alms. I have taken some advice from Murray. He says I should blend in more.'

'Oh, does he indeed?' she says.

'And I am wondering whether I'm being put under too much pressure to conceive,' I continue. 'Maybe it would do me good to have a rest from it.'

'A rest?' She looks appalled.

'Maybe the pressure is not helping matters,' I whisper.

She nods. 'I had wondered that too,' she says. 'And in fact I have something that might help. I bought a tonic for you in the Canongate.'

She opens a drawer and produces a brown glass bottle with an ornate globe-shaped stopper. 'This is good medicine. It will make you healthy.'

'I am healthy,' I say.

'It will help you conceive,' she replies.

'Where did you get it from? Did the Scots send you?' I sit up and take the bottle gingerly and remove the stopper. The liquid inside is thick and smells sweet and spiced.

'I procured it myself,' she says, 'from an apothecary. It has honey in it, and cinnamon from the Orient. We need to expedite the process of conception. Everything hangs in the balance until you give the Scots an heir.'

Kirsten Sørensen is not going to help me at all, I realize.

'Thank you,' I tell her, putting the bottle on the table beside my bed. 'I will take a dose of this every morning. But I will hide it under my bed, so His Majesty does not see it.'

She smiles, a rare crack in her facade.

'You are a good girl, Anna,' she says.

When she leaves, I sniff the contents of the bottle again. Almost delicious. I take it to the window and pour the whole lot out. If I'm to get my hands on a tincture to keep me from getting pregnant, I'm going to have to procure it myself.

When James visits me that night, there is a dark excitement to him. He stands at the door, still in his outdoor cloak and boots.

'Magnificent news,' he says. 'The witch who tried to kill us has been caught. Miraculous news.'

He looks half-drunk. I get out of bed, shivering, and go to him. He gleams, beads of sweat on his brow.

'Come to bed and tell me about it,' I suggest, trying to sound soothing.

He lets me take off his outer garments as he talks.

'She was spotted in the Canongate and hunted down. Baillie Seaton has a well-deserved purse of coin.

I am shivering even more now, and I drag him into bed beside me, so that we can warm ourselves under the blankets.

'Have you seen her?' I ask.

'I will visit her soon,' he replies. 'For now, they're preparing her.'

'Is she here? In Holyroodhouse?' I cannot stand the thought.

'It's the best place for her. She can't escape. She'll be guarded day and night.' James's voice has a dangerous energy. 'She's being held in one of the barns until we can examine her thoroughly.'

It takes me straight back to that terrible night they burned Doritte Olsen. And the morning she sprang back to life. But James is restless, getting the blankets into a tangle, pouring himself wine, slurping it, eyes darting all around the room.

'Is it not a risk to have her so close?' I ask. 'She could bewitch us.'

'Reverend Thompson has been informed,' he says. 'He will muster up a praying party to stand over her. Recite the Word of the Lord in her presence. Block out the Evil One. Kirsten can join the praying party. Not you, Anna. You should not get close.'

'Perhaps we should pray now,' I whisper.

'Later,' he says. 'I am thinking now. The Devil wants to get to me. Through you – through Denmark – he has come closer to me than he's ever dared. It is something of the Nordic territory that has enabled him. Its bleakness and its backwaters have provided a breeding ground for sorcery. I will write to Dr Hemmingsen first thing, informing him of the development.'

'We of the Danish court are not wicked, not at all. We are God-fearing, just as God-fearing as you,' I tell him. 'I beg that you bear this in mind.'

'I do not doubt your godliness, my love,' he says. 'But it is easy to become ensnared in the Devil's trap, even unwittingly.'

I must reassure him. He cannot think of me as the source of some plague of wickedness.

'I'm frightened,' I say.

'We should hang a cross at the window,' he replies, looking around the room edgily.

'I will do it myself,' I tell him. 'Perhaps we should not have our union tonight, not with a witch under our roof.' I pat his arm. His doublet is the one with the marguerites embroidered on the sleeves, the one I embroidered before we met, and I get a flashback of Doritte Olsen burning.

'Oh, we must,' he says. 'We must take every opportunity we can, for the bloodline.'

He moves towards me. His feet and hands are cold. His

eyes flit, nervously. His breathing is rapid, his breath stale. I let him kiss me, trying not to wince. Firmly he pushes me down. He does it quickly and quietly, with his jaw clenched like an animal. It feels different, as though he is stabbing me. He keeps his eyes closed, not looking at me once. It's not me that excites him. It is his battle with the witches.

February 1590
From Dr Neils Hemmingsen,
in Copenhagen

To His Majesty King James the Sixth

Your Majesty,

I believe the Danish side of the investigation to be concluded. All of the witches in Copenhagen Prison have confessed to taking part in the conspiracy to destroy the Danish fleet with weather magic. They did not freely confess, but did so after being put to extensive torture. We also had the women examined by the Trier Witchfinder, who used pricking to find several marks upon their bodies that looked like common moles or warts, but were in fact Devil's Marks, from which the Devil had suckled. And when these parts were pricked, the women gave no sign of pain at all.

The women also admitted visiting Mistress Doritte Olsen in the dungeon at Kronborg Castle, using magical methods of travel, the day before she was burned at the stake. All of the women have said they did convene with witches from Scotland at various locations, where they conducted malicious magic, intended to stop any royal crossing the German Sea. They said the Devil came to them in various animal forms. They were instructed by the Devil to assist him, in return for riches and favours.

They said the Devil aims to weaken you by any means possible.

All have been sentenced to death by fire, and I await your further instructions.

Your servant, in God

Chapter Twenty-Nine

JURA

*Holyroodhouse
March 1590*

There are no charmes to save me from this. This is the work of the Divvil himself. It has been two or three days, for I've slept and seen the sun rise and set through a wee window, and there is no worse sight than the dark coming when you are trapped.

There has been food brought, and water, and a stinking blanket, which means they do not want me to starve or freeze. There are straw bales to sit and sleep on.

And no one has told me anything.

They are not rough with me, like they were when they took me. A kirk minister has come and looked me up and down. He held a torch, all the better to see me in the gloom. His lips were in a snarl of disgust, but there was something else too. His eyes were wide and dark. He was afraid of me.

Different men take it in turns to guard the door. I am not shackled, which is what I've heard they do to prisoners, but I could not get past those men. They are broad and tall, and I think they would have their dirty way with me if they could. They don't have the fear in their eyes that the kirk minister did.

I would ask someone what's going on, but mibbie I'm safer saying nothing.

What would Ma do? Should I ask for Da? Or for Aunt Mary? What would they do?

I know what Master Kincaid has said, to get me into this fix. It will be the snowdrop bulbs – I have no doubt of it.

On the third day the minister comes back. He says his name is Reverend Thompson, and he puts a stool in the middle of the room and tells me to sit on it. He puts a torch in a stand next to us. He speaks to me softly, like I'm a stray kitten that he is trying to tempt into a sack. The stool is low, like a milking stool. I am just about squatting, with my knees raised. I don't know what to do with the blanket: cover my chest or my legs. In the end I place it over my knees. I smell of old piss and shit.

'Tell me,' he says, his nostrils flaring at the smell, 'why you chose the Devil over God. For I am a man of God and it is beyond my understanding.'

'I'm as feared of the Divvil as you are, sir,' I say.

He closes his eyes. His face is stony, licked orange from the light of the torch. He looks like a man who has never known joy.

'Tell me, have you ever used sorcery?'

I sit up straight. 'I'm a healer,' I say. 'I use charmes to help the sick.'

'Sick people like Hazel Kincaid,' he says. 'The daughter of your master, Baillie Kincaid. She was afflicted by a rash on her face that vanished after you uttered a spell.'

'I used a poultice,' I tell him.

'But there were magic words,' he goes on.

So Hazel Kincaid has been telling tales on me. 'Sometimes magic words help,' I say.

The door opens and another man comes in. Everyone bows. He is smaller, with a long nose and a red beard.

He stands in front of me, breathing fast, his breath whistling up and down his nose.

'Who is your master?' he asks me. 'Not Baillie Kincaid, whose home you ran away from. Who is your real master?'

'I have no master now,' I tell him. 'I work for myself.'

'Everyone has a master. Even I have a master, and I am the King of Scotland. My master is God.'

My heart thumps. Surely this slight fellow is not the king – the man in the procession, who rode the horse. Where's his crown? He looks diminished without his robes.

He continues, 'I have an enemy, you see. An enemy who wishes me harm precisely because I am God's direct servant on Earth. And that enemy is the Devil.' He narrows his eyes. 'Is the Devil your master?'

I sink to the floor, put my forehead on the cold stone, prostrating myself. 'Your Majesty, I am God's servant too. I fear the Divvil just like everyone else.'

'What magic were you doing with the ribbons?' asks the minister.

How do they know about my ribbons? They must have been through my possessions, the things I left behind. 'Love spells,' I say, mortified.

'Did you curse the Danish fleet?' asks the king. 'The *Gideon*. It was nearly destroyed in a storm, despite the best shipbuilders and craftsmen and sailors working on it.'

'No, the opposite: when we heard that the Danish princess was lost at sea, I dipped a stone into the ocean to bless her,' I tell him.

In the silence that follows I hear the swallow of throats, the sniff of bulbous noses, the rasp of beards being scratched.

'And what was the nature of this *blessing*?' asks the king.

'Just some words, a prayer, a special smooth stone to calm the ship's journey,' I say.

'So you have the power to change the weather?' says the king, and his voice is hard.

My knees ache from kneeling, but I cannot move now.

'It was merely a blessing. A guid wish.'

'And what knowledge do you have of the witches of Denmark?' He spits out the words.

'What witches of Denmark?' I ask, confused.

'You have been to Denmark, have you not? Or did they come to you? Did you fly? Did you convene with Ane Koldings of Copenhagen?'

I blink. There is a terror in him, he twitches with the energy of it, infecting the minister. They both blink and nod and growl at me.

'You speak of fantasies,' I say. 'Folk cannie fly.'

The men confer. I hear mutters that I cannot make out. Then the King speaks, loud enough for me to hear.

'We will starve the truth out of her. Do not let her sleep.'

The king and the minister leave. The guards stay. Will they really starve me? My stomach growls at the thought. I am still not better from the fever. My body feels in that weak way, as though it has been in a fight and the sleepless night has made it worse. Now this: mad accusations of flying witches. Surely they cannot be serious. Someone will talk sense into the king.

I get back onto the stool. One of the men comes close to me, checking on me. He says nothing, then returns to his post by the door.

What will they do with me? I think I've an idea. I've had

long enough to consider it. I've seen harlots whipped at North Berwick Green. Will they shave my head and cart me to the Canongate Tollbooth? Will they nail my ear to a post for the day? Healing is not a crime – everyone knows that. This must be what Mary meant when she warned me that cunning women were being hunted. I should have asked her more about it, instead of brushing her off.

I shiver, then startle at the loud bang of the door being thrown open. The guards are beckoned outside and I am alone in the room. I wonder how long it will be before they return. Perhaps they are changing the watch. But they do not come back inside. Instead a lone man enters the room, short and fat and red-faced, closing the door behind him and adjusting his eyeglasses. It is Master Kincaid.

He walks towards me, looking terrifyingly high-and-mighty. The guards remain outside. He has told them to stay there, I know it. He stands in front of me, glowering.

'You tried to poison me,' he spits.

'That's not true,' I reply. I hold my head high to him. I will not let him see how terrified I am. He would enjoy it too much.

'You tried to kill me and then you ran away. And you sat in my own house, with those wicked ribbons, cursing everyone.'

'I didn't try to kill you, I tried to dampen your sinful sexual appetite,' I say. 'And I will tell the king about you if he asks.'

He lifts his hand as if to slap me, then stops. He taps his foot, studying me. 'You have lost your looks already, lassie,' he goes on. 'A few days in a cell will do that to a lassie. I've seen it before, in all the thieves and whores I've had whipped. But if you show me a kindness, I might speak to His Majesty on your behalf.'

Every part of me recoils. He is already reaching under his cloak.

'You are far more wicked than I am,' I say. 'I'd rather spend a day in the stocks than be made to touch you again.'

This time he does slap me.

Chapter Thirty

KIRSTEN

Holyroodhouse
March 1590

There was a once Great Pestilence that spread from country to country, killing millions of people, rich and poor alike. It made its victims' bodies swell up and they vomited blood, and their flesh would rot whilst they were still alive. Those days are long gone, they say. We pray that pestilence will not come back. But a new plague is upon us. A plague of fear; a disease of ideologies. Doritte Olsen knew it. The women and men of Trier knew it.

It is early evening and the grounds of Holyroodhouse are bathed in a turquoise twilight, that luminous light that fills the sky when winter is making way for spring. Crosses have been stabbed into bushes and rowan branches have been slashed from any trees in the vicinity and slung beside doorways. It's a night when wolves will howl. As I make my way from the main building out into the open, a deer scampers across my path, startled by my footsteps. I pull my shawl closer and hurry towards the lanterns. My girdle book swings at each step. A group of courtiers – Danes and Scots – have been gathered up as a praying party, led by Reverend Thompson. I have never heard the like, but King James is intent on us holding a vigil near the witch. The prayers must smother her and keep the Devil away. The request to come was in fact a summoning. We were not asked to volunteer. But I would have come anyway. I need to glean as much information as I can.

As the night thickens, we come together and form a circle. We are right outside the barn at the back of the Holyrood estate, where they are keeping the witch, beside the poultry and the Highland cattle. Terror hisses around our little circle in whispers. *She is inches away – are we safe? Hide your face beneath your shawl; if she sees you, she will tell the Devil what you look like.* I wonder if the king is teaching us a lesson: *Look what will happen if you are tempted by sorcery. You will end up like her.*

The girl in the barn is doomed. My fear is who she will name when they begin their inquisition in earnest. Ane Koldings named eleven others, all innocent men and women, after they stretched her across their torture rack like a wet bed sheet on laundering day. She named people she had never met.

I need to know who this girl is and who she knows. The Canongate is a small place. North Berwick is even smaller.

Reverend Thompson clears his throat and regards our group.

'We are gathered here,' he says, in funereal tones, 'to take our places in the great war against evil.'

The group gasps, clutching their fine cloaks to their chins. We double down in prayer. The sky opens and spits of rain begin to fall.

Lord, grant us your holy spirit to protect us. I imagine the prayers reaching the girl's ears. I hope she prays along with us.

We pray as the rain grows heavier. We pray as the temperature drops and the moon rises over Arthur's Seat. The deer comes back and watches us, sheltering under a tree. *Is that the Devil come in animal form?* We pray harder. Earnest and trembling and soaked with rain.

Finally, after an hour or more, the fragile leaves of our prayer books are too soaked to carry on.

'We have done well, but our vigil cannot end here. We will need a night-watch,' Reverend Thompson cries through the rain. 'We need a man or a woman of God to remain here and pray over this woman; listen to any confession; channel the Lord's peace into her.' I can barely make out his face in the weakening torchlight. 'Who will volunteer?'

There are gasps of horror. 'We can't stand out here all night,' says one of the Scots ladies. 'We will catch our deaths. We might see the Devil himself. Can we not pray in the chapel? Or in our chambers?'

'Our prayers must be heard by this wicked woman,' says Reverend Thompson. 'She is being kept here whilst statements are made from those who were affected by her wickedness in North Berwick. She must hear our strength. Our faith. The night-watch will pray in the room where this witch is being held. The night-watch will be given a comfortable chair and will have the safety of the guards watching over them.'

'I am sure no one will volunteer for that,' says the Scots lady. There are murmurings of agreement.

I put up my hand. 'I volunteer,' I say. 'God help me.'

Reverend Thompson spends several minutes instructing me on what I should say whilst I pray. We are standing against the barn now, sheltered from the rain by the thick walls. Everyone else has fled, their lanterns disappearing until there is nothing left to see.

He wipes the rain off his face, unembarrassed by the fact

that he is not praying over the woman himself. Perhaps he is afraid of her.

'Don't mention evil or suffering, for that will excite her,' he says. 'Concentrate on the Holy Spirit. On humility and patience. Let her be in no doubt that we are a force of His strength. She may commune with the Devil somehow. He may even sneak in, taking the form of a rat or a bat or a bird. That deer might be the Devil, and it might come back and peer at you through the window. But do not be afraid, Mistress Sørensen. And remember, the guards are just outside the door.'

I am not afraid. The Devil has been hanging around us for weeks. I am no more afraid of him in a cunning woman's cell than I would be in my own chamber. It is the men who rule us that I am afraid of.

He shows me into the barn and a great fuss is made of bringing me a chair and a blanket. The girl is pale and stocky and her hair is lank, and the room stinks. She does not look human. She sits on a hay bale, frozen, as though she thinks we are about to do her some grave ill.

'We come in peace,' Reverend Thompson says, holding up his hands. 'This godly woman simply means to pray over you in order to bring something of the Lord into this room.'

She looks up. 'The Lord stopped looking after me a while ago, sir,' she croaks.

'The wickedness in her!' He shakes his head in disgust. Can he not see that she has been beaten? Can he not see how she cowers?

'I will take it from here, Reverend,' I say. 'Your supper will be getting cold.'

He nods, looking relieved. 'May God be with you, Mistress Sørensen,' he says. 'Just call on the guards if there is any trouble.' He nods one more time and slithers out of the room.

The girl and I regard each other for a few heartbeats.

'I will pray if you like,' I say. 'Or I will be silent. You may talk if you wish and I won't judge anything you say.'

'Do you think I am a witch too?' she asks. 'You've no fear of me. You're not trembling like the rest of them.'

'I've no fear of you,' I say. 'I think that when women are accused of wickedness, someone usually means them harm.'

She nods, slowly. 'Someone does mean me harm. The baddest man I have ever met.'

'Who is he?' I ask, but of course I already know.

'Baillie Kincaid of North Berwick,' she says. 'I would not give him what he wanted, and now he is getting his revenge.'

Ah, he has got worse over the years. I say nothing, merely bite my tongue and wait for her to speak again. She waits a moment or two before she does, her eyes roaming up and down me, taking me in and deciding whether she can fully trust me or not.

'Miss,' she says, 'can you bring me some water? Some food. Even just scraps. They're starving me.' She calls me Miss, but she's much younger than me. Her voice is powder-dry. I walk to the chair that has been placed in the corner of the room, dripping rainwater as I go. I think of the others, retreating to the banqueting hall for warmed wine and sympathy. Of Reverend Thompson, herding them and telling the Scots ladies that he is relieved a Dane volunteered.

I sit down, feeling the cold wet seep through my skirts. I must find out what she knows, and who else might be in danger.

'I can try to get you some food,' I tell her. 'But first, can you tell me how you came to be here?'

'They've asked me about sorcery,' she says. 'But I don't understand the questions they ask. They talk of witches in Denmark. Do you know of these witches?'

'I know no witches,' I reply. 'But you live on the Canongate, did you meet any cunning women there?' My heart is in my mouth.

'My aunt,' she says. 'Does the king think cunning women wicked?'

'He does,' I say. 'There are fears that the Devil has got into the minds of some cunning women. What is your aunt's name? What is your name? No one has told me your name.'

'I am Jura Craig, Miss, daughter of Auld Mistress Craig of North Berwick. My aunt is Mary. Some folks call her Auld Mary, but she's mibbie fifty years old or so, so she's neither old nor young, but she does read cards. Is that Divvilment, Miss? Her house is in the Canongate and I've been living next door.'

Is this a trick?

I ask her to repeat what she has said, and she does.

'Can you get a message to my aunt?' she asks, and then she keeps on talking. But I can't hear her. My ears ring. My throat swells. My heart pounds.

Chapter Thirty-One

KIRSTEN

North Berwick
Twenty-four years earlier

Dawn cracks the Firth of Forth open like a nut. One moment we are in the inky blackness of the dead hours; the next, a slice of sunlight divides sea and sky. *Firth* comes from *fjord*, Papa says. *Our Norse ancestors fell in love with these lands.* Papa was always too romantic. He should have been more honest about the cruelty some people are capable of.

We are in North Berwick. We have made a pilgrimage to St Andrew's, following the old route, and now we are on our way back. We are not supposed to be doing this: John Knox, the great reformer, ordered the destruction of the cathedral at St Andrew's and nothing remains of it but ruined stone. But Papa's friends knew where the relics had been hidden. Hundreds still walked and sailed the trail, and Papa wanted to make the journey, as his father had done before him. He is pleased with himself that he is managing to do this. He wears his pilgrimage like a crown.

One day, when we are back home in Denmark, Papa will convert to Protestantism, so that both he and I can advance at court. But we do not know that yet. Today, as I stand outside the North Berwick Inn, shivering in the morning chill, all I know is a sunrise of silver and gold, and the glory of Scotland's east coastline of pale sands and grassy hills and creamy tides. Beside me, on the beach wall, a gull preens his wing with his beak, then regards the wide beach, pausing his screeching and swooping to give himself a moment of rest.

I am collecting sea-shells before breakfast and our departure back to Edinburgh. I am too old, at sixteen, to be collecting sea-shells. But it is something I have always done. I like the soothing whirl of them. Oysters and mussels and scallops and whelks. We are in Scotland because Papa believes there's a fortune to be made in the malted-barley trade. He has been meeting maltmen and learning their craft and is setting up trading deals. He believes it's vital to see the world, and learn new languages, even for a girl, which is why I'm with him. He'd begun teaching me Scots even before we got here. But travelling unsettles me. Collecting familiar things brings me comfort.

The damp sand masks the stranger's soft footsteps until he is a few feet away. If I had seen him, and not been too busy hunching over the tide's bounties, nose wrinkling at the iodine scent of seaweed, I would have gone back inside. When I stand up and notice him, he has a look of open curiosity about him. I am old enough to know that look is dangerous.

'Hello, lass,' he says.

I understand the language fairly well by now and wish him a good morning.

'Where are you from?' he asks. His clothes are well made, the trim on his cloak is perfectly edged. He smells of alcohol fumes.

I feel uncomfortable now and start edging back to the inn. Papa will be getting up and wondering where I am. I walk ahead of the man as he calls out to me: asking me my name, why am I here, am I a pilgrim, should he report me to the minister? When we get to the inn, just as I think I am safe, the man puts his hands on me, so fast I can't react, and drags me into an alley.

Afterwards, there is sand and blood under my fingernails and my hands are caked in dirt. Mama would have shaken her head and asked what on earth I had got up to. The man is gone, the sweep of his fine cloak having disappeared around the corner like an eerie trick. I am squatting on the ground next to weeds. The earth is damp and rank from the horse piss that trickles down the alley from where the animals are tethered at the top.

I think time passes, but I don't know how long. My ears ring. I break out in a cold sweat. I hear the clack of pattens from around the corner and stand up shakily, thinking someone else has come to cause me further injury. The woman, when she appears, is short and broad, with eyes the blue of the Firth of Forth itself, and under her brown bonnet are curls as white as its waves, as though she has risen from the sea.

When she sees me, she stops dead in her tracks. 'This is not a place to stand about,' she says. 'Are you lost?'

When I open my trembling mouth but give no answer, she frowns, her face creasing into deep, weathered lines.

'Was that man troubling you? The man who I passed a minute ago on the sea front?' When she realizes my kirtle is askew, she takes a step back. Her jaw drops. 'Did he hurt you?' she asks.

I feel my head admit it, in a heavy nod.

The woman takes me gently and bundles me into the inn, ignoring the innkeeper when he tries to have her thrown out.

She leads me upstairs to where Papa is readying himself for breakfast, brushing his cape.

'Daughter,' he says, looking alarmed, 'what has happened?'

The woman talks rapidly, and they have a conversation about me as I stand at the door. She is telling him I am harmed and he looks puzzled, as though someone has told him that his understanding of the entire world is slightly awry.

I am put back to bed, and Papa goes off to find the man who was seen hurrying away from me, righting his breeches. The woman sits down in a chair at the side of the bed.

'Your father should leave it be,' she says. 'He should not take trouble to Stuart Kincaid's door. He thinks himself a man of importance. Others think it too.'

She brings me water and, as I sip it, she puts her hand on my shoulder. It is a soft touch.

''Tis not your fault,' she says.

An hour or so passes, then Papa returns. He looks defeated.

'I cannot report him,' he tells me. 'He knows we are pilgrims. Our crime is worse than his.'

The woman goes away, then comes back later that afternoon. She brings a grey liquid in a cup. 'This will make sure nothing sticks,' she whispers. 'But don't tell your da.'

Papa informs her that we are leaving in the morning to go to Edinburgh. He may have to leave me there awhile, as he no longer thinks it's safe to take me travelling with him. She tells him I can stay with her sister in the Canongate.

'North Berwick was too small a place for Mary. She can read cards and see the future and there's more call for that in a big town than in a place like this. She will watch over your lass.'

As they talk, making their arrangements, I try to think clearly through my daze and work out what happened to me. Did I beg for it somehow? Is that why Mama was always so insistent on chaperones? Why did I not scream? I wonder these things for a long time, until I am a grown woman, old enough and wise enough to realize that some men simply do what they want.

I have never collected sea-shells since that day.

When we got to the Canongate, Papa found Mary and paid her to cook and clean for me, and a tutor to keep me occupied in needlework and language lessons whilst he went away to meet bottle-makers and ship owners. He wrote from the Highlands and then from England. His absence stretched into weeks, months. I taught Mary to read, using Papa's letters.

Mary knew I was with child before I did. She asked, gingerly, one morning as I sat, ashen-faced and nauseous for the third day in a row.

'Have you a sweetheart?' she said.

I shook my head, thinking she must have assumed me lovesick.

'Have you been with a man?' she asked.

At first I did not understand what she meant. Then I realized what Kincaid had truly done.

'Did my sister not give you something to take?' she asked.

She had, hadn't she? I remembered the unpleasant drink. I had left it on the side-table. It had been too bitter to swallow. I didn't know what she meant about stopping something from sticking.

I was sick then. Again and again, as though my body was trying to rid itself of everything inside it. But even though I heaved, the thing inside my womb was stuck fast.

Mary said there were two ways of dealing with it. She could give me medicine to bring back my menses, but that would kill the baby, or I could have the baby.

Kill the baby – I had never heard such wickedness in my life.

'It is not yet a proper bairn,' she said. 'But you are a bairn, and plenty before you have taken the medicine. It's safe.'

Safe? And what if it is not safe, if it makes me sick, or worse?

I was sixteen, still young enough to feel the joy of a sea-shell on a beach and old enough to know the wickedness of some men. Truthfully? I did not really believe Mary. I thought if I prayed or wished hard enough, the problem would go away.

It did not.

I had the baby just before Papa returned to collect me. He knew she was mine the minute he saw her. It was painful, watching him put the puzzle pieces together, looking from her downy head to mine, the scent of milk and baby-breath heady in Mary's kitchen.

'We can't take a baby back to Denmark,' he said.

'I can't keep her,' Mary replied. 'That's too much to ask. And anyway the Canongate is a foul place to raise a child.'

So we all got in a cart and travelled to North Berwick, to her sister, who lived in a cottage by the sea and was known for having a soft spot for waifs and strays.

I had called her Jura, after the Scottish island. They liked the name so much they kept it.

Statement from Baillie Stuart Kincaid, taken by the scribe of His Majesty King James at Holyroodhouse, in the year of God 1590

When Mistress Jura Craig came into my household, I assumed her wholesome and sound, but instead a series of ungodly things happened. As a God-fearing man, I should have paid more attention to the happenings under my own roof, and beyond, but backsight is a marvellous thing.

Firstly, the weather turned most ferocious. We'd been blessed with a magnificent summer, but the storms that came with the arrival of Mistress Craig threatened the harvests. Even the horses were nervous of her. Folk say her mother practised the magic arts, but I knew nothing of this when I took her in. It was women's gossip.

I left the household on business – the king's business – and when I came back it was as though everyone was under a spell. My daughter was in raptures over Mistress Craig; it appears there had been some kind of healing done to her skin. My daughter is not a vain girl, but it does not take much to tempt a woman from the good path. My wife was in thrall to her and had sent Mistress Craig out to cure the women of North Berwick of their complaints. Honest, God-fearing women. If I had known, I would never have left them, knowing how Eve was deceived by the serpent.

The next part of my statement is delicate as it covers

Miss Craig's transgression of wantonness. I have sought counsel on this matter from Reverend Thompson and I am assured it is not wicked to talk of these matters, for I was not at fault.

Mistress Craig was wanton from the first day. I should have recognized this, but it was the last thing on my mind. She would insist on coming to me and delaying in my study, to discuss all manner of trivial household matters. She went out at all hours of the night, even in foul weather, in which she seemed to delight, for I never saw her merrier than in those days when there was torrential rain. I believe she tempted our neighbour's son, Master Robbie Bathgate, and when he rejected her advances, that was the point at which she lost her self-control.

I fell very unwell one morning around the seventh of December last year after consuming my usual breakfast posset. Normally this is prepared by our cook but later, when I conducted my own enquiries, I found it had been prepared by Mistress Craig herself, as Cook had a brace of rabbits to deal with. I spent many hours in a most wonderful dream, where I met a young man who promised me that I could see the world if I joined him on a cart driven by cats, with said cart being able to travel great distances in a short time. Well, I leapt on the cart, this being a dream rather than real life, and in no time we were flying through the sky and landing in various places. Bordeaux in France, then mountainous places, then Geneva, then a place I did not recognize, but now believe to be Copenhagen, where the man took on his true form – which was the Devil himself, with forked tongue and a tail and cloven *feet. At this point I invoked the name of God Almighty and demanded to be returned to North Berwick. The Devil laughed and said he was too busy, but sent his servant to see me home, and that servant was my own servant, Miss Jura Craig. I saw her face in that dream as clear as I saw it when she came to my bedside with a jug of water.*

I swear this is a true account, by the mercy of Almighty God and His chosen king, James the Sixth of Scotland.

Chapter Thirty-Two

ANNA

Holyroodhouse
March 1590

I think I may be with child.
 I have felt sick, these past two days, which I know to be the first sign, for I have been schooled endlessly in matters of the womb. I feel like I can taste the rot of the streets outside. I crave sea air. Oh God, what will Henry say? It would destroy everything.

I cannot be with child. I am due to bleed in the coming days. I will know then. I will have to work out what to do.

A blackbird sings on the chimney above my fireplace. His song is so light and carefree I always stop to listen. Sometimes he flutters down to my windowsill. I have put out seeds. I miss Aksel. I miss Henry when we are not at our lessons.

The tailor has delivered a whalebone farthingale hoop fixed with bolsters of cotton at the hips, and two new overskirts – one in emerald Bruges satin, one in violet taffeta – wide enough to stretch over it. It is twice as wide as any hoop I have ever worn.

Kirsten detests it. I like it a lot.

'Your mama would think you foolish for copying such a ludicrous fashion,' she says.

I'm four feet wide at the hips now. It's marvellous. I've practised sitting and walking through doors at a diagonal. It's like a game, a dance. She's come to get me ready for James. She sets about the task of removing the gown with great sighs and a shaking of her head, untying ribbons and heaving herself about my skirts.

'I am just like the Scots now,' I tell her, the hoops dropping to the floor with a clatter and a thud. But truly, it is more than that. I enjoy the new width of me. I have always been taught to be small. I'm enjoying the feeling of being larger-than-life.

'We will never be like the Scots and that is a blessing,' says Kirsten.

She has been pricklier than usual ever since spending the night praying over the North Berwick witch. She appeared late for breakfast and I had to get Hanne to dress me, which meant I was late for lunch too.

'The Scots are unfathomable,' she goes on, hanging the skirts up.

'What news of the witch in the barn?' I ask her. 'Are you to pray over her again?'

'I should hope so,' she says. 'It is my duty,' she adds hurriedly.

'Is she terrifying?' I whisper.

Kirsten looks out of the window. She is in a sweat from the task of undressing me. The blackbird is hopping on the window ledge, looking for his supper. 'Have you named the bird?' she asks.

I pause, embarrassed. 'Peckin. For he is always pecking.'

She nods. 'And do you talk to him? In the way you talked to Aksel?'

'Sometimes,' I admit. 'Although I do not tell him anything important.'

Kirsten sits down on my bed. 'They might accuse you of being a witch for talking to a bird.'

I flinch. 'That is a wicked thing to say,' I tell her.

'But it is true,' she says. 'All it would take would be for someone to spy on you and see you talking to a blackbird and they would say he was your familiar, or the Devil in disguise. They would not burn you, for you are Danish royalty. But if you were not – say Hanne was seen talking to Peckin, and say the meat hanging in the outhouse went sour or there was an outbreak of pox, then she might be blamed.'

I frown, irritated at Kirsten for such horrible talk. 'But who would say such a thing, if it were not true?'

'Your fear of witches is misplaced,' she continues. 'Your fear of the girl in the barn is misplaced. You were terrified of Doritte Olsen because you were told of her wickedness. But do you truly believe women can cause storms?'

'The Devil can cause them,' I reply. 'And he uses the weakest amongst us to do his work.'

'Mistress Olsen was not weak,' says Kirsten. 'She was one of the strongest people you will ever know of. She was tortured and burned to death and she remained dignified throughout. She did not reappear at the port at Kronborg when the *Gideon* sailed that morning. That was your fear manifesting. Fear can make us imagine all kinds of nonsense.'

'What are you telling me?' I ask. I feel even more nauseous now, as though the room is spinning. My world is turning upside down. 'Are you a witch too?'

'Oh, Anna.' Kirsten shakes her head in scorn. 'There are no witches, at least not in the devilish sense. Mistress Olsen was a healer. She could no more conjure a storm than you could. The storm at sea was the work of nature, not the work of women. Mistress Jura Craig in the barn is a healer too. If you are to rule Scotland fairly, you must understand these things.'

I think Kirsten needs to shut up before someone hears her. 'Fetch the hairbrush,' I say. 'James will be here soon.'

She nods and her face puckers back into its usual knot. I believe Kirsten has been waiting to say these things for a long time.

'Tell no one of this conversation,' she whispers. 'But we must continue to have it. James of Scotland is becoming a dangerous man. A threat to ordinary women. You might be the only person who can talk sense to him.'

She leaves, making sure my farthingale and its skirts are hanging impeccably. I stand at the window. Peckin is off somewhere, gathering his twigs or perched on a wall, watching the world swirl under his feet.

Kirsten Sørensen is many things. Difficult. Demanding of perfection. Secretive. But she is loyal. I have no reason to doubt anything she has ever said.

James, when he visits that evening, sees the new farthingale hanging up and laughs, but in an admiring way.

'Well, little Anna, I shall like to see you in that, my queen,' he says.

I have no wish to be his queen. I laugh back, disguising my horror with a smile.

'Whatever pleases you, sir,' I say with a curtsey. We get into bed.

'Oh,' he says, puzzled, looking at my bed-table. 'Has the sugar-man sent more *scorchets*? I had not asked for any. I wondered if it was too much of an indulgence.'

'He must have done,' I reply, trying to sound as innocent as

I can. 'But it's only a small indulgence. A reward for a long day serving God.'

'Hmm,' he says. 'Perhaps you are right.'

He does his usual things. Afterwards, I lie back and think. I have work to do. If my bleeding does not arrive, I will have to find someone to help me.

Chapter Thirty-Three

KIRSTEN

Holyroodhouse
March 1590

I still have all the letters Mary sent me when Jura was a little girl. They're folded into my trunk. Perhaps I should burn them in case the Scots ever search our chambers when we are out.

I pull one out from the bottom of the trunk. One of the first:

September 1568
The Canongate

Dear Kirsten,

I hope my handwriting is readable to you. I have just returned from a week with my sister in North Berwick; as it is so stifling here in town I needed the sea air. The bairn is bonnie and doing marvellous. She is clambering all over the place and her hair is getting aye long now. Her favourite thing to eat is bread soaked in milk, and she is aye putting her hands in her mouth. Oh, she looks like you, Kirsten; when she does not want to do something, she screws up her face and she is your spit.

> *I have given my sister the money you sent and she was grateful and said thank you very much.*
> *Your friend, Mary*

I close my eyes. What did she look like? Blonde wisps curling around the nape of her neck. A wet, pink fist. Like me, waking up each morning to the rhythm of tide and gull, but hers were thousands of miles away.

I knew they would teach Jura their ways. Charm and song and wish. Trying to take a little control of the world, with chalk marks and feathers and herbs, for poor people have no real power. I kept writing to Mary, to keep myself within their world so that I was never forgotten. My letters were my own charm.

I think I wrote back immediately, but I did not say any of those things. Instead, I would have described Kronborg and the court that Papa had set his sights on. The smart cottage he had bought near the castle, and the malt that had begun to make its way from Scotland to Demark via the trading line he had set up. I wrote in plain words, so that Mary could understand them. I wrote in plain words in the hope she might read the letters out to Jura on her next visit.

I remember how my arms ached for my little one. I still can't smell milk or vanilla or cinnamon without thinking of her, the scent of her pale skin. I remember the promise I made: *one day I will return to you.*

And here I am.

Chapter Thirty-Four

JURA

Holyroodhouse
March 1590

They bring pilliwinks. The guard tells me the pilliwinks are coming and at first I don't know what he's talking about. I had thought it some daft joke, or a code, or nonsense. They bring them first thing in the morning. They wake me up, crashing into the barn, the king and the minister and some other men. The king is carrying a small black clamp.

They strap my arms to my sides with leather belts. They load the fire with logs. They bring jugs of water and wine for themselves. The woman who came to pray and promised me water has not been back. The men take off their cloaks and their hats and rub their hands together. The orange glow of the flames dances around the room. We could be in hell. It couldnie be any worse than this.

'Will you confess to any wickedness before we start?' asks the king. 'And save us all the upset?'

'Confess to what?' I ask.

'Tell us how you worked with the Danish witches. Tell us methods you used to raise the sea-storms.'

I shake my head.

'If you confess, we will bring you hot food,' the king says. 'I will arrange it myself. And hot water with which to bathe, and soap and new garments to wear. A fresh blanket.'

One of the men takes my right hand. I ball my fingers into a fist, but he unpicks my thumb. Another man approaches with the pilliwinks. Even before they begin, I scream. The cold metal latches onto my thumb. Then one of the men twists a key on the device and the clamp bears down. I scream again and the king comes over to me.

'Get her to stop screaming,' he shouts. 'Get her under control.' He is sweating and red in the face.

The man untwists the key and I look down at my thumb. The clamp has left a furious slash across it.

'Did you send a storm to drown the Danish fleet?' the king asks.

'I did not,' I say.

'Pilliwinks!' the king shouts and the clamp goes down again.

This time he does not stop me screaming. I scream even though my throat is raw. I scream even when I am slapped to stop. I scream even when they release the clamp again.

'The Devil is in her,' cries one of the men. I think it is that minister. I hear someone apologize to the king for the stench of my piss.

'The Divvil's in all of you,' I cry. I am nothing but pain. My thumb. My throat. My arms, where the belts bite into it.

'Pilliwinks,' cries the king.

'No!' I shout. Everything in the room stops, save for the crack of the wood on the fire.

'Do you have something to confess?' asks King James, his face so close to mine I can see the ginger hair in his nostrils, the beads of sweat running down his nose.

'What will happen if I confess?' I ask him.

His eyes shine. 'A fair trial,' he says.
'I have done nothing wrong,' I plead.
He wipes the bead of sweat from his nose.
'Pilliwinks,' he says.

The First Confession of Mistress Jura Craig, taken at Holyroodhouse by the High and Mighty King James the Sixth of Scotland on the thirtieth day of March in the year of Our Lord 1590

I visited the Auld Kirk Green near the beach at North Berwick at midnight, sometime in September last. It was my habit to visit this part of the town in the middle of the night because that was my meeting place with the Divvil. I've known the Divvil for a long time, and I ask him to help me when I have a problem that needs solving. He helps me cure ailments and get rid of pests, and keep milk fresh for weeks and settle any scores with folk who cross me.

That night the Divvil did come, on a horse and cart lit with candles, which did not flicker even in the wind. He said he would take me on a magnificent journey if I fancied it, and this time the rewards would be far greater than ever before. I got in the cart, and we flew through the air to Copenhagen and met with witches there. We all vowed to help the Divvil in his campaign against His Majesty.

When I returned to North Berwick, I tied knots in a purple ribbon and dipped it in the sea to raise a great tempest to meet the Princess Anna's fleet. When Mistress Jane Kennedy drowned in the ferry-boat in the Firth of Forth, I knew that was a most *tremendous sign of our success. At kirk, when everyone was praying for Princess Anna, I had my fingers crossed in my lap.*

I want now to live a life free of sin, at God's mercy.

Chapter Thirty-Five

KIRSTEN

Holyroodhouse
April 1590

What am I to do? I have thought of every possibility. *Tell Anna everything. Tell King James everything. Tell Jura that I am her mother. Tell Kincaid that Jura is his daughter.*

None of these things is the right thing to do. Not yet. They feel wrong when I churn them around futilely in my mind, like cream that won't whip properly.

In the end, I take a risk and go and visit Mary. I creep out of the palace and onto the Canongate. All it takes is a plaid shawl and a basket and I blend onto its canvas of horses-and-carts and urchins and chicken-sellers.

It feels surreal, visiting the place where I lived and gave birth all those years ago. A place that has become an address, words on parchment, that I sent letters to. The stairs are the same; worn and narrow. The door has not been painted in all these years.

Mary answers the door immediately, looking distraught.

'It's happening,' she says. 'They came and took Jura. She was living next door. I wanted to get a message to you at the palace and tell you she was living close by, but I was feared of getting you into trouble.'

'I've seen her,' I say. 'Kincaid has accused her of witchcraft.'

'His own daughter,' she says. 'Jura has no idea. She ended up working as his maid and ran away from him. He tried his nonsense on her too.'

'He is vile. Wicked beyond words. He does not deserve to know that Jura is his daughter,' I tell her.

'And she can't ever know that Kincaid is her father,' Mary says. 'For he has traumatized her enough. If she were to know that evil man is her da, I don't think Jura would ever come to terms with it.'

'Does she believe Mistress Craig to be her mother?' I ask.

'She has never questioned it,' replies Mary. 'She has a gift of healing and she believes it comes from her ma. Jura adored her. She went to Kincaid after her ma died, and now look what has happened. Her da is no use. Lost in the drink.'

There's a sharp tug in my belly where once there was a baby. I thought I did the best thing for Jura. Now I realize I've failed her.

'You must stop all spells and magic and fortune-telling,' I tell Mary. 'Keep yourself to yourself. You are lucky the king's men did not come knocking at your door as well. They may well do so. They are interrogating Jura and she is already confessing to all manner of nonsense. She is in terror. If they ask for names of her accomplices – of any other cunning women she knows – she might give yours.'

'She wouldn't do that,' says Mary.

'It's torture,' I tell her. 'She has no control over what she will do.'

Mary fetches a bottle from a high shelf and pours us wine. It is probably her best wine, but it tastes like vinegar. I thought so often about this house, back in Kronborg, that I felt if I stepped outside the palace door it might even be there. I could trace the path up its stairs to its long, dark hall. The kitchen where the firepit reeked. Now I'm here, and everything I dreaded since I saw Mistress Olsen burn has come true, but is far, far worse.

We drink from chipped cups, the only sounds in the room being Mary's gulps and the crack of the firewood under the cooking pot.

'I think you're going to have to disappear,' I tell her.

'I was afraid you might say that,' Mary replies. 'But where will I go and what will you do?'

'I will try to think of a way to help Jura,' I say. 'But you can't stay here. You need to get as far away as you possibly can.'

'I can't go back to North Berwick,' she says, looking agitated. 'They know me there.'

'North Berwick is not far enough,' I tell her. 'You need to head south. Into England. Just until these hunts die down.'

'But I wanted to get to know you again,' says Mary. 'For years all we have had is letter-writing. Am I to lose you again?'

'Only for a while,' I respond, pulling out a purse and handing it to her. It has a year's worth of my saved-up coins in it. 'Leave as soon as you can. Burn any letters I sent to you, for they might search these rooms. Remove all traces of yourself and future-telling and me. Then find a cart heading south and get onto it.'

Chapter Thirty-Six

ANNA

Holyroodhouse
April 1590

Henry is to teach me tennis. He has persuaded James that I must learn the skills of the game in order to better enjoy my summers here. Soon the tennis courts will be filled with ladies, and would it not be superb if I could hold my own against some of them?

James agreed. Henry thinks he agreed because Henry's tennis is supposedly the best at court. I think it was because he's so distracted by the woman in his custody that nothing else matters.

We play on the bottom court, furthest away from the palace. We are watched, of course, with so many people standing by, applauding my efforts batting the ball to and fro, that we can't make any decent attempt at conversation. But as he coaches me, we manage snatches. I still have not bled. I wait for it: the heaviness is there, but the blood does not come. Is this what pregnancy is like?

'There's a woman being kept in the barn,' I say.

'Yes, they are convinced she can tell them about the plot against the Crown,' he says. 'They think Bothwell is behind it all and he has amassed an army of witches. They think she will know who the Scots witches are.'

'But can that really be true? A peasant woman involved in something so deadly?'

Henry picks up the ball again and shows me how I should be serving. 'They are terrified of Bothwell. They think he has spies and allies in every village in Scotland. At the very least, this will serve as a message to him that James sees no one as innocent.'

We play a little longer. Long enough and badly enough for those watching us to get bored and distracted. He comes and talks to me again.

'I admired you in your farthingale the other evening at dinner,' he says.

I laugh. 'Kirsten detests it,' I reply.

'When we are finally together, there will be no Kirsten, no James, just the two of us,' he tells me.

'Murray thinks I'm the perfect wife, so it will only be a matter of time before James asks me to marry him.'

'You suit Murray's purposes because you turn a blind eye to his relationship with James, and you have not made a fuss so far. But I believe James will wait for you to conceive,' Henry says. 'No matter what Murray thinks, James needs children. I think failing to conceive is your best chance of getting out of this.'

My stomach lurches. *What if it's too late?*

After the game, Henry says he'll walk me back to the palace.

'I would rather walk awhile around the gardens,' I say.

'I will come with you,' he offers. But I say no. We can't be seen spending too much time together. Besides, there is something I want to look at.

There are bushes behind the barn where Mistress Craig is

being held captive. I creep into them, with my tennis racket in my hand. If anyone asks, I will say I am searching for a lost ball. The branches brush my face and arms, but I carry on. I find a gap in the barn wall, just as wide as my hand. I crouch down and look through it. She's there.

If Mistress Craig were really a witch, surely she would do more than lie curled up on a hay bale? Her hair is spread across it, her clothes filthy and streaks of dark blood across her.

I'm breathing so hard I think she might hear me.

She sits up, slowly, as though every bone aches. Then she says something. Her voice is high and sweet, like Aksel's was. She is chanting – it is a spell! But then I hear her speak to God, which I know a witch would never do.

'Lord God, high in the heavens, help me today,' she says. 'And all your heavenly creatures – the selkies and the angels – help me too, if any of you can hear me.'

It is the strangest prayer I have ever heard.

I should leave. She is peculiar. Even if she does speak to God. I am about to turn when there is a commotion. I duck away, but I can hear men's voices in the room and out the front too. Lots of them. The wooden handle of my tennis racket is slick with sweat. I should not have come. And now I am stuck, for I can't wander out when there are so many people outside.

Her scream soars above all of it.

'No, sir, you are not to come at me again with these wicked devices.'

'But we must get further details from you.' It is Reverend Thompson, I am sure of it. Dread slithers through my guts. It is the tone of his voice, the curl of menace about it.

'The things I say when you hurt me are not true,' she cries.

'It's the pain. You would say anything too, if you were being hurt.'

'I would not,' says the reverend. 'For the Good Lord would guide me through it.'

There is an awful-sounding scuffle.

The next voice I recognize immediately, and sickeningly. James, my betrothed, the man who shares my bed.

'I rather think you enjoyed the pilliwinks, Mistress Jura. It made you sing beautifully. We have brought them back today. And we also have a rope, which we will put about your neck and pull tight until you tell us who else is involved in the plot to destroy me. And we will not stop until we have every name. But first, let me introduce you to a friend of mine, who has travelled many miles to assist me today. This is Dr Hemmingsen, all the way from Copenhagen. He has great experience in interrogation.'

I can't help but look. They are unconcerned, anyway; the last thing they are worried about is being seen, so caught up are they in the task that is unfolding.

Dr Hemmingsen, who must have come to this barn straight off a ship, for I had no idea that he had arrived or was even on his way, is unloading the contents of a leather case onto a table.

'The Devil's mark is usually found on the breast or the privy parts,' he is saying. 'I have the pricker here.'

The men crowd around the table.

'I am fascinated by this,' James says. 'Talk me through it as you go.'

Two men are holding Mistress Craig down on the hay bale, hunkering down on her. She starts wailing, screaming like an animal. I feel bile rise in my throat.

'She will have to be stripped,' Dr Hemmingsen tells them,

his voice as cool as well-water. 'In Copenhagen the Witch Pricker had a woman assisting. Can a woman be fetched? A midwife or some such?'

'We've no time for the fetching of midwives.' James's voice is the opposite of Dr Hemmingsen's. It is all ablaze. I can imagine the spittle frothing at the corners of his lips. He toys with his amulet. I imagine him running his fingers across the flower-engraving.

There is a flurry of movement around the girl. I should run away. I should stop them. Instead I stay where I am, crouched, unable to move. I see a naked leg, a naked arm. I have never seen another woman naked before. I barely get to see my own self naked. I am always being dressed or bundled into underskirts. I doubt James has ever seen me fully naked, and now he is staring at this wretch. He looks utterly transfixed.

Her legs tremble. She whimpers.

Dr Hemmingsen clears his throat. 'The breasts look to be without mark. One of the women in Copenhagen had a third teat.'

The men in the room gasp.

'And under torture she confessed that the Devil himself did suckle upon it most frequently,' Dr Hemmingsen adds. 'I see no abnormalities to Mistress Craig's breasts at all. But this is where the bodkin comes into its own.' He goes to his case and brings out a long, sharp object. 'A witch will have an area on her skin which the Devil has marked and made his own. A witch cannot feel any pain when this area is pricked, nor will any blood be drawn.'

'Don't hurt me, sir,' Mistress Craig cries.

'Hush, hush,' soothes Dr Hemmingsen. 'I am not in the business of causing excess pain. I will use it gently. If you lie still and let me know when you can feel the bodkin, that will suffice.'

It goes on for several minutes. She squeals and sobs and begs. None of the men say anything. The only sound is from her. The pauses between her cries are so silent that if I made a run for it now, they would hear the crack of branches.

Finally Dr Hemmingsen speaks. 'We will have to examine the privy parts now,' he says.

Mistress Craig has stopped whimpering. Her silence is worse than her noise.

'Ah, look,' Dr Hemmingsen finally declares. 'A dark spot, here on the top of the thigh. It looks like a mole, but when I placed the bodkin on it, she gave no indication of pain.'

The men crowd around. One holds a lamp overhead. I can see her face, screwed up in agony. Her mouth is moving silently.

'Is that it? The Devil's mark?' James sounds awestruck.

'It is indeed,' says Dr Hemmingsen. 'The Devil has suckled from Mistress Craig at this very spot. We will leave her now. But we should come again tomorrow to find out what else she knows. I felt the confession you obtained with the pilliwinks merely scratched the surface.'

'It is good that you are here,' says James. 'We need the guidance of your expertise. Praise God Almighty.'

'Amen,' says Dr Hemmingsen.

I wait for the men to leave. They take their time, for there is the packing of Dr Hemmingsen's case and the righting of Mistress Craig's dress and kirtle, which Dr Hemmingsen insists on doing, as if to make himself feel civilized again, and the tidying up of chairs and hay bales.

She curls up again, pulling a blanket over herself.

I feel like I want to say something to her, but I can't. It's another violation. I don't want her to know anyone saw that, let alone a spying stranger. Let alone the woman who shares her bed with the man who ordered it, who stood and watched it as though it was the most wondrous thing he had ever seen.

At three o'clock, when I am safely back in my chamber with tales to the maids of what a wonderful game of tennis I enjoyed, James sends me a note, saying he has urgent business with Dr Hemmingsen, who has just arrived from Copenhagen, and not to expect him to visit upon me this evening. I am to have dinner in my apartments with Kirsten, as there are serious matters to be discussed in the dining hall.

At four o'clock my stomach cramps and, when I use the chamberpot, my menses have come. *I am safe. I have survived another month.*

I will not always be so fortunate. I will need help to stay unpregnant.

Chapter Thirty-Seven

KIRSTEN

Holyroodhouse
April 1590

What are they doing to Jura? The wondering is torture itself.

James has scarcely been seen. He is down in that barn with that awful doctor. Anna is abed again with menstrual cramps, but how can I worry about the lack of a royal heir now?

I keep remembering Mistress Olsen's bloodied thumbs.

Are they doing that to Jura too? Dr Hemmingsen will have methods. He has travelled thousands of miles to deploy them.

What did Baillie Kincaid do to Jura, to make her run away? How did she reject him, to make him so angry with her?

Wicked man. It triggers the memory of what he did to me, amongst the weeds and horse piss. I remember the look on his face. His sneer of disgust as he watched me beg him to stop. I still have nightmares about it. It's why I never married. Why I never sought another man after Peter. By the time Kincaid and Peter had finished with me, I had had enough of the ruthlessness and selfishness of men to last me a lifetime.

And now Kincaid is here, right under my roof. He's done very well for himself over the years, rising up in the ranks and never being found out for the rogue he is. But time has whitened his whiskers and greyed his face, and hunched his shoulders and given him something of a stoop. A slowness. It is fascinating to watch.

Eight o'clock sharp this morning in the banqueting hall and Kincaid is enjoying his breakfast very much. I doubt they have endless jugs of fresh cream and finest heather-honey with their oatmeal in North Berwick, so he's making the most of his time here. He has been a guest of His Majesty since he brought Jura Craig to the palace gates. A cat who's brought a mouse, entrails spilled, to his master's doorstep. He's here for the fine food and the great wines and the revenge.

The breakfasting at Holyroodhouse is always boisterously loud, with mainly the men attending, feeding their hangovers with clatters and shouts. The court ladies tend to avoid the early-morning socializing; they are too intent on trying to squeeze into their farthingales, and keen to get some respite for an hour or two in their peaceful chambers. But I have been breakfasting of late. Kincaid has utterly failed to recognize me, but it gives me the opportunity to observe him and eavesdrop on his plans for each day. And I have edged closer and closer to where he sits. An observer might even think I have taken a fancy to him.

Reverend Thompson, who is sitting beside me, interrupts my train of thought.

'Mistress Sørensen, I hope you're recovered from your night in the barn,' he says. He butters his bread thickly and puts two hard-boiled eggs on his plate.

'The Lord was with me at all times,' I reply. 'I could feel Him standing at my side.'

Reverend Thompson nods, but he is only half listening. His small eyes scan the room, looking to see if anyone more interesting or more important than me might come in and take the empty chair on the other side of him. His eyes flit past the tables, up onto the walls, where crosses now hang and circles have been etched in chalk to ward off evil. It's impossible to avoid them – a constant reminder that we are in danger.

'Are you sending any more prayer parties out to the barn?' I ask.

The minister sniffs, considering the first of his eggs. He takes a spoon and gently taps on the shell until it cracks. He unpeels it deftly, wiping his hands on his kerchief when he is done.

'Dr Hemmingsen considers it unwise to put innocent people in the same room as sorcerers,' he says. 'In Copenhagen no one went near them, apart from the guards. In fact he was quite scornful when I told him we had prayed over Mistress Craig.'

I pick up an egg myself, even though I hate eggs. 'Dr Hemmingsen is quite the expert, it seems,' I comment, picking my words carefully. 'But he is a scholar, not a man of the Church.'

Reverend Thompson splits his egg and sprinkles it with salt and eats it, one half followed by the other.

'Dr Hemmingsen is the king's most trusted advisor on this matter,' he says. 'But you are right. His approach is academic.' He gives little away, apart from a slight furrow of his brow. I wonder if Reverend Thompson feels threatened by Dr Hemmingsen, and by James's absolute trust in him. How he felt when Dr Hemmingsen was scornful of his attempt to keep the Devil away with prayer.

'Faith,' I say. 'Faith is what will see us through. We can draw as many circles on the walls as we like, but we are at war with the Devil. It will take our humanity, not just our learning, to win this war.'

He picks up the other egg and considers its smooth, brown

shell before raising his eyes to meet mine. 'You have no fear of the sorceress in our barn, do you, Mistress Sørensen?'

'My only fear is failing God,' I reply.

'And would you pray with her again, if I asked you? Preach to her?'

'If you felt it the best thing to do,' I say.

'I think it might be appropriate,' he agrees. 'They have found a Devil's mark upon her. Under her skirts.'

Oh God, they have violated her. 'Then we need as much protection as we can get,' I say. 'The Devil will be close, hoping to get to her again.'

'Quite,' he responds. 'They will ramp up their interrogations now – I heard it from Dr Hemmingsen himself. He means to use more torture on her to get to the bottom of her connection to the Earl of Bothwell. When they are finished, go and preach to her, Mistress Sørensen. Preach louder than the Devil himself.'

He does not attempt to eat his second egg. His buttered bread lies uneaten. He has lost his appetite. He is afraid of her. He is afraid of seeing her tortured and damaged. He fears not the Devil in her, but his own reflection in her eyes. He does not want to see his own complicity, the brutality of his king. He can't look her in the eye.

'I will go,' I say.

The Second Confession of Mistress Jura Craig, taken at Holyroodhouse by the High and Mighty King James the Sixth of Scotland on the seventh day of April in the year of Our Lord 1590, by interrogation with an Iron Spiked Boot, manufactured this same week at the Canongate by Melville Blacksmiths, by Appointment to His Majestie

> *I convened many times with the Divvil, on the instruction of Bothwell, cousin of King James. Bothwell wants the throne and thinks King James a terrible king, a weak man. Bothwell came riding into North Berwick one day and found me on the shore and promised me all manner of riches if I met his friend, the Divvil. But he could not act alone, for we needed the power of witches in Denmark and Scotland in order to carry out his most marvellous plan. Bothwell was furious when the storm failed to drown the Danish fleet and there is more sorcery afoot now, bigger and more terrifying than the world has ever seen.*

Chapter Thirty-Eight

ANNA

Holyroodhouse
April 1590

I feared Doritte Olsen. I feared the Devil. Now I know what wickedness truly is, and it shares my bed.

I can't tell anyone. I've seen what they do to women. They will stop at nothing. No part of a woman's body is truly her own. But I should have realized that, when they handfasted me to James Stuart and did not ask me whether it was something I even wanted.

James announces that the delayed masque will now take place. Reverend Thompson is appalled and says we ought to be praying instead, but James wants to show off to Dr Hemmingsen.

'We will not let the Devil spoil our traditions,' he says. 'This masque has been months in the preparation. And the story it tells is one of the power of good over evil.' There is no point in arguing with James anyway — not even if you're Reverend Thompson, or anyone else. James is right about everything. He believes in the divine right of kings; his absolute monarchy over everything, from the peasants in the streets to the men in robes and the women under his roof.

I am glad we are having the masque. It means everyone will

be distracted, watching acrobats and drinking wine, and I can visit Jura Craig again.

I slip out of a side-door when everyone is milling around in the banqueting hall. Torches blaze on stands all around the room. James and Murray are side by side. Murray looks dazzling in a white satin doublet. They can't take their eyes off each other. Are they as in love with each other as Henry and I are? I suppose they must be, and yet they can be bolder in public.

I have an hour before we sit down. I've made sure not to wear the farthingale but to dress in deep-purple skirts, so that I am not seen easily as I pass from the buildings into the grounds. It is light enough to see where I am going. I can hear the guards at the front of the barn. They are drinking something strong, no doubt passed from the banqueting hall. I can tell by the way they are laughing. When I get to the back of the barn, I light my candle.

She is lying on the hay bale again. This time I say something to her.

'Mistress Craig,' I mutter, keeping my voice low, 'can you come to the wall?'

She lifts her head, looking around her as if she imagines there's a ghost in the room.

'Who's there?' she asks. 'No one is to hurt me again. They promised me no one would hurt me again.'

'I won't hurt you,' I say. 'I know what they did to you.'

She sits up slowly, looking around her to see where the voice is coming from.

'I'm at the window,' I say. 'Do you see the candlelight? Please come over.'

She hobbles. James has brutalized her. I move my head, so

she cannot see my face. I wish I could trust her, but I know I can't. I put my hand up to the window.

'Who are you?' she enquires.

'A lady at court,' I tell her. I soften my accent as much as I can so that she does not recognize it as foreign.

'Can you help me?' she asks. 'Have you come to rescue me? The men want me to have a trial. They say God will know if I tell the truth, but when I try to tell the truth they don't believe me.'

I take a deep breath.

'I will try to help you,' I say. 'But I need something from you too.'

'I have nothing,' she replies. 'Is this a trick to get me to say more things about the Divvil and storms?'

'It's not a trick. I know your craft is nothing evil. Can you help women?'

'What do you want?' she says. 'Can you get me out of here? Tell them it's nonsense. Get someone to look at my foot. Look what they did to it. They put it in irons and they would have clamped them closed if I hadn't begged. It's full of cuts. Can you bring me a clean linen to bind it with? Some vinegar. I need to make a poultice or it might go bad.'

'I can't just let you out of here, but I'll get you clean cloths,' I tell her. 'And tell me what I might take to stop a pregnancy.'

She falls silent.

'Are you with child?' she asks. 'For some would say it's the Divvil's work to interfere with that.'

'I'm not with child yet, but it will happen if I don't do something to stop it,' I reply.

'There are cunning women in the Canongate,' she says. 'Any one of them will give you what you need.'

'I can't go to the Canongate. Court ladies are not allowed.'

The wind stirs the bushes. I will be caught if I stay out here too long.

'And you will help me, in return?' she asks.

'I will do everything I can,' I promise her.

'I will tell you what you need to take,' she says, 'but first I need you to bring something to me. If you don't help me, I'm not helping you.'

'What do you want?' I ask, my irritation rising. I didn't think she'd try to strike some sort of bargain with me. 'But you have to know that I don't possess the power to let you out.'

'Then I need something precious. A gold ring. I need it for protection. One of the king's. And a white ribbon. Pure as you can find. Of silk or satin.'

'Is this witchcraft?' I enquire, horrified.

'Do you know nothing, lassie?' she says. 'Gold is for goodness. For the highest level of protection. White ribbons are for hope. I'll offer them to the selkies. There's nothing of the Divvil in it.'

Oh God, I don't understand what she means.

'Is it for a spell?' I ask.

'Yes, but a good one,' she says. 'And then I'll tell you exactly what you need to protect yourself. Nothing as fancy as gold. Simple plants. Easy to pick. They will be growing around here, for sure.'

'You mustn't tell anyone I came,' I say. 'Do you promise that, if I bring you these things?'

'If I get the chance to protect myself, I'll get out of here,' she says.

She's talking nonsense. Of all the things she could have asked – for me to pay the guards or drug them, or beg in her defence or fetch someone – none of these things. I can hear her breathe softly in the darkness. Is she simple-minded? Does she not understand the way of the world? Or does she know things about magic that ordinary people don't?

'I'll fetch you what you want,' I tell her.

No one at the masque has noticed my absence. Some dancing has begun, whilst we await the players taking to the stage.

Kirsten stands at the edge of the crowd, aloof as ever, but more handsome than I have ever seen her, as if she has spent an age getting ready. No wonder she couldn't care less about my dress tonight. Her corset is low, her breasts bulge slightly above it. Her hair falls in tight curls from her combs. There is something exaggerated about her face – a brightness to her lips and cheeks, a paleness to her nose. Dear God, Kirsten Sørensen is wearing face-paint! One of the many things she scorns, along with farthingale hoops and low necklines. Why ever is she doing this? Her brow is furrowed as if she is watching someone. I follow her gaze. She is looking at the North Berwick man, Baillie Kincaid.

Surely she can't have her sights set on him? He looks like a horrible white toad in a coat that's too tight. But she has. Every now and then she tilts her head and flaps her fan as if to catch his eye. He is deep in conversation with other men, stuffing slices of roasted hog into his mouth.

Kirsten Sørensen is a puzzle I will never work out. I am debating about interrupting her when I feel the lightest touch on my arm.

It is Henry.

'Madam, will you dance with me?' he says.

'Is it allowed?' I ask.

'It's a masque,' he replies. 'Anything is allowed. Have you seen James in the last few minutes? I think if you looked, you'd find he's disappeared off with Murray for a while. The masque won't begin until they're back. That's why everyone is dancing.'

'Then you should keep Anna of Denmark entertained,' I tell him.

He takes my arm. 'You are my Anna,' he whispers. His lips brush my ear and linger on my neck, but no one is looking. The thrill of it is like a lightning storm all the way to my stomach, and below.

'Talk to me again,' I whisper back, making sure to touch his ear with my lips when I do so.

'Oh God, Anna,' he says. 'We're in public.'

'But no one's really looking,' I say. We're at the back of the room and it's true. There's so much wine and laughter and shadow that we could hide for minutes. Everyone's memories will be blurred anyway.

Henry takes me to the middle of the dance floor. 'If we dance in plain sight, it won't look like we're trying to hide anything,' he tells me. Every time he speaks, his lips brush my ears, the side of my head. He puts one hand on my waist and we begin to dance. His other hand clasps mine. Our fingers clench each other's tightly, as though we are hanging onto each other for dear life.

I don't want the dance to end. I want to lie with him. I want his hands on my skin. I know he can make me forget all about James. I'm melting into this moment. Henry has enveloped me. Nothing else matters; nothing except cedar scent and skin on skin, and hearing him breathe.

Later there is the masque and singing, and wild costume and somersaulting and cartwheeling. They will talk of the spectacle for months. But all I will remember – all that will ever matter – is my dance with Henry.

Chapter Thirty-Nine

JURA

Holyroodhouse
May 1590

Men come and go with water and bowls of food. But they do not look me in the eye or talk to me.

Reverend Thompson waves incense every day, trailing it around me, trying to make the room too holy for demons to linger in. I sit in a silver cloud. They have drawn five-pointed stars by the fireplace and the door. I am not allowed to be in the dark, they have now decided, not even at night, for the Divvil loves the darkness. The room is a haze of smoke and candlelight. More kirk than dungeon. They mutter when they are near me: *Dear Lord, protect me.*

They made me tell the most terrible tales. I don't know where the stories even came from, for I have never imagined such nonsense. But what else could I say, when they were forcing those tales out of me with their torture? They are the wicked ones, not me.

'Speak and I will offer you salvation. A fair trial.' That is what the king promised me, whispered in my ear. 'Speak and we will be merciful. Speak and God will forgive you.'

And so I spoke their truth. And now I wait for their mercy. Their fair trial.

Neither of the two women has been back. No gold ring. No ribbon. No protection. The two women talk with the same accent. Neither of them is Scots. They are ladies from the Danish court. I think they can help get me out, but I'm running out of time.

I want to go back to North Berwick. I want Ma, and air so fresh that each gust of wind is a slap in the face, full of the salt spit of waves and gull-shriek and the grit of sand.

I will come back to you, I promise North Berwick beach.

The door swings open and two men come in and make me stand up. They put me in a clean white cap, grabbing my hair and pushing it into place. They take me up into the blinding light of the morning, one leading the way and the other following me with a long stick in his hand. I had forgotten what mornings are like. The ferocious birdsong and the smell of fires being laid and breakfasts cooking. It smells the same in this palace as it does anywhere. I have started to feel sick again. Now they are feeding me, my stomach can't hold much food and I have the heave of nausea and dread.

We stop at a large set of doors, and I am shooed up the steps by the same two men, the long stick never far from my head. The doors swing open, and they walk me through a hallway with ceilings high as a kirk, into a large room with huge windows set with criss-cross leaded glass. The king sits on a carved wooden chair on a platform in the corner, looking more king-like now, as he is draped in a white fur cloak, his beard groomed to a sharp point below his chin. Beside him is Dr Hemmingsen, the man who did the terrible things to me. The room smells of polish. In the other corner are white flowers in a vase. *White is for hope.*

I fall to my knees.

'You made me confess all sorts of things that are not true,' I cry. 'You were going to break my legs.'

His Majesty rubs his beard. A large, jewelled ring gleams on his hand, fat and red as a cherry.

'Mistress Craig, I have brought you here so that we can make a full account of all the events that led up to the plot to drown the Danish fleet. Call the witnesses,' he says. 'We have a confession from you, but we must also hear from those directly affected by your wickedness.'

'What witnesses?' I ask.

The door opens again and two more guards appear, flanking two people: Robbie Bathgate and Hazel Kincaid.

The king calls Hazel 'Mistress Bathgate', and then I see that Robbie has his arm around her, in a way that makes it clear they're now husband and wife. He's married her. Hazel wears a neat white cap, and her gown is the colour of fresh, clean hay. Robbie still looks like the impish poulterer's laddie he always was, except that his face is leaner. Or perhaps it was always lean; there was not much light in the darkness of Berwick Law.

They bow.

Look at the state of me. Greasy and ugly, and broken and wicked. I am lower than a dog. I remember Robbie pressing his fingers up against me, trying to get under my clothes. And Baillie Kincaid, lust in his eyes. Look at me now. I want to cry, but I'll not do so in front of Robbie Bathgate.

'Do you recognize this woman?' says the king.

They nod.

'I am speaking to him,' says King James, pointing to Robbie. Hazel flushes, her rash flaring.

'What did this woman do to you?' asks the king.

'She cursed my father's poultry, Your Majesty, right in front of me,' he replies, his voice cracking. 'And then the chickens fell sick and died.'

'I didn't mean anything by it,' I say. Everyone looks at me.

'Do not interrupt the witness. You will have your turn,' the king says. 'And what manner of curse did she make?'

Robbie frowns. Hazel nudges him. His face lights up again.

'She wished them dead,' he continues.

A scribe by the king's side is scratching relentlessly onto a parchment, his quill quivering.

'And did she make any motion or movement, or did she touch the poultry?' King James asks, leaning back in his chair and crossing his legs.

'I think she moved,' said Robbie. 'I think she pointed at the hens—'

Dr Hemmingsen interrupts. As soon as he speaks I have a flashback of him looming over me, talking calmly as he poked and prodded me, and I think I might be sick. 'I am an expert in these kinds of supernatural events. Now when Mistress Craig pointed at the hens, did you notice any change in her?' he asks. 'Was she talking to anyone else – perhaps an invisible demon? Perhaps the Devil himself?'

Robbie's shoulders tremble. Hazel pats at her rash.

'There have been confessions in my country – Denmark – from witches who admit to communicating with the Devil.' Dr Hemmingsen says it quite casually, as if it was a very ordinary observation. 'And of witches communicating with demons, who may take the form of animals or sprites, or even remain invisible.'

'There might have been a cat,' Robbie says, 'in the vicinity.'

The king sits up straight, nodding at Robbie to continue.

'She might have spoken to it,' he goes on. 'A black cat I'd never seen before.'

'There was no cat,' I shout. 'He's making things up.'

I feel a smack across my arm that is so hard I lose my balance. The man with the stick glowers down at me. I straighten myself. *You must remain calm*, I tell myself. *The Danish women are going to help.*

'There is no shame in your testimony, Master Bathgate' says King James. 'Do not be deterred.' His voice is soft. 'I am interested, too, in whether Mistress Craig danced or jumped, or did anything unnatural, as she uttered this curse?'

Robbie's head swivels from the king to his new wife. He does not look at me.

'I think she danced,' he said.

Everyone in the room inhales sharply.

'That does not surprise me at all,' comments Dr Hemmingsen. 'And was the dancing unnatural?'

'It was like nothing I have ever seen,' croaks Robbie.

By the end of the morning I have danced a jig. I have conversed in growls with a cat. At one point, both my legs left the ground and did not land back there for a count of three.

'As though she was in full flight,' the king tells the scribe. 'And how many dead chickens?'

'Thirty-eight,' says Robbie, and I think that is the only truth he has told in this room.

'Robbie Bathgate is a liar,' I scream. 'Ask him what he tried to do to me up Berwick Law. He tried to have his way with me.' I am rewarded with another thump to my arm. I wince, but I will not cry in front of Robbie. When I open my eyes, Hazel is glaring at me.

Then it is her turn. And she tells of how I cured her face, only for the rash to come back worse; of how she lay in bed at night and heard me dance and stomp in the room above her; and of how I would come back from night-travels with sand and pieces of shell in my pattens.

'From North Berwick beach?' asks the king. 'From storm-raising?'

Just for a moment Hazel looks doubtful. Her face clouds.

'I hear,' says King James, 'there are covens of witches. You were not part of a coven, were you, Mistress Bathgate?'

Hazel shakes her head so vigorously that strands of her hair escape from her cap. 'I am a God-fearing woman,' she replies.

'But you asked Mistress Craig to charm the rash off your face,' says the king.

'I asked for a poultice,' she weeps. 'And now my face and my arms are covered with the same rash, twice as red. Mistress Craig drew strange markings on the floorboards under my bed with a chalky stone.'

King James asks for a cup of small beer. There is a lull whilst it is brought and he drinks it. Hazel clutches Robbie as though her life depends on it. The king hands back his cup and turns his attention to Hazel again. 'The forces that have worked against the Crown are strong, and powerful,' he tells her. 'Stronger than one woman, one witch. I believe my cousin, the Earl of Bothwell, is behind it and may have met witches in person. Tell me more about Mistress Craig's night-time trips to the beach.'

Hazel tells him that she saw me coming home at dawn, my pattens soaked with water and seaweed. That she is such a good woman herself that she prayed for my soul every night. But it was no use. One night, when the moon was at its fullest, she saw me come down from the sky into her garden. I interrupted her sleep with cries of Bothwell's name.

The king is satisfied at that. He strokes his beard and nods.

Next, Robbie Bathgate's ma and da are fetched. Poulterer Bathgate, between his stutters and his bowing, asks if there will be compensation for his dead flock.

'Is justice not compensation enough?' the king replies.

Finally Baillie and Guidwife Kincaid are fetched. She is wearing her best navy wool dress. He looks thunderous.

'She tried to murder me,' he tells the court.

I consider whether telling everyone about his raging prick is worth the smack on the back I will get.

'Did you not notice you had a sorceress under your roof?' asks Dr Hemmingsen. 'Was there not a hint? Missing herbs from the kitchen? Unusual beasts prowling around the house?'

Baillie Kincaid shakes his head. 'She was devious,' he responds. His wife nods.

'Her mother was the same,' Guidwife Kincaid says. 'The strangest woman I ever did see. They say she kept spell books under her bed. With drawings of serpents and skulls.'

The king complains that the room is too dark and the candles need replenishing. Dr Hemmingsen looks at the Kincaids, intent.

'You are uniquely positioned,' he says, 'to give an insight into Mistress Craig's daily habits, which may give us clues of the daily habits of a sorceress. Never have I interviewed anyone who has had an accused witch as their maid.'

Baillie Kincaid nods gravely, and his chest swells.

'Your observations may go down in history,' adds the doctor.

'Well, perhaps there were one or two habits,' says the despicable Baillie Kincaid.

The fresh candles blaze.

The guidwife steps in again. 'She was lewd,' the mistress says. 'She was a temptress.'

'No!' I cry. 'It was all him.'

The king leans forward. 'She tried to tempt you, didn't she, Kincaid?'

'Often,' says Baillie Kincaid. 'As though she was possessed.'

'It's true,' shouts the mistress. 'She had my husband under some kind of spell from the minute she walked into our house.'

'Dear God, she bewitched him,' mutters Dr Hemmingsen, scribbling so fast in his notebook that I think his quill will snap.

Eventually they have said all they can possibly say. But I will not break. I will not let them see me weep and wail. I stand as strong as I can. Ma, you would have been so proud.

The king sits back as though he has consumed a great feast and his belly is about to pop.

'Mistress Craig, we seem to have built up a full picture,' he tells me. 'Is there anything you wish to say?'

'I have been tortured and lied about,' I respond.

King James laughs. 'Dr Hemmingsen,' he says, 'what do you make of this?'

'It is exactly as I thought,' he replies. 'It chimes with the testimonies from Denmark. And look, here, in the *Malleus Maleficarum* it says that those accused who do not cry during their trial are most certainly witches. Your Majesty, this woman has not shed a tear.'

Chapter Forty

KIRSTEN

Holyroodhouse
May 1590

Dear Kirsten,
I have made it as far as Southwark, London, which is south of the River Thames and has a playhouse theatre, bull- and bear-baiting rings and taverns. It reminds me of the Canongate, but is much bigger and means it's easier to keep myself to myself, as you say I must. I am anonymous here. I am doing as you said. I'm not future-telling for customers, but it is very difficult not to do what comes naturally.

Write to me as soon as you can with news of Jura Craig. Don't spare me the details. I want to know everything.

I know you'll try to get to her.

Are you going to tell her you are her real mother? I pray to God that you never tell her who her real father is. That is something she should never know.

Mary

*

I burn the letter as soon as I have read it and memorized the address. It goes in the fireplace, along with all the letters I have ever received from Mary.

It is too dangerous to keep them.

Of course I can't tell Jura I'm her mother. If I did that – even if I swore her to secrecy – she might tell them in desperation, and they'd think I was a witch too and no doubt drag me into their fantasies of a sorcery plot. I was there when the storm brewed around the *Gideon*, after all. And as for telling Jura that Baillie Kincaid is her father? Well, that's the last thing I'd ever do. If I thought he'd believe me, or try to rescue her, perhaps it might be worth the risk, but he has already told the King of Scotland she is a witch. He is the worst man I have ever met.

At least Mary's safe. Men went back to Jura's house and questioned her neighbours, but all they found in Mary's apartment were the remnants of her last meal and a cat that was taken away and drowned in case it was bewitched, the poor mite.

Nothing linking her to me, thank God, or they would have been straight up to my rooms and I would be in that barn with Jura, having my private parts searched and my thumbs wrenched.

I've heard snatches from the trial. Witnesses who saw Jura curse and fly through the sky. But I must stay calm – I don't have long. I have a half-formed plan in my mind, but it will only work if I act quickly.

First, I have Anna to deal with too.

When she danced with Lord Henry the other night, I had to admit it: a more suited pair I've never seen. Which makes it all the worse that they can never be together.

'Have you written to your mama lately?' I ask her as I get

her into her day-gown, battling the farthingale ribbons and the huge whalebone cage.

Anna sucks her cheeks and studies her reflection in the looking-glass.

'I write to her every week,' she says. 'There's no news to tell her that is different from last week's news. All she wants to hear about is whether I'm with child.'

'That's unfair,' I reply. 'She would love to hear about the masque. You certainly seemed to enjoy it. I don't think I've ever seen you so happy as when you were dancing.'

'I'm allowed to dance,' she says, closing her eyes as if to try to make me disappear. 'And James was too busy.'

'You're allowed to dance,' I agree. 'But not too much. And when you dance with a handsome young man, you are not supposed to whisper to him or seem delighted, or smile and close your eyes.'

Her eyes fly open. 'It wasn't like that,' she replies.

'You'd had lots of wine and weren't aware of yourself,' I tell her. 'But if you carry on like that, someone's going to notice. You're not here to choose a husband – a husband has been chosen for you. If you embarrass James, he'll take it badly. Very badly. He's not the sort of man to suffer being made a fool of.'

Anna bites her lip and says nothing. No rude retort, no denial. No embarrassed apology. I can't blame her for feeling besotted with Lord Henry. It's natural. But she can't let her feelings guide her actions. If James gets wind that she is in love with another man, Anna and I will be cast off to Hellebæk Abbey on the next ship, and I will be powerless to help my daughter.

At last Anna is dressed and powdered and perfumed and ready for the morning.

'What are your plans for today?' I ask her.

She picks up her fan, a white lace one that matches the ruffles on her sleeves, and gives her reflection a final admiring glance. 'Studying,' she says. 'Then watching tennis.'

She does not mention Lord Henry's name, even though it is written all over her face. I curtsey as she leaves, then go about the business of tidying Anna's chamber, picking up her discarded nightgown and opening the window to air the room. The blackbird flutters down, looking for his crumbs. I feed him some leftover crusts from Anna's breakfast tray and watch him demolish them.

Smart little blackbird, finding the right window amongst the thousands in this town. You've got to have your wits about you, Kirsten Sørensen. No one is going to rescue you. You must do it yourself.

I go to my own chamber and get myself ready for the day. I don't have Anna's youth or beauty, but I have some vermillion from the apothecary in the Canongate, and a decent emerald-green dress that reveals a fair bit of bosom. I match my earrings to my dress and survey myself in the looking glass.

I could almost be accused of looking like a courtesan.

I put on my best boots and go and see if I can find Kincaid.

I finally catch him in the hour after luncheon when the palace is at its quietest with praying, and whatever else they all get up to. James and Dr Hemmingsen are consulting each other in the library after hearing a day of nonsense tales. Kincaid is hanging around outside the library, as though he is at a loss for something to do. Perhaps he is hoping to be invited in. Perhaps he has been waiting for me.

I descend the staircase slowly and deliberately. He watches me.

'Baillie Kincaid,' I say, 'I believe I owe you a debt for finding the witch who tried to drown me.'

'Mistress Sørensen, I believe?' he replies. 'I was simply doing God's duty.'

I hide my smile with my fan. He enjoys that. Enjoys thinking me shy.

He holds out his arm. 'I fancy a daunder around the gardens to get some good air,' he says. 'Walk with me awhile.'

There's no good air in this town, and certainly none around Kincaid. I take his arm so easily I wonder if there might be something wicked in me. Why do I not recoil? Why am I not afraid?

I think it is my anger. It has overcome every other emotion.

'The hawthorn blossom is said to be glorious at this time of year, but I've not yet seen any,' I say. 'I'd love to take a walk in the gardens and see how spring is coming to life. Denmark is so glorious at this time of year. I'm sure Scotland is too, but I haven't had the time to notice.'

'You've been occupied,' he murmurs, 'with looking after your Danish princess.'

'It's an honour,' I say. 'But I do like to take an hour or so to myself every now and again.'

'Hawthorn blossom,' he muses, pretending to know where it might grow. 'Come with me and we shall seek some out.'

We walk through the main doors and the guards bow to us as we go. We pass some men working in the gardens and a couple playing tennis. Despite his tendency to accuse women of unspeakable things, Kincaid's actually a man of few words.

'Have you ever been to Denmark?' I ask.

He chuckles. 'I've never even left Scotland,' he replies. 'But I know Haddingtonshire better than any man, because I've travelled the length and breadth of it, collecting the taxes. I know every inn, every merchant, every farmer, every blacksmith.'

'My goodness,' I murmur, trying to sound impressed.

'Oh yes,' he goes on, encouraged by my tone. 'I know everything that's going on in Haddingtonshire. In fact you should visit one day. You should tell your princess about our beaches and our sunny weather. She should enjoy a visit very much.'

'But is it safe? I'm rather terrified of your witches,' I say.

'Oh, goodness, of course it's safe,' he says, stopping abruptly. 'You would be in the safest of hands. You would stay at Seton Palace and play pall-mall and golf.'

'Yes, that is all very well, but what protection can you offer the Danish princess?' I ask. 'She has only ever stayed in Leith and Holyroodhouse. If she is to travel, and that is indeed on our agenda, then I need to know she will be protected.'

'I am the most well-connected man in Haddingtonshire,' Kincaid says. 'Nothing happens in Haddingtonshire without my knowledge.'

'Then I am reassured,' I respond, squeezing his arm as tightly as I dare.

He takes a deep breath in, savouring my grip.

'You are distracting me from the hawthorn blossoms,' he whispers.

'Then I apologize. Let's take a tour of them before anyone notices I'm missing,' I say.

'Of course, of course.'

We find a fine display of hawthorn trees on a path leading up to Arthur's Seat.

'This country is quite magnificent,' I tell him. 'And all the better now that I think I have found a good companion. Now let's return to the palace.'

'Indeed,' says Kincaid. We walk back to the beat of his laboured breathing. He clearly walks rarely these days. Time has not been generous to him. I fill in the gaps with chatter, which is not something that comes naturally to me, but today it seems to.

'It's wonderful to see spring has finally arrived,' I tell him. 'After such a dark winter.'

Kincaid nods, looking around him. 'Spring has truly come,' he says. 'The season of renewal and hope.'

It's true. It has been a long, hard winter, full of demons. But the days are getting longer, the nights shorter. The fields and woodlands are full of creamy blossom. I smile at him. Kincaid smiles back, assuming I am simply happy to have spent time in his company.

If only he knew.

Chapter Forty-One

ANNA

Holyroodhouse
May 1590

I know which ring I need to take. Something innocuous, one James won't notice. Something he might easily have dropped on the floor of that barn, should it ever be discovered. It could be discovered, easily. They might decide to search Jura's body again. He sometimes wears a thin gold band on his middle finger. Perhaps Murray gave it to him. But he does not wear it all the time.

James keeps his jewellery in his inner bedchamber. A place I've never been invited into. He visits me. It has never been suggested that I might visit him.

That evening I tell him I want us to spend the night in his room. I whisper it to him, in his ear. 'I would like the change,' I say. We are at dinner with everyone. It has been difficult to get a word in. He's been so engrossed with Dr Hemmingsen that he's barely touched his salmon. 'I would like to be in your chamber tonight.' I avoid Henry's eye as I say it.

'Let's not discuss this now,' James replies, looking embarrassed, although no one would have overheard me.

'But I would like to see where you sleep,' I continue. I am emboldened by the knowledge that I will have medicine soon, to help keep me unpregnant. I have already found a white ribbon amongst the dozens in my dressing room. No one will even notice it's missing.

James puts his hand over mine. Henry looks away.

James isn't wearing the ring tonight. 'My chamber is my sanctuary,' he says. 'I would rather keep it private.'

And so I sneak up there alone. Whilst they are all foraging the best cheeses from the cheese-plates and beckoning the servants for more red wine, I make my way up the stairs, as if to my own chamber, growing angrier at every step of my foot on the cold stone slabs that James's inner bedchamber is his sanctum, and my inner bedchamber is not *my* sanctum, because he visits it.

I pass sconces and portraits and blossom in vases. I pass under high ceilings and flit across leaded-glass windows, up two flights of steep staircases, until I am near our apartments. I thought someone might stop me. But I only see the occasional watchman. Finally, at the top of a corridor, I turn left to James's quarters instead of right to mine. No one is around.

I open the door into his bedchamber, ready with an excuse on my lips that I thought I had seen someone and I was following them. But there's no one here. I stand in my betrothed's sanctuary and it takes only a few moments to understand why I am not permitted here. This is a bedroom for two. Both sides of the bed are made up with pillows and robes. There are books stacked on each bedside table. Two pairs of slippers, side by side. And, unmistakably, Murray's robes, embroidered with his crest, hang on one side and James's robes on the other. They live as spouses. The spicy scent of patchouli hangs in the air.

I go to the dressing table. It's stacked with combs and brushes and perfume bottles and parchments. I open one note and read it: *Thinking of you.* Oh, they even leave each other love notes. I see sketches of James that Murray has done – naked and near-naked in all of them. I even recognize the light patch of hair on James's chest, the amulet he wears to ward off witches.

I don't have time to get upset about it. Or jealous that Henry and I cannot have this kind of privacy, this luxury. I rummage in the drawers and find the ring, in a black velvet box. I take it out of the box and put it into my shoe. It digs into my foot all the way back to the dining hall and, when I sit down – my absence noticed by no one except Henry – I pretend to be enchanted by the dessert of French jellied apricots, even though they are as hard as little stones.

James will never, ever love me. He cannot. He is enraptured by his true love, Murray. I can see why too. Perfect tendrils of blond curls. Big arms. Such a strong jaw. I can never be the person James Stuart desires. And he is not the person *I* desire.

That night he comes to my chamber, waking me up, for it is after midnight and I have only just got to sleep. Kirsten is abed, and Hanne scuttles about the room hanging up his robe before disappearing. I wish I could disappear too.

James gets into bed beside me.

'Dr Hemmingsen is keeping me late, but we have a task to do,' he says. 'We are months now, without a royal heir.'

'The Lord will bless us in time,' I respond.

'But we must assist him, Anna,' he continues, with a mirthless laugh. He fingers his gold amulet as he speaks.

I have drunk too much wine, and my whole body feels heavy and bruised about the hips and waist, from the ties and knots of the great farthingale. I shiver. James occupies himself with my nightgown, which has layers and layers of cotton, and loses patience trying to take them up.

'You will never get with a child if I can't find where to put myself,' he complains.

I pull up the nightgown myself, feeling shamed. Thank God it's dark. He busies himself. Thank God it's quick.

James is in better fettle, once the deed is done. He lies back on the cushions. He looks different when he reclines. His face is slacker, more relaxed.

'This is turning out to be the most spectacular witch trial Scotland has ever seen,' he says. 'The witnesses have talked of fantastical events.'

I remember him in the barn, looming over Mistress Craig, and try not to feel sick.

'And who will judge her?' I ask.

'I will judge her,' he replies. 'I have been keeping records of everything she confesses. I'm writing up my notes with the aim of producing a pamphlet, or even a book on the matter, for it is of the most significance. Dr Hemmingsen agrees. But we still haven't got to the bottom of it all. Mistress Craig is vague on the subject of Bothwell. She knows him, but she hasn't disclosed everything. He and the Devil still have a grip on her. I can feel it in my bones.'

'So you believe Bothwell to be behind all of it? That he has truly made a pact with the Devil to overthrow you?'

'Without a shadow of a doubt,' he says. He sits up in bed, his passion for the subject far greater than the passion he has just shown for me. 'Bothwell couldn't defeat me otherwise. He's sold his soul. These witches are merely his puppets. One thing this ordeal has taught me is that we cannot be certain of anything.'

He turns to me. He puts his fingers to my throat, tracing a line from my chin to the frills at the top of my nightgown.

'My pamphlet will spread the word about the threat we face. But that's not for you to worry about. You have only one task, and that is to carry my child. At the first sign of a pregnancy I will make good my promise to marry you. God be with us, Anna.'

Chapter Forty-Two

JURA

Holyroodhouse
May 1590

Reverend Thompson brings the Danish woman again. 'May your faith guide you, Mistress Sørensen,' he tells her.

'The Lord is protecting me,' she answers. 'I can feel His presence surrounding me. Every living soul deserves the chance of forgiveness. She deserves the Lord.'

He refuses to meet my eye, his face in shadow as he leaves, righting his collar and brushing at his robes. Mibbie he's brushing the incense-dust off them or mibbie he's brushing me off them – the knowledge of me sitting here day and night. He'll not want that thought clinging to his fine clothes. I hope that whenever he smells incense, the minister remembers me, and what his king did to me.

Mistress Sørensen sits down and settles her psalter on her lap. She opens it as though she is about to pray with me, but then thinks better of it and closes it again.

'I wanted you to come back, but I never thought you would,' I say. 'Especially after all the lies they are telling about me and my divvilment. Wild tales.'

'Quite fantastical,' she replies. 'Quite incredible.'

'You don't believe them, do you?' I ask, studying her through the incense-fog. A log cracks on the fire. The wind stirs the bushes outside.

'It is not for me to decide,' she answers carefully. 'I'm only here to pray for your soul.'

'Why do you really keep coming back?' I ask. 'For you're not really praying with me, even though that's what you're telling the minister.'

She bites her lips and looks about the room. 'Perhaps we should pray, then,' she says. 'If that's what you want to do.'

'I can pray all night if I want to,' I tell her. 'But I would rather you told me how I might get out of here. You must be close to the king. Mibbie you can talk to him and tell him that what he's doing is wrong. Sinfully wrong. The Lord will judge him.'

'You can't say things like that,' she says. 'It is not for the likes of you or me to tell the king that he will be judged by God. King James sees himself as God's chosen representative on Earth.'

'But you want to help me, don't you? It's why you've come back. You know they've been hurting me and it's not right. You know I could die in here, and your conscience is telling you to help.' It's true. I can feel the life slipping out of me. I can feel myself getting weaker. My bones ache with sleeping on the hay bale. Even my mouth aches from all the begging.

Mistress Sørensen is quiet for a minute, closing her eyes. I study her face. It's neither bonnie nor plain, big nor small. She has frown lines etched into her forehead that make her seem unhappy, but apart from that she looks as ordinary as they come.

And my life depends on her. This woman may be my best chance.

'There are things I can't tell you yet,' she says. 'And I need you to trust me, if you're to stay safe. If anyone asks, all we ever do together is pray. Do you understand?' Her voice shakes.

Well, I want to ask a hundred questions now. What can she mean?

'Are you going to speak to the king?' I ask her.

She shakes her head. 'I'm not going to speak to the king,' she says. 'He wouldn't listen to me if I did.'

'Are you a cunning woman?' I ask. 'Is that why you want to help?'

She shakes her head again, looking irritated. 'I've never had a desire to be one, but perhaps I should have thought about it. Perhaps if I'd tried casting spells, my life would have been easier, but I've never done that.'

Mibbie she should try, I think, but I don't say that.

'So how can you help me?' I ask.

She shakes her head. 'I'm not sure yet. But you must trust me that I'm trying.'

'And why are you trying to help me, Mistress Sørensen? For it would be far easier for you to walk away and forget all about me.'

I watch her suck her cheeks and consider the question.

Finally she nods, as if agreeing with herself that she is giving the right answer.

'We don't know each other, you and I,' she says. 'And we are very different. But we have more in common than you know. And it's my duty to help you. That's all you need to know, and if you tell anyone of this conversation, then I won't be able to help you. Do you understand me?'

I've never seen anyone look more serious. 'Aye, I understand you,' I reply.

We're interrupted then by a rustling at the wall. I don't want to be interrupted. I want this Danish woman to stop being a puzzle and start explaining things. But Mistress Sørensen jumps at the noise and breaks her gaze from me.

'Who's there?' she calls.

At first I think it must be an animal in the bushes outside the barn. A deer or somesuch, but then I see the flicker of a face, so fleeting you might miss it altogether.

'Oh,' I cry. It slips out before I can stop it. 'It's the other Danish lady.'

Mistress Sørensen bolts over to the wall as fast as a rat.

'Anna, is that you?' she demands, in a most imperious, scolding voice. 'Anna, I can see your face. What on earth are you doing here?'

The other woman sounds just as scolding. 'Never mind what I am doing. What are *you* doing, Kirsten? You're supposed to be praying, not talking about how you can help a prisoner.'

Anna. Surely the woman at the wall cannot be the Danish princess? The one I prayed for, with my smooth pebble in the sea. The one I bound to myself with ribbons as I watched her pass in her silver carriage. The one I am accused of trying to kill. I scurry across to speak through the hole. Surely the lady who has been begging for my help hasn't been the Princess of Denmark?'

'Princess Anna. If this is really you, then you must know that I never tried to drown you,' I tell her.

She brings her face closer to the gap. I can see her clearly. Fine skin and long eyelashes and shiny hair. She shakes her head. 'I know you didn't try to drown me,' she answers.

'Then you must tell them,' I say. 'Tell the king and the minister. Tell them Baillie Kincaid is a liar and that I have never harmed a soul in my life. That I was trying to save you with my charme, not kill you. The whole thing is nonsense. How can they even believe such a thing?'

I can hear both women's shallow breathing in the silence that follows.

Finally Mistress Sørensen speaks. 'King James won't listen to her. He's obsessed,' she says. 'Like a dog with a bone. The fleet almost perished and he has decided someone is to blame.'

'He is paranoid that his cousin Bothwell is trying to get rid of him,' says Anna. 'He is unbearable.' She shudders.

'Is that why you don't want to have his bairn?' I ask the princess, before realizing that I have spoken out of turn.

Anna gasps.

'What's this?' demands Mistress Sørensen. 'Are you with child?'

'Nothing of the sort,' replies Anna, her voice quivering. She is afeared of Mistress Sørensen. Imagine a princess being afeared of anyone. But her voice quivers, like all the air has gone out of her chest.

'Then why are you here?' asks Mistress Sørensen. 'Hiding in the bushes and telling strangers you don't want the king's child. This is utterly reckless. If you're caught, you'll be accused of conspiring with this woman. With Bothwell. They will burn you as well. Or cut off your head like they did with the king's own mother. They're terrified.'

'Mistress Craig was helping me to avoid a pregnancy altogether,' says Anna. Her voice gathers strength. 'She said she would advise me on how to do it safely, if I helped her. She doesn't want much, Kirsten. She only wants some objects that she thinks will protect her.'

'Spells and superstition,' cries Mistress Sørensen. 'Don't be so foolish. Get away from here before someone sees you. Before a guard decides to take a piss behind the barn or the minister comes back, or they decide to interrogate her again.'

'I'm going nowhere until Jura Craig tells me what medicine

I need to take to stop getting pregnant,' Anna replies. Her pale eyes bulge at me. Because the fact is, Kirsten, that I do not want to have a baby with James Stuart.'

'But that's your duty,' admonishes Kirsten. 'It's not about what you want. It's about our countries.'

'But I'm in love with Henry Roxburgh,' Anna says. 'I want a husband who desires me, and I want to wake up each morning looking forward to the day instead of dreading it.'

'You should have come and told me this, instead of looking for potions,' chastises Mistress Sørensen.

Anna laughs, a cold little laugh. I can see her shaking her head. Biting her lip. I had no idea a royal princess could be so unhappy. She brings her hand up to the gap in the wall and passes a gold ring and a pure-white ribbon through it. Oh, fine, fine gold! I've never seen the like. I take them, being ever so careful not to get them covered with dirt and dust.

'Someone will miss this ring,' I whisper.

'I doubt it,' Anna says.

'Where's this ring from?' Mistress Sørensen's voice has panic in it. She takes the ring from me and studies it. 'I've not seen it before. Did you steal it from somewhere?'

'Well, it has to be the king's,' I say, 'or the charme won't work.'

'What are you doing?' hisses Mistress Sørensen. 'Is this ring one of James's? For if it is, there will be fearful trouble if you're caught.'

'He won't miss it,' replies Anna. 'He has more rings than fingers and toes to put them on. He has more servants than he knows what to do with. He even has another lover, Kirsten. He shares his bed with Douglas Murray.'

'Kings have lovers, Anna – it is a tale as old as time,' says Mistress Sørensen. 'But queens do not. Queens entertain themselves in purer ways. You have your pick of amusements: art and masque and song. You could be the happiest woman in Scotland.'

'Only if I marry Henry Roxburgh,' she responds.

I put the ring on my own finger and place the white ribbon in the palm of my hand. Pure silk. A ring from the hand of the king. I have never touched such treasures. I will have to keep them well hidden.

Mistress Sørensen breaks off arguing with the princess and watches me. 'It is all superstition,' she says. 'Jewels and ribbons offer no protection.'

'You would be surprised at how much protection they can offer,' I tell her.

'You should not do any spells whilst you are in this barn,' says Mistress Sørensen. 'If you're caught, it will make everything even worse for you.'

As if they could get any worse.

'Let her tell me what plants to pick to stop a pregnancy,' begs Anna. 'I can't live like this, thinking I might have James's child.'

'I made the princess a promise,' I say.

Mistress Sørensen closes her eyes. 'I suppose it does not matter for the moment, if you do not get with child. That can wait. What matters most now is helping Jura. She is in immediate danger. I wanted to help her myself, but I'm not entirely sure I can. Anna, I am asking you: can you help too?'

Chapter Forty-Three

KIRSTEN

Holyroodhouse
May 1590

The questions start rattling out of Anna as soon as we arrive back in her chamber. She shoos Hanne out, the poor girl; she was only trying to keep the fire going, so I take to the task myself, so that I can at least keep my back to Anna. I don't want her to see my face.

'What on *earth*, Kirsten?' she asks. 'Why ever are you promising to help that woman? We can't interfere.'

'There are things you don't know,' I tell her.

'You're far too secretive,' she says. 'It has to stop.'

'I never wanted to drag you into it. But you have dragged yourself into this by hanging around the barn,' I reply. The fire gets going. The flames lick up the grate and get too hot for me to stand next to. I step back and sit down on the chair nearest the fire.

Anna sits in the chair opposite. Her latest embroidery is draped over the arm: a white kerchief decorated with fine-spiked green leaves. She has such a neat stitch. She arranges her skirts over her knees and looks at me expectantly.

'Dragged myself into what?' she says.

'You already know that I have a history in Scotland,' I tell her. 'And that is why I was chosen to come here with you.' She nods, her lips tight. 'Well, my connection is to North Berwick. Where Jura Craig is from. Where Baillie Kincaid is from.'

'Ah,' she says. 'Do you know them?'

'I do, although it has been a long time. Jura Craig is my daughter.'

Anna's face opens in shock. 'That can't be right,' she whispers.

So I tell her my story.

By the time I am finished, the fire is starting to die down again.

'I must tell James,' Anna says. 'He'll put everything right.'

'He might do that,' I agree, 'or Dr Hemmingsen might believe me to be a witch, as well as my daughter. And how long before James starts wondering if you're a witch too? That we've all been conspiring against him together. We can't trust any of them. And if you truly want to get out of this marriage, I'm of no help to you in a prison cell, or burned for treason.'

'You'd help me?' She looks like a child again.

'The reason I needed us both here in Scotland was to give me time to find my daughter and warn her, and Mary, that the witch hunts were coming, and to get them somewhere safe,' I tell her. 'Mary is in London now. If I can get Jura to safety too, then that's the best thing I can do for her. After that, we can decide what to do about your betrothal.'

'Then that's what we'll do,' replies Anna. 'It's up to us to help each other now.'

She picks up the embroidery and examines it.

'I'm making this for Henry,' she says. 'It's cedar leaves in the snow. Am I ridiculous, Kirsten, for falling in love with him?'

'Does he love you too?' I ask.

'Yes,' she says. 'I know it.' She takes up her needle again. 'How have you not gone out of your mind, Kirsten, knowing the danger your daughter is in?'

'Because she needs me,' I reply. 'As do you. Now, what were those plants Jura told you to pick? You can't be seen hanging around the kitchen garden. I'll fetch them.'

'Thank you,' she says. 'Thank you, Kirsten. I don't know what I'd do without you here.'

'Then I'll give you a piece of advice. You cannot risk being caught. Not with the herbs, and not with Henry. Not near Jura Craig. I depend on you, Anna; and Jura is depending on me. We are bound together. Do you understand? This is not solely about you.'

'I understand,' she answers, but her fingers are already playing with the kerchief, her gaze breaking from mine, to make it perfect for Henry Roxburgh.

I hope Anna does understand.

Chapter Forty-Four

JURA

Holyroodhouse
May 1590

The men take me back before King James again. Back to the high-ceilinged library with the criss-cross glass windows and the white flowers, which are wilting now but no one has changed them. They say the trial is not over until the king has decided it's over.

I am made to sit on the floor in front of him and Dr Hemmingsen as they ask me questions and mutter amongst themselves. The king plays constantly with his amulet. *Gold for the highest level of protection.* He's protecting himself from sorcery – from me. The questions get wilder and wilder.

'How high can you levitate?' Dr Hemmingsen asks me.

'Could you make that baton fly,' asks the king, pointing to the man with the stick.

'If I could, would I not fly out of here?' I reason, and the man with the stick taps me sharply on the back.

'Don't antagonize her,' warns Dr Hemmingsen, considering his book. 'According to the *Malleus Maleficarum*, she could summon a demon, and there are plenty of places a demon could enter this room by: the fireplace; that open window over there; even the gap under that door.'

The king tosses an apple core to a servant.

'Fetch Reverend Thompson and the incense, just to be sure,' he says.

Eventually Dr Hemmingsen places the book on a table, gentle as if it were a Bible, and comes down to where I am sitting. He bends down, his mouth brushing my ear. He smells of wine that has gone vinegary.

'There is one thing that troubles me,' he says. 'And that is that you cannot have acted alone in Scotland, in the plot you have confessed to, with the witches of Denmark. There were several of them over there. How many of them are in Scotland, hmm? Who inducted you into sorcery? Who are you in league with?'

He takes off my cap, watching as my hair slides heavily onto my shoulders.

'You are a comely girl,' he goes on, playing with the cross around his neck, 'but you will not bewitch me. Name the members of your Scottish coven.'

'Name them,' echoes the king. 'Or we will put you back in the leg-crusher.'

'Go and fetch the leg-crusher,' says Dr Hemmingsen to the man with the baton. But no one moves, yet.

This is the moment I was waiting for. The moment Kirsten Sørensen said would come.

'I can give you one name. But that is the only other witch I know,' I say.

The room falls still, save for the glow of the candles, so bright they almost hum.

'Name the witch,' says the king.

'He is Baillie Kincaid,' I tell them.

'Nonsense,' replies the king. 'Fetch the leg-crusher.'

'Wait,' says Dr Hemmingsen. 'Listen to her first. I have heard stranger things than this in Copenhagen, trust me.'

The king sits back, looking at me with narrowed eyes.

'Baillie Kincaid sent the storms,' I say. 'He stood on North Berwick beach. I saw him and another man – mibbie Bothwell – when I was out on my walk one night. He has decided to turn it all on me, and it has worked.'

The king shakes his head. 'How do we know she's not lying?' he asks.

'We don't,' says Dr Hemmingsen. 'There's only one way to find out. Fetch Kincaid. We will get to the bottom of this accusation, one way or the other.'

They find him quickly enough and bring him in. Kincaid has a smart air about him, wearing a fine new doublet I've never seen before, which looks like it was bought from a Canongate tailor.

'Kincaid, Mistress Craig has made a grave allegation against you,' says the king. 'That you've conspired with my sworn enemy, Bothwell, and that you were involved in the storm-raising yourself.'

Kincaid's face turns a frightening shade of purple and I think he'll explode. He turns to me with so much rage I'm glad there are guards in the room.

'Of course this wicked whore would say such things about me,' he spurts. 'But I am your most loyal servant, Your Majesty. Have I not worked hard, every day of my life, to keep order in Haddingtonshire?'

'You have indeed,' replies the king. 'But you understand that we had to ask.'

'Tell me something,' says Dr Hemmingsen, 'because I am struggling to understand it. How did you manage to have this witch living under your roof for so long, yet not realize she was casting spells against His Majesty? You talk of finding ribbons and chalk marks, and toing and froing in the dead of night, and of women being cured of their ills and of poisonings. And yet you had no idea? You had no notion to report her? Hold a trial in Haddington?' He turns to the king. 'For a baillie – a man of the law – it seems bizarre that he had no notion of a treason conspiracy unfolding under his very roof.'

The king plucks another shiny red apple from the bowl and passes it from his left hand to his right as if it were a ball. 'It is her word against his,' he says. 'And the baillie is a trusted man.'

At that moment there is a stirring near the door.

Kirsten Sørensen walks into the room. She sweeps into a low curtsey.

'If you'll allow me, Your Majesty, I have something I must say about Baillie Kincaid,' she says. She doesn't wait to be asked, but walks to the front where Kincaid is standing. She has her hands balled into tight little fists. There will be fingernail marks in her palms. Her skirts are a flash of pure white above the grey flagstones.

'Mistress Sørensen,' says the king, 'whatever do you have to say about Baillie Kincaid?'

'It is grave, Your Majesty,' she responds.

Kincaid gawps, the glare of the sun through the window making his pocked skin glisten. Everything feels dangerous.

'He made a confession to me. That he is connected to Bothwell and knows more about the sorcery plot than he pretends to.'

'This is abhorrent,' says Baillie Kincaid. His forehead has a sheen of sweat now.

James ignores him and addresses her. 'Mistress Sørensen, are you aware of the seriousness of what you say?'

The court scribe opens a fresh page in his writing journal.

'Bothwell has promised Baillie Kincaid a promotion if Bothwell is made king. Kincaid asked me to be his mistress and promised me great riches if I am.'

'These women are conspiring against me,' Kincaid cries.

Mistress Sørensen turns to face him. Her hands are no longer balled up into fists, but are on her hips, firm and square.

'I am a senior lady of the Danish court – Princess Anna of Denmark's most trusted attendant. Are you daring to question my loyalty?'

A cloud passes over the sun and the room falls grey. The only flash of colour is the red apple, now dangling dangerously from the king's hand. It will drop onto the flagstones and smash, if he doesn't remember it's there, and the servant will have to scrape it up, pulp and pips. Dr Hemmingsen pulls at his ruffled collar like it's strangling him.

'Your Majesty,' begs Baillie Kincaid.

Dr Hemmingsen puts up his hand. 'There is only one way to determine the facts of the case,' he says. 'And that is to have Baillie Kincaid interrogated.'

The king sits up straight and puts the apple back on the tray. He rights his robes. 'We will do exactly that,' he says to Dr Hemmingsen. 'Mistress Sørensen, thank you for your disclosure.'

They take me back to the barn and give me a plate of meat and eggs and bread. Washed down with milk, too. They mean to keep me strong. I might tell more tales. But they would never have believed me if Mistress Sørensen hadn't walked in. She was so convincing, I half believed her myself.

The day passes. The cloud that descended earlier settles in.

My belly bulges with meat and milk. *What will they do next?* 'Tis true. Gold does give protection. The ribbon and the ring, well hidden under the dirt in a wee gap in the corner of the barn, are working their magic.

Night comes. I sleep better than I have done in days.

Morning comes. I am served a breakfast, then a lunch. Then I am summoned once again to stand before the king.

'There's news,' the guard says as he walks me up the stairs. 'Big news.'

Baillie Kincaid is there, hands tied behind his back. But he is not alone. Beside him are the guidwife, and Hazel and Robbie. The guidwife's hair has been shorn. Her scalp is bright with scabs. I get a flash of her standing in her hallway, proud in her pristine cap, and I feel ill.

'Extraordinary confessions,' Dr Hemmingsen tells the king.

'Repeat them for the court scribe,' says James.

Kincaid has said they are all in the plot together. What torture was done to him, to get him to say that? He has rope-burns about his neck. All his weight is on one foot. They have strangled him and put his leg in that clamp. My heart beats wildly and I can feel my entire body tremble.

Dr Hemmingsen clears his throat and licks his lips, then begins to recite what Kincaid said, under torture.

'"We all met at night, at North Berwick kirk. We called ourselves the North Berwick Witches. Sometimes the Divvil himself would come, in the form of a sea creature or a horse, and sometimes he would send his demons. We would kill cats and dogs, and sometimes babies. In return, the Divvil gave us tokens of his appreciation. The Bathgates' flock would lay and lay, even in the darkest days of winter. We would find small treasures, such as brooches and rings, under bushes or beneath the fungus of trees. Bothwell heard about us, through his network of spies, and one night he came along and made a deal with us. We would help him stop Anna of Denmark setting foot on Scottish soil, and he would pay us very guid coin and give us all guid lives as his servants, when he became king. We celebrated lustily, and Bothwell did all manner of things with our women, and we enjoyed it too – the guidwife especially.'"

When Dr Hemmingsen says that part, Guidwife Kincaid shakes her shorn head so fast that her brains must surely rattle inside it, but he carries on.

"'I, Baillie Kincaid was the leader in all of this. By day I was one of the Crown's most trusted bailiffs. By night I was a spy.'"

I did not think Kincaid had such imagination. But then I remember how I felt when they showed me that leg-crusher and I know: when you are terrorized, you will say anything.

Baillie Kincaid, the story continues, was clerk of the coven. He kept a register of all who attended and wrote all of their acts down in a great ledger.

'Guidwife Kincaid was the last to confess and only did so after we shaved off all her hair and pricked her with a needle, and found her Devil's mark, which did not bleed when pricked,' says Dr Hemmingsen.

I look at the guidwife, her face alight with humiliation, bristles of hair at her crown.

'This is all lies,' shouts Baillie Kincaid. 'Torture is no way to get a confession.'

Dr Hemmingsen stands, his notes in his hands. 'The interrogation methods are well established. Torture is how we extracted Mistress Craig's confession,' he says. 'Are you saying you lied to the court about her?'

'What will you do with us?' begs Hazel. 'If we confess to it all, and say how sorry we are and we were tempted by the Devil?'

'Will there be mercy?' asks Robbie Bathgate. 'I can do the stocks – they don't scare me – but if I go to prison, I can't be there long as I'm needed back at the farm.'

'How long might we go to prison for?' asks the guidwife.

The king stands up. 'You have confessed to a sorcery plot,' he says gently. 'You have confessed to treason. This is not a matter of stocks or whippings, or even prison.'

'He will burn us at the stake,' says Baillie Kincaid.

'I will retire with Dr Hemmingsen to consider what to do with you all,' answers the king.

Hazel starts wailing. That is exactly what they want. They want us screaming and begging.

Now it's time for me to do the thing that the Danish princess has told me to do.

I put up my hand. No one notices.

'Excuse me,' I shout. Now everyone is looking at me. 'I need to say something,' I tell the king.

'Do not listen to her,' says Baillie Kincaid.

'I think we should,' urges Dr Hemmingsen. 'She is valuable.'

'It's for the king's ears only,' I say.

Everyone looks at one another. The room is silent, except for Hazel's whimpers.

'Come over here and tell me what it is you want to say,' replies the king.

Chapter Forty-Five

ANNA

Holyroodhouse
May 1590

T he entire palace is on edge. *Kirsten Sørensen interrupted the trial with astonishing news.* They all saw her and Baillie Kincaid taking their promenade the other day. Now it turns out that Kincaid is the Devil amongst us. James and Dr Hemmingsen are still in the library, deciding what will happen next. Whatever they resolve, it will be spectacular. In the meantime James has sent all five prisoners to the Canongate Tollbooth. There are too many of them now. They need to be locked up properly: iron gates and shackles.

Kirsten is outrageous. Risking herself like that, telling lies like that.

'You would have done the same,' she says, 'if your child was in peril.'

I suppose I would, but I'm a world away from worrying about that now. My mouth still has the bitter aftertaste of my new tincture. Herbs and berries from the kitchen garden, and some that grow wild near the bottom of Arthur's Seat. Honey to make it palatable. A small cupful each morning. It has turned my stomach, but Jura said I would get used to it. *The lassies in North Berwick swear by it.*

How is Jura managing in a proper prison? Is she in chains? Time is running out for her. James will want all of Scotland to know how he dealt with Bothwell's plot. Kirsten and I have spent the last hour pacing the gardens. She's too agitated to sit still, now that Jura is out of reach, up on the Canongate. I should try to keep her calm, stop her panicking, but I can't. The consequences of her wild claims are too horrific. I can't comprehend it.

'And now they all stand convicted,' I tell her. 'Five people, none of whom have ever cast a spell in their lives.'

'That's not my fault,' she insists. 'I only named Kincaid. He started all of this. It's on his conscience, not mine.'

But it should be. Kirsten should know, more than anyone, how stories can grow fantastical when people are interrogated.

I arrive late to my lesson with Henry. I nearly call it off altogether to stay with Kirsten, but I need to be next to him and feel his comfort.

The study is warm with the closeness of a wet spring as we sit at our books. The court ladies have all been saying it's marvellous how well my language has improved. How impressive a tutor Henry must be. It's incredible what people will believe. If only they knew that we barely look inside the pages.

He holds my hand under the table.

'I think they'll burn the witches when the rain clears, and when they've had time to get word out,' he says. 'I think they'll want everyone there.'

'Don't talk about it,' I reply. 'I've seen a witch burn before. It is the most horrific thing you can imagine.'

I look out of the window at the grey sky. Why are Scottish springs the colour of lead? Can Jura see out of a window?

Onto the Canongate and the merchants' houses, and the rattling carts and the salt-sellers and the butter-sellers. Alive with life. Is she wondering if this is her last day on this Earth?

What did she say to James? I hope it was enough to save herself.

Henry strokes the palm of my hand with his finger. 'I've been planning what we'll do when we get out of here,' he says.

I grasp his hand tighter. 'Tell me,' I urge him. 'I've made sure I can't get pregnant. I'm taking medicine that stops it.'

'I'll come and get you from Hellebæk Abbey. You'll be there no longer than a month – however long it takes me to make the journey. I'll come with a horse and cart. You'll need to watch for me. When you see me, make your escape that night and I'll be waiting for you. We'll travel as far away as we can. We can settle anywhere you want.'

'Ánslo,' I suggest. 'And we'll have to bring Kirsten.'

I don't tell him that Kirsten might be about to witness the execution of the daughter she barely knew. How will she live with herself, knowing that her story led to Kincaid's wife and daughter and her husband also being convicted?

Perhaps Kirsten will stay at Hellebæk Abbey. Perhaps she will see it as a just prison sentence.

Henry squeezes my hand. I close my eyes and bask in his warmth and try to push away all the wickedness and fear that hangs in the air, amongst the closeness and sickly sweet rot of the Canongate. I let my head fall towards his shoulder and rest there.

'When we are finally together we will hold each other tightly each night in bed,' I say.

Suddenly he jumps away from me. His movement upsets the books on the table and I sit up, dazed. My hand is damp from where he held it. I look up to see what has happened.

James is standing at the door. He has been watching us. And by the shocked look on his face, he has seen and heard everything. He takes a moment to compose himself.

'I came to tell you I have decided that the witches are to burn tomorrow,' he says. 'I came to tell you to ready yourself. They'll burn up at Castlehill and I want you to go up there ahead of it, in the silver carriage, and entertain the kirk ministers. I want you there in your best gown, Anna, to show everyone that we will not be beaten. But I see you are too preoccupied to care about my efforts to protect you.'

Chapter Forty-Six

JURA

The Canongate Tollbooth
June 1590

The women prisoners' cell is underneath the great bell-tower of the Canongate, whose bell is pulled on the hour, every hour, and that is what will drive me to madness. Not the other lassies – prostitutes, vagabonds and coin-counterfeiters – for they are all just lassies down on their luck. Not the shared shit-pail or the thin pottage. Not the fact that we are stone-cold at night, and shackled if we make too much fuss about anything. Not the fact that King James of Scotland has decided we are to burn.

The loud, predictable bang of the Canongate bell goes right through me. I dream of ways to silence it. I wrap cloths around my head and stuff rags into my ears and still it reverberates. You can't think, when there is a bell ringing above you every hour.

Mibbie that's why they do it.

Hazel and the guidwife won't look at me. I no longer exist to them. They've occupied a space at the other side of the room and sit, talking between themselves, on their best behaviour, to avoid the big guard with the whip and the wee guard with the shackles. Hazel Kincaid, *Hazel Bathgate now*, is a stronger lassie than I would ever have given her credit for. She holds her head high and takes her mother in her arms from time to time. She won't let anyone near her.

I tried to talk to her, once. 'I am no more a witch than you are,' I say. 'You must know that now.'

'You're wickeder than a witch,' she hissed. 'You put chalk marks by my bed to curse me. And you will burn in hell, whilst me and my ma will go to the glory of God.'

The glory of God. I wonder what that must be like. A place of love and redemption and angels blowing trumpets, and perhaps Ma is there waiting for me.

The other women avoid us. They're afraid. Who wouldn't be?

Another clang. I sweat and shake in my own body stink. It has been decided that we will burn tomorrow. We are to be washed and dressed in clean smocks before we are carted up to Castlehill. I wish they would do it now.

The door swings open and one of the guards surveys the room. When he spots me, he nods and beckons. I stand up, thinking they are coming to take us for our baths, but he shakes his head at Hazel and the guidwife.

'Just you,' he says. 'King's orders.'

I follow him down two flights of narrow stairs into a small semi-circular room, set with a desk and chairs and parchments and quills, that looks as though it must be where they scribble down everyone's sins and sentences.

When I see who is sitting at the desk, I fall to my knees.

His Majesty has come himself. He is without robe and crown. Without that snivelling Dr Hemmingsen. Two men I have not seen before stand beside him, hunched under the low ceiling, until he tells them to leave the room.

'Get up, Mistress Craig,' he says. 'I can't talk to you if you are grovelling.'

I stand up, shakily, and sit on the chair opposite him, embarrassed of my stink. Mibbie he does not notice, or mibbie he has other things to worry about, for he looks me straight in the eye without flinching or wrinkling his nose.

'I've thought over what you told me in private in my courtroom,' he says. 'In fact I have thought of little else.'

He blinks and I notice how fair his eyelashes are. Under all that paraphernalia, he's just a man.

That afternoon in the courtroom, after everyone had been sent out, it was simply me and him too. The king had sat back in his chair and sighed.

'What do you have to say to me?' he'd asked, looking wary.

'That I'm not wicked,' I'd said. He'd rolled his eyes. 'Merely a humble cunning woman. But I do know things, sir, and I know why the Princess Anna of Denmark has not got with child yet, despite the fact that you attempt it each night.'

His jaw had dropped.

'How do you know what goes on in my private chambers?' he'd asked. 'Do you have spies?'

'I don't have spies,' I'd said. 'But I've guessed right and she will not get with child, for something is preventing it happening, without you even knowing.'

That had been enough for the king. He had shaken his head and shouted to the guards to come and take me away.

But now he's back.

'What is this thing you talked of? This thing that has prevented a conception?' the king asks. 'For I have reason to believe my betrothed has a motive to never want to produce a royal heir.' His hands reach for his gold amulet again and I watch him caress it.

'It's there,' I say. 'In your hands. Take off that charme and have a proper look at it.'

I noticed it first that day he was hanging over me as those men did their unspeakable things. The gold charme. *Gold for the highest level of protection.*

'This? This is to ward off the Devil,' he says.

'Well, it might do that – I have no idea,' I reply. 'But it will stop Anna of Denmark getting pregnant. It has a Christmas rose carved onto it. No foetus will quicken with a Christmas rose near it.'

He brings the charme up to his face to inspect it.

'The Christmas rose drives out evil,' he tells me. 'Dr Hemmingsen gave it to me.'

'I dare say it does,' I say. 'For Dr Hemmingsen is a most learned man and I'm sure he gave it to you with the best intentions. The Christmas rose is a powerful plant. Too powerful. Any healer – cunning woman, physician or apothecary – will tell you the Christmas rose purges everything, from madness to sickness and pregnancies.'

He drops the charme. It hits his chest with a light thud.

'The Christmas rose is so powerful that even a carving of it on an amulet is a purge,' I add. 'Especially if it's been made as a charme. You don't know what incantations were said over it, by its maker. It could have been a witch who carved that. And you wear it when you are bedding the princess, do you not? In fact you never take it off. Not even during your intimacy. It hangs over you both as you try to conceive.'

'How do you know this?' he asks.

'I'm a cunning woman, sir. There are things we know that we can't explain. But I'm not a servant of the Divvil. I'm a woman of guid intention and guid knowledge. I was accused of wickedness by my master, Baillie Kincaid, for his own impish reasons – to get as close to you as he could – and it nearly worked. And it will be on your conscience if you send me to my death after the knowledge I have given you. You might never produce an heir unless you take off that charme. And what a gift that would be to your enemy, Bothwell. If I was truly his servant, do you think I'd have told you all this?'

He sits back and I do the same. A surge of exhaustion washes over me, weightier than I've ever felt. It's like a tidal wave, heavy with silt. The last lick of a dying storm.

The king's chair is small and rickety, and he looks desperate to be out of it and away from this room – away from me and my stink and whatever wickedness I may, or may not, be about.

'When Kincaid reported you to me, I believed well and truly that you were a witch,' he says. 'But now I realize he is the man behind the conspiracy to destroy me.'

I can't disagree with him, even though I know Kincaid could no more conjure up a storm than conjure up fire or ice. I can only beg for my own life. And Kincaid tried to have me killed. He would have watched me burn at the stake and he would have taken satisfaction from it too.

It is that sure knowledge that makes me nod in agreement to the king and reassure the man that he has conquered evil. And mibbie that will damn me to hell. Mibbie I will never see the glory of God, and Ma will wait there for eternity for me, but I would rather live to see another day.

'All right, then, you can go,' King James says. 'It wouldn't be right for me to keep you here any longer. Perhaps you might make your way up to Castlehill to watch my enemies burn. Perhaps not. Perhaps you've had enough of this town and you'll want to head back to North Berwick.' He takes off his amulet and hands it to me. 'Take it. I don't want it near me.'

'Aye, sir, you don't,' I say. 'The Christmas rose is a powerful thing.'

He straightens his collar.

'Are the others to burn too then?' I ask. 'The guidwife and the Bathgates?' Surely he will not condemn them. Surely he will save his wrath for Kincaid alone?

'They conspired with Baillie Kincaid,' he says. 'I believe that, as their servant, you were not trusted to be in their coven. A man like Kincaid would only conspire with his closest allies, not with the girl who sweeps his rushes. Dr Hemmingsen disagrees,' he adds, peering at me. 'Dr Hemmingsen believes you are all involved. But he is not responsible for handing down the sentences. I am.'

What can I say? If I start to argue their case now, I'll be back in that prison cell before I know what's happening. Upstairs, the four of them are counting down the hours. Downstairs, there are carts that could take me miles away from here.

So I say nothing. I just nod.

The king strides out of the door, leaving it open for me to go. I hear him telling the guards I am to be allowed out. I hear the shock in their voices. I hear them agreeing and scurrying after him. I will leave in a minute. Once I have gathered my thoughts.

He believed it. He accepted that his amulet is cursed. I am stunned. But he is a superstitious man. A paranoid man. He is ripe to believe anything. Och, I might be a daftie. I might believe in sprites and pray to the selkies, and have been stupid enough to end up where I've ended up, but a carving of a plant won't stop a baby from being conceived. If that were true, we cunning women would have a much easier life.

But there are some things that can't be put down to mere coincidence, aren't there? I touch my waist where the gold ring hangs now on the white ribbon.

I think the charme has protected me.

I had asked the Princess Anna about King James, when I realized who she was. When the three of us were trying to work out what to do. For I was never going to help her with her herbs, if she didn't help me.

'Tell me something about the king that only those closest to him could ever know. I need him to be frightened of me, but I also need him to think I can help him,' I'd told her.

And that is when she'd said how superstitious he was, right down to the fact that he was wearing something around his neck to ward off witches.

'Is that the sort of thing you mean?' she'd asked. 'It's an amulet carved with a special flower.'

I'd remembered it myself, hanging over me. My mind had reached back to Ma's medicine books. Their detailed drawings that I pored over nightly to learn her ways.

'Aye, that might do it,' I'd said.

Chapter Forty-Seven

ANNA

Edinburgh Castle
June 1590

Castlehill – the highest point for miles. I get out of the silver carriage. Kirsten takes my arm. Scotland stretches before us in horizontal stripes. Grey sky falls to Fife farmland. Beneath that is the silvery snake of the Firth and then a patch of green Edinburgh field, and finally the Nor Loch below, which defends this ridged city from attacks.

The earthy smell of rain is everywhere, mingled with the scent of unwashed bodies and butchers' stalls. Even the wind that comes off the sea and slaps our faces has the tang of fish markets. There is nothing fresh here. Everything is tainted.

The kirk elders have arrived, and they are in their smartest cloaks. They have combed their beards over their high white ruffles and brushed the dust off their tall black hats. The burgh baillies have come from the shires, far and wide. The lairds have come from their mansion houses. They have arrived from North Berwick and Calder and Dalkeith. From Linlithgow and Penicuik and Prestonpans. From Gilmerton and Livingston. They have come to see how King James deals with diabolism. They have come to show their godliness. They are listening to the stories of bodkins and racks. Of shin-crushers and thumb-screws. Some of them come with tales of women dancing under the moon in their own villages. They are here to learn lessons and spread the word. They will take their lessons home with them, and this is how the witch panic will spread.

We file into the Great Hall for roasted hog on a spit. The feast will last as long as the drizzle. When the skies clear, they will lift the tarpaulins over the pyres that are keeping the logs bone-dry. The North Berwick witches are in a cell somewhere below our feet, where no one can hear their curses.

There are four North Berwick witches. Mistress Jura Craig's account is being rewritten. James has decided she was never a witch and that Kincaid tried to blame her to get into Holyroodhouse, where mayhem would have ensued if he had not tried to boast of it to Kirsten Sørensen.

Kirsten remains tight-lipped on the matter, but that's just what Kirsten's like. She has saved her daughter.

'Look,' she says, righting my skirts for the hundredth time, 'you are covered in dust. These floors and walls are filthy. You should have worn a darker colour. I was wrong to put you in cream. It's not a mistake I'll make again, if we ever come back to the castle.'

If we ever come back. The only certainty consists of the next few hours. After that, I don't know what's going to happen. I've not seen Henry since James walked in on us. Then James left the study and he was not at dinner or any other meals. He has not come to my bed.

I feel sick as everyone gorges themselves on pig and fig and caraway biscuits. Reverend Thompson sits next to me, so close I can hear the wet click of his mouth. He has been down in the cells with them. James sent him there to hear any last words.

'I'm sure the spectacle of the burnings will act as a deterrent,' comments the minister opposite him. 'Edinburgh has never seen the like. The king is proving that he has no mercy, when it comes to those who dare to plot against him.'

'Or is this merely the beginning?' another man muses, reaching for the almonds. 'We have uncovered one single conspiracy. How many more covens are out there, plotting against the Crown?' He looks at me, as though I might have the answer.

'We'll be far more vigilant now,' says another. This one is not a minister, but has the air of a councillor. 'When the king's pamphlet on demonology is published, it will be an important study text.'

I turn to Reverend Thompson. 'What did they say, Reverend, when you sat in the cells with them?'

He stops chewing and stares at his plate. 'Very little,' he replies. 'Just the usual pleas of innocence. The women were the most vociferous—'

We are interrupted by a sharp tap on my shoulder. A servant passes me a note. The ministers continue their conversation as I open it. Oh my God, it is from Henry.

I am in St Margaret's Chapel. Come as soon as you can.

I stand up and address the kirk men. 'I will spend the next hour in the chapel in private prayer,' I tell them. 'I will be praying for the souls of the condemned.'

They stand, relieved to be rid of me.

Reverend Thompson's eyes meet mine and flicker for a moment before he stares down at his plate again. For the rest of the men at our table, the North Berwick witches are a merely a concept. An aberration. But Reverend Thompson has sat with them. He knows they are our brethren and sisters, our flesh and blood. And he looks troubled by what is about to unfold.

*

St Margaret's Chapel is across the square from the Great Hall. Torches flicker on the path. The rain has eased. They will burn them soon. The chapel door is open. The scent of incense and beeswax and dust takes me back to the chapel at Kronborg. I close my eyes and open them again. St Margaret's is the tiniest of chapels, just a few feet wide, with the afternoon gloom falling through the small arched windows.

Henry.

He's sitting on the pew nearest the altar. He turns when I walk in the room.

'Make sure the door is shut behind you,' he tells me.

I walk over and sit next to him. 'I've been worried sick,' I say.

He smiles, but it is a terrible-looking smile, loaded with bad news.

'What is it?' I ask.

'Anna, I am going to have to tell you something, and you're going to have to be incredibly brave,' he says.

My heart stops.

'I am not staying here. I'm being sent away from Holyroodhouse. James is sending me back to the Scottish Borders. I leave in an hour.'

Oh, so that's how James is going to deal with it. I might have guessed, I suppose. The King of Scotland can share his bed with his lover, but a Queen of Scotland cannot.

'I'll come and visit you,' I promise him. 'Whenever I can.'

'You won't be allowed,' he tells me. 'James is banishing me, Anna. That's our punishment.'

'But I'll sneak away,' I say. 'I'll find a way of seeing you.'

He shakes his head. 'You don't understand. If we breach the banishment, he'll have me killed. It won't happen in public. It won't be an execution. But James will have me killed. He's told me.'

Panic rises in my throat. My armpits tingle with sweat. My heart thuds.

'Then come and find me in Denmark.'

'James won't let me run away. I'm going to be watched at all times. He wants me to keep an eye on Roxburghshire for him. Guard it from Bothwell. He is sending men to assist me, but really they will be spying on me. If I try to get to Denmark, I won't make it as far as a port.'

'I'll talk to James,' I insist.

'He can't be seen to be weak,' Henry replies. 'If we run off together, it will be the ultimate humiliation.' I suppose it would be. 'We don't have long,' whispers Henry.

The sun has come out from behind the rain clouds. It lights up the arched windows. We sit, still not touching, as the tender rays spread across the chapel. What a golden afternoon we shall have. The colours of Fife and Edinburgh will shift from grey to yellow. The spring wind will sing into the sails of the ships on the Forth like a hymn.

'There's a carriage waiting for me down at Castlehill,' Henry says. 'I only stopped here as a detour. We need to say our goodbyes now.'

Now? But how? There are so many unspoken things that I don't even know where to start. How can I say goodbye, when I have not even told him yet how I felt when I first saw him – how he lit up the room with his smile? Or how the thought of him keeps me going each day. I think of Henry when I wake and when I go to sleep. I open my mouth to start telling him everything, but he stops me.

'There's not enough time for us to sit here and tell each other all the things we want to say,' he says gently. 'Instead shall we hold hands and imagine ourselves back by the lake at the Bishop's Palace in Ánslo? I know it sounds like a strange thing to do, but I think we were at our happiest there.'

And that is what we do. As the sun heats the cold stone walls of the chapel, and the sailors on the Forth grasp their cauls and give thanks for the good weather, as Reverend Thompson remembers Guidwife Kincaid's gut-wrenching cries, her head scarred with bodkin pricks, and Jura Craig makes her way to freedom, Henry and I sit in silence, for we have nothing to say sorry for and nothing to regret.

Instead of words, Henry takes my hand in his and we rediscover our warmth and our touch. Our fingers, which were meant for each other's. Our hands, which grip and stroke and search each other. Our loving touch, which has never ended in a consummation, and never will. Our shared sadness. And in that fullness – that *emptiness* – we both go back to that small, peaceful place in Ánslo, the *hytte* beside the lake, with the taste of *akvavit* on our lips and the scent of winter in the air. We stay there, under the pines, until Henry lets go of my hand for the last time, stands up and bows and leaves the chapel.

Chapter Forty-Eight

JURA

Edinburgh Castle
June 1590

I walk up the hill, in the opposite direction to Holyroodhouse, clutching the gold amulet in my hand. I take it as far as a jeweller's and walk out of there with a purse of coin. I keep the king's gold ring, though. And the white ribbon. I think I'll keep them for a very long time.

I pay my toll at Netherbow Port. I trudge upwards and reach the linen stalls of the Land Market and buy a new shawl, thick enough to keep me warm at night, and drab enough that when I place it over my head and shoulders I disappear and look like any of the other guidwives hurrying up the hill to see the witches burn. When I reach Castlehill the crowd heaves. People and horses and carts and carriages, all thronging in the narrow street.

The rain has stopped. The sun appears. Ma, it's going to be a belter.

I push through the throng, my elbows and hips nudging the way. I know I shouldn't, but I must. Is it wicked of me to want to watch Master Kincaid die? To watch Robbie Bathgate howl, the way he watched me howl.

I think I've come a long way from worrying about what is right and what is wrong.

I find a space, near where the four stakes stand high, and I nearly heave, for that could have been five. A whisper goes around the crowd. *They're bringing them out soon.* The rain holds off. Oh, that sun is bright and warm and heavenly. It has been so long since I felt the sun on my heid that I begin to weep. And then the tears really do run: for stolen kisses at Berwick Law and the taste of Tipsy Laird, and for the vile things Baillie Kincaid did.

'Don't cry for them,' a man next to me says. 'They're evil.'

And that is the trouble with accusations, is it not? That if one person says something against another, and the accuser is more powerful than the accused, what hope is there?

I am here to watch Robbie and the bailiff burn, but I am here to deliver a swift and merciful end to Hazel and the guidwife. Ribbon magic is easy to do. Such a colourful display at the Land Market. Purple for royalty, as I know now, and green for fertility and black for death, which you must not normally meddle with, except in cases where a death is long and lingering and an end would be a blessing.

Under my shawl I knot two black ribbons together. One for the mistress and one for her daughter.

When they bring the prisoners out, everyone gasps and cranes their necks and lifts their bairns up to gawp. Their hands are still bound and now they all have ropes around their necks. They are all clean and shorn and wearing pristine smocks. The men are first, stumbling and petrified. Canopies that have been draped over the wood piles to keep them dry are dragged away. The women are pulled out next, with Hazel screaming.

Shh, I whisper, pulling on a black ribbon. *Calm yourself down.*

The people around me begin to mutter and twitch. 'She is young,' says one. 'They cannie burn a young lassie.'

Oh, but they can. They can, and they will.

They are separated out, Hazel and the guidwife never taking

their eyes off each other, as if they are tied by an invisible thread. The guidwife is saying something to her daughter that I cannie hear, but I hope she is telling her that she is no witch, that she will rise to heaven and they will see each other there in no time at all. The glory of God. Amen.

As they are tied to their stakes, I knot the black ribbons again. *Welcome your deaths, for God's glory is a better place than Castlehill.*

The men writhe against their posts already. The women are still. Behind each stake one soldier remains, each with a hand on the rope holding the women's necks.

I knot the ribbons again. *Let the soldiers give you swift deaths. Let the soldiers garrotte you before you burn.*

The guidwife leans back, her neck exposed, white and pure as a swan's. Her soldier pulls hard on the rope to her neck. Instantly she collapses.

Everyone around me gasps. 'She's gone already,' someone says.

I look across to Hazel, who is standing with her eyes closed. *Oh, Hazel. Plain and scratchy. Desperate to be bonnie and bold. You were so full of light that night the guidwives came over and we all sang the ballad of Tam Lin – your rash all gone and your voice as clear as a bell. I have never seen a lassie shine so bright. I could feel your hope radiate from you. Hope of being a fine guidwife to Robbie Bathgate.*

Hazel does not fight the rope either. She goes quietly and easily, as if she has fallen asleep dreaming of being the finest guidwife in all of North Berwick. Off she goes, off to find her Ma, in God's glory.

The men are different. When the ropes are taken to them, they choke and wheeze. The fires are lit, one after the other. The wood has stayed dry, and it explodes in a bright blaze. The women remain limp. Their souls are in God's welcoming arms now. But the men scream – terrible long screams that take for ever to die out.

Finally a hush falls over smoke-filled Castlehill, terrified and solemn; the hush of death, as hundreds bear witness to the power of King James of Scotland.

I leave as quickly as I can, to get ahead of the surge of folk scurrying back to their homes and shops and kirk pews, where they will pray fervently that the Divvil never visits them, offering them his tempting prizes in exchange for their souls.

I buy some more belongings at the Land Market. A new kirtle and undergarments and a new cap, then enough food to last me a few days. A sack to carry it all in. It's heavy, but I don't plan on walking too far, just down the steep closes to the Grassmarket, where the traders are finishing up their business for the day and the place is heaving with the last sales of the horse fair and the cattle fair, the taverns spilling with traders and drovers.

I don't know where I'm going, but I know I have to get as far away as I can.

When the hand grabs my shoulder, I jump.

At first I try to get away, but the person is tight on my tail and I've not walked or run for a long time.

'Don't run, I need to talk to you.'

I recognize the voice. It rises above the Grassmarket loud enough and grand enough and foreign enough to make heads turn. I stop in my tracks.

'Mistress Sørensen,' I say.

'Now you are a free woman, come and have an ale with me,' she replies.

*

We are the only women in the alehouse and I want to get out of there, but she takes my arm and fights our way to a table.

I want to ask Kirsten Sørensen a hundred questions about why she rescued me, but I find that I just stare at her instead.

Two ales are poured for us, and if the landlady wonders why a well-dressed woman is drinking with a filthy wretch like me, she keeps her questions to herself.

'I think I owe you my life,' I say. 'Because if it wasn't for you, I'd be dead.'

She sups her ale and makes a face like she has never had cheap ale before.

'If it wasn't for me, you'd never have been born,' she says.

Chapter Forty-Nine

KIRSTEN

Holyroodhouse
June 1590

After Jura was born, in that little apartment in the Canongate, I held her all night and whispered her promises as she slept: *The whole world will be yours to take. I will always keep you safe.* They were the promises of a new mother, full of hope and exhaustion. As the days went on, and Papa wrote saying he was coming to collect me and that he had such high hopes for us back at Kronborg, I knew I could not keep my promises. I would have to pass the child to Mary and hope that Mary would be as good a mother to Jura as I would have been.

I have surpassed that, have I not? I have destroyed lives to let Jura keep hers. God will judge me, I know it. And even if I must rot in hell with Kincaid for the rest of eternity, I will do so willingly, knowing I have saved my daughter. I might not have been able to be a mother to her when she was growing up, but I was there in her hour of need.

In the aftermath of the witch-burnings, Holyroodhouse is silent of masque and music and dining-room chatter. The mood suits me. Jura is on her way to find Mary in London. I gave her the address.

Anna has not decided what she is going to do.

As the bodies charred, King James and Dr Hemmingsen rode down from Castlehill and went straight back to their writing. The barn has been swept out and rooms have been set aside at the Canongate Tollbooth especially for witches.

James plans to travel to London to stay at Queen Elizabeth's court soon. There are conversations to be had about who will be the next monarch of England. There are no more Tudors. James is the rightful heir, but it needs to happen without riot or outcry.

Anna is deciding whether to go with James or take a ship to Hellebæk Abbey. James wants her to marry him. Her affair with Henry Roxburgh served to show him how desirable Anna is. She has taken to her chamber, refusing all visitors except me, but in truth no one but me has tried to speak to her. Certainly not James. I don't think it's because he's too busy with his pamphlet. It's because he knows the decision is hers alone to take. He doesn't want a reluctant queen.

It's been a week now. A week since the burnings, and a week since she was forced to say goodbye to Henry. I've come to her room more times than I can count. I've got a list of the Leith Port sailings.

I rap firmly on Anna's chamber door and walk in.

'There's a Danish ship leaving tomorrow,' I tell her, handing her the timetable. 'If we are going to go, I'd rather go sooner than later. There's no point us hanging around here.'

She looks up from where she's lying on the bed. Her face is blank.

'Do you regret any of it?' she asks.

'Something happens to you when you become a mother,' I say. 'You will do anything to protect your child.'

'Perhaps I will never know what that feels like,' she says.

'I think you would be a good mother,' I tell her. 'You have so much love. And more than that: you understand how the world works. You understand the dangerous times we are in.'

'When will it end?' she asks. 'When will James be happy that enough witches have been rounded up and killed?'

'It won't end for a long time,' I reply, trying to sound as gentle as I can. 'And if you run back to Denmark there's nothing you can do. You will become powerless. If you stay here, you might be able to give him some counsel.'

'James would never listen to me,' she says.

'He will if you come to him willingly, as his queen,' I suggest. 'He will need a strong woman at his side if he is to take the English throne. They will see him as a foreigner. He needs someone who understands what that's like.'

'We can never love each other as a husband and wife should,' she says. 'He loves Murray, and I love Henry. James has made sure I won't see Henry again. I hate him for that.'

'James could have had Henry executed for treason and he didn't,' I answer. 'I think he does love you in his own way.'

'But I'm not sure I believe what he believes. I don't agree with his type of religion. His hatred of witches. His strictness.'

'He thinks women are more vulnerable to the Devil than men are,' I say. 'Perhaps you can show him we are not.'

I tell her I will fetch her some wine and take my leave. Her chamber is stuffy and miserable and I can't bear to be in it, trying to sympathize with her, when I don't know if I will see my daughter again. I feel as though I am back on the *Gideon*, lurching from one uncertainty to the next, seasick. I fetch the wine and some ginger biscuits. Anna does not even lift her head to thank me. Her psalter lies on her bedside table beside the bowl of her *scorchet* confections.

I hope she finds comfort in it.

If we are going to Hellebæk Abbey, it is the only book she will be allowed to read.

Chapter Fifty

ANNA

Holyroodhouse
June 1590

The Danish ship sails tomorrow at noon. I've folded and unfolded the timetable so many times the ink is fading into the creases. We could have a cart summoned at first light. Kirsten has agitated all week. Every night I hear her creak back and forth across her chamber into the small hours, when I finally fall into a few hours' sleep.

It's late afternoon now, and at Hellebæk Abbey the nuns will be gathering for dinner. It will be a peaceful meal. Gulls will rise over the spire, swooping down the cliffs, eating the stale crumbs of yesterday's bread. There will be no stiff collars or wide-hooped gowns or accusations of witchery. No marital duties. I will never have to carry an heir. I can think about Henry in peace there. No one will question why I am quiet or sad or in deep thought. They'll assume I'm sorry I failed to become Queen of Scotland, when really I'll simply be grateful that I loved and was loved. That I held a warm hand and saw a smile full of kindness, and know what it is when the taste of two people's lips becomes one taste.

At the lake at the Bishop's Palace in Ánslo, summer will be in full swing. What must it be like? The woodlands alive with the flowers and plants and creatures that slept as Henry and I met. Oh, life is short and sweet. One minute you think you have the whole world ahead of you; the next you wonder where it has gone. Kirsten would laugh at that and tell me I am too young to have such thoughts, but I've lived a different sort of a life from her. We've been side by side, but entirely separate. And now our paths are interlinked. Whatever I do, she is bound to me.

All these years and Kirsten never even hinted she had a child.

To have waited it out and come here, then found her and almost lost her. To have stood up in court in front of the king and made up a story to save her daughter's life.

To never be able to tell her daughter who her father was.

I think Kirsten Sørensen is the most extraordinary woman I have ever met.

If I go with James to Whitehall Palace as he negotiates the union of the crowns, I can easily spare Kirsten for a couple of hours each day of our trip. She and Jura could spend time getting to know each other, and they could visit the playhouse theatre and take walks in the parks and by the river. Perhaps, in time, when it is safe in Scotland again, Jura and Mary could come back. They could live near Kirsten, wherever she is.

The floorboards creak again.

Kirsten comes in with the wine on a tray. 'I'm ready to go to Hellebæk Abbey, if that's what you want,' she says. 'My bags are packed and so are yours. We can only take what we can carry, so we should wear our heaviest capes, even though the weather's been decent of late.'

'They only have two robes at Hellebæk Abbey,' I tell her. 'Winter and summer. Imagine that. What will we fill our days with, when there's no dinner or walks to dress for, or fans to match with gloves and slippers?'

'We'll fill our days with prayer and thought and hard work,' says Kirsten. 'You'll have to learn how to wash dishes and scrub floors and cook, but you'll enjoy it. There's pride in honest work.'

I can't remember ever seeing Kirsten scrub a floor or wash a plate, but that's just what Kirsten's like – always putting the people she loves at the centre of her thoughts. It took me a long time to realize that.

I get off the bed and go to the window. There are carts lined up at the bottom of the road. How long will it take Jura to get to London? Will she be there already? I envy her the life she'll have. Perhaps she'll fall in love.

'Will Jura and Mary have enough coin to live on?' I ask.

Kirsten stops, looking puzzled that I should even care.

'I worry about it,' I say. 'They can't work as cunning women, can they? It's too dangerous. Rents might rise. What if they want to get out of the city when it's hot and stifling? What if there's a fire or a plague? Who would look after them?'

'They can write to us at the abbey,' she says. 'We can help them by sending them money, if they need it.'

'And Mother Abbess would pass over their letters, would she? How do we know she wouldn't give them to my mama first?'

'In giving up your betrothal, you give up control of many things,' Kirsten replies. 'You think you're merely a pawn in their game, but we have more privileges at court than we realize.'

'Please help me get dressed,' I say. 'I want to talk to James.'

He meets me outside the library. He looks as if he has barely slept in days. There are dark circles under his eyes.

'Dr Hemmingsen and I have almost finished writing up our notes,' he says.

I nod curtly to show I am not interested in talking about witches. 'Walk with me outside,' I say. 'You need fresh air, and I want us to speak freely.'

We walk through the gardens, past plants that stop pregnancies and bushes that ward off witches. If I go through with this, I'll have to stop taking the tincture. I'll have to bear his children.

But if I can't have Henry Roxburgh, perhaps that is the next best thing.

'I don't want to go to Hellebæk Abbey,' I tell him. 'I am not cut out to be a nun.'

'Your mama will be relieved,' he says. 'And so am I.'

'Are you?' I stop in the middle of the pathway.

He takes my hand. It's a simple gesture, but it surprises me. Usually James touches me out of duty.

'You have taken on this challenge – this betrothal – with huge dignity,' he tells me.

'Hardly,' I say. 'I fell in love with another man.'

James shakes his head. 'Our betrothal is not about falling in love. It's not about romance. It's about uniting two countries. It's about giving Scotland a queen, and I think you have the qualities of a queen. It's no wonder Henry fell in love with you. You are brave. You survived that storm. I need that quality in a wife.'

'You are asking me to make a huge sacrifice, in order to marry you. You are in love with another man. He shares your bed.'

'And if I were not king, I might be able to live with him in private,' says James. 'And not worry about heirs or thrones, or plots to destroy me.' He runs his fingers through his hair.

For the first time in my life, I think I might even feel sorry for him.

'I will be your wife,' I say.

James smiles, and I believe he is genuinely happy.

A new day dawns, and noon comes and goes. The Danish ship will have set sail by now, gliding down the Firth of Forth towards the German Sea. Perhaps Mama will see it in a week or two as she glances out of her window across the Øresund strait, but she will never know how close I came to getting on it.

I sit down and write Mama the letter she has waited months for, telling her that I will be married within weeks and crowned Queen of Scotland at Holyrood Abbey by the end of the year. I recite the plans for the wedding and the coronation, even though she knows them. She helped to oversee them, after all. I will wear a robe of purple velvet trimmed with fur, and my crown will be set with pearls, diamonds and a ruby. I will be paraded around Edinburgh in my silver coach. Children will throw confections and girls will perform dances and psalms will be sung. Speeches will be delivered, exhorting the virtues: prudence and justice and temperance and fortitude. It is a day that will go down in history, when Anna, Princess of Denmark becomes Anna, Queen of Scots.

I put down my writing set, because the day is ticking on and soon it will be time to think about what to wear for dinner. And Kirsten will come in again any minute and do what she does best, deciding what shoe and what fan, and tutting at my farthingale again.

The little blackbird Peckin drops by and takes some seeds from the windowsill. Bless you, Peckin. Fluttering about town with not a care in the world. Well-fed and well admired. Some might say I am like a well-plumed bird too, but they don't know the half of it.

I sit down on my bed and stop in my tracks at a faint noise. At first I think it is the gentle notes of a clavichord, the way Henry used to play for me. But then, as I listen, I realize it's just the wind. It will always be like this, won't it? I'll be in the middle of something and then a hint of Henry will catch me out. A laugh, a song, a curl of dark hair. Right now, the memory of him is so vivid I still think I could reach out and touch him. Is he doing the same, down in the Scottish Borders? Thinking of me and reaching for my hand?

The idea of it catches in my throat and the tears come again. One day Henry will have faded and I'll have to try hard to picture him. But today I sit on my bed and cry for him. For the unspoken words. For the other life we could have had, if we had not been born to the positions we hold.

And if I close my eyes, I can see it. I really can. There we are, in Ánslo, look: the two of us laughing and drinking *akvavit* without a care in the world. We are by the *hytte* at the Bishop's Palace, watching the sun set gloriously over the lake. The pines are lush and the night is sultry and the scent of cedar lingers in the air.

HISTORICAL NOTE

This is a story based on historical events and whilst some of the characters are based on real people, others are entirely fictional. The North Berwick witch trials of 1590 were a notorious episode in early modern Scotland and there has been a renewed interest in the history of witch hunts and the persecution of people – mainly women – as writers and historians examine these events from a feminist perspective.

I was inspired to take a fictional look at the marriage of King James VI of Scotland to Anna of Denmark when I learned that it was not only the catalyst for his personal involvement as judge in the North Berwick witch trials, but also the inspiration for his book *Daemonologie*, which endorses the practice of witch hunting and calls for witches to be punished most severely. The North Berwick witch trials are included in James's book in a section entitled 'Newes from Scotland'.

They took place at a time of significant political turbulence and religious reformation in Scotland, when King James was trying to assert his power. When the fleet carrying Anna of Denmark to Scotland was hit by a storm, the weather events were blamed on witches in Denmark, a country that was experiencing a surge of interest in sorcery because of the large and ongoing persecution in nearby Trier in Germany, which was the epicentre of witch hysteria at that time. When King

James travelled to rescue his new bride, he spent time in Norway and Denmark, where he heard these allegations at first hand. He became keenly interested in the idea of sorcery.

Meanwhile a housemaid in North Berwick called Geillis Duncan came to the attention of her master when she was sneaking out at night and appeared to have the ability to perform miraculous cures. She was put to torture, where she confessed to being a witch and named numerous others, men and women. One of these, an Agnes Sampson, who was also put to torture, said that people were involved in a plot to create the storm. The accusations spread to the upper echelons of society and finally to King James's cousin, Francis Stewart, fifth Earl of Bothwell, an ambitious and troublesome man who was thought to lie at the heart of the plot. This was the first major witch trial in Scotland, and the first time a monarch had been the target of a murder plot by witches. *Daemonologie* became an authoritative guide for anyone concerned with witch conspiracies, to protect themselves from the Devil, and it set the framework for the witch hunts that followed throughout Britain.

The King's Witches is a fictional retelling of the North Berwick witch trials from the perspective of women – both real and imagined – who were at their heart. Very little is known about Anna of Denmark's view of the matter, and I was intrigued by how it might have affected her: not only to fear for her life from sorcerers, but to witness her husband persecuting men and women. In real life, Anna was just fourteen years old when betrothed to James, but my fictional Anna is a little older, at seventeen. Kirsten Sørensen is my imagined Danish lady-in-waiting who might have her own link to Scotland. Jura Craig is based loosely on Geillis Duncan.

The King's Witches begins with the start of a trial marriage, or handfasting, between the royal couple, and the proxy ceremony. Whilst there was indeed a proxy ceremony, because James did not travel to Denmark and Earl Marischal stood in for him, the marriage was actually legal from the start. The handfasting tradition – of a year and a day's engagement – was common in Scotland and even in the Scottish court at the time, with any child automatically legitimized if the couple agreed to become legally married. The real marriage of King James and Anna of Denmark was a long and successful one, with three children who survived infancy. There is no historical record of her having any affairs, although it is understood that King James had relationships with both men and women. Douglas Murray of Kirkbrae is my own fictional character. I have also taken some liberties with the dates of some events in order to fit my story into its own timeframe.

It is thought that between 1400 and 1782 around 40,000–60,000 people in Europe were killed due to the suspicion that they were practising witchcraft, peaking between 1560 and 1630. Most of those who were killed were women over the age of forty. In March 2022 Nicola Sturgeon, then First Minister of Scotland, apologized for the historical persecution of witches.

ACKNOWLEDGEMENTS

I am incredibly grateful to the brilliant team of people who have helped create this book. Thank you with all my heart to Maria Rejt, Madeleine O'Shea, Alice Gray, Michael Davies and Kinza Azira at Mantle, as well as the Pan Macmillan team – Gillian Mackay, Rebecca Needes, Mary Chamberlain, Marian Reid, Moesha Parirenyatwa, Chloe Davies and Natasha Tulett – and Charlotte Day for the stunning cover. All my love and thanks, as ever, to Viola Hayden at Curtis Brown for your wisdom, guidance and support.

There is a wealth of historical research available on the reign of King James VI of Scotland and his consort Anna of Denmark, particularly regarding the storm of 1589, but I was particularly inspired by the article 'Witchcraft Against Royal Danish Ships in 1589 and the Transnational Transfer of Ideas', by Liv Helene Willumsen of the University of Tromsø.

There is also a growing body of research and analysis of witch trials, and I was grateful for the information in the Survey of Scottish Witchcraft by the University of Edinburgh, as well as the Witches of Scotland campaign for justice for those accused of witchcraft led by Claire Mitchell KC and Zoe Venditozzi.

Launching a novel-writing career is an enormous challenge and I am indebted to the authors, bloggers and booksellers who have supported me. There are too many to name, but in particular, thank you to Dan Bassett, Janice Hallett, Tina Baker, David Bishop and the 2023 Debuts as well as Fran Woodrow, Joanne Baird and Caroline Maston.

Thank you to Bob McDevitt and all at the Bloody Scotland crime writing festival for giving me a platform to showcase my work and for the amazing work you do to champion Scottish writing. Thanks also to the Edinburgh International Book Festival and Scottish Book Trust and libraries across the country.

I am grateful to the friends and family who have supported my writing – the Fab Fringers, Ruby and Tom, and Sarah. And to Paul, for inspiring me to achieve the very best I can.

Lastly Dad, David Foster. With love and thanks for all that you do for your family, this book is for you.